"Let me walk you to the door."

"Just a minute," Veronica answered, placing a restraining hand on his. "Whoever heard of the perfect date without the perfect good-night kiss?"

Jay cupped her face in his hands and tried to keep the kiss as light and undemanding as the evening had been, but it was no good. As soon as her tongue swept over his upper lip, Jay opened his mouth to take it inside, savoring the sweetness like a famished man approaching the banquet table, too hungry for decorum, a victim of a greed he never wanted to know. He supposed that if he could make a conscious choice it would be not to love her, not to want her so intensely. But all that was academic now. He couldn't stop loving her and desiring her any more than the sun could set in the east....

ABOUT THE AUTHOR

Katherine Coffaro lives in Santa Cruz, California, with her husband and two children. She holds a Ph.D. in biology and has done research in invertebrate immunology. Now she devotes herself full-time to her writing career.

Books by Katherine Coffaro

Sunward Journey

KATHERINE COFFARO

Harlequin Books

TORONTO • NEW YORK • LONDON
AMSTERDAM • PARIS • SYDNEY • HAMBURG
STOCKHOLM • ATHENS • TOKYO • MILAN

Published December 1984

ISBN 0-373-16081-X

Printed in Canada

Chapter One

Veronica Dubcek seldom had either the time or the inclination toward self-pity, but on this particular Christmas Eve as she sat alone in her living room watching the San Gabriel peaks turn purple in the early setting winter sun, she was awash with the sentiment. It colored her thoughts a melancholic blue-gray, that dull muted shade of the ocean on a foggy day when the sky lacks brilliance and the sun seems to be in some other galaxy. The feeling had sunk down to her bones, enervating her of a vitality capable of registering upon the senses of even the most casual observer.

She had never spent a Christmas Eve alone in her life, and as welcome as the prospect of time to herself and her studies had seemed when the children elected to visit her parents in Nevada, there was now something intrinsically sad about the whole thing, and Veronica wished she had taken her mother's advice to come with the kids. And there had been other options to avoid solitude on the day before Christmas, but likewise she had declined them all, convincing herself she preferred to be alone. She thought of dressing and dropping by a party one of the other secretaries at work was giving that evening, but the energy to rise from her seat wasn't there, so she continued to look out the window. By the time the highest peaks of the mountains were as dark as the despair in her heart, Veronica's depression began to take the form of anger, an emotional transition not unprecedented in the past.

Of all the days to kill himself, why had her husband chosen Christmas Eve? Didn't he know he would destroy the holiday season for those closest to him for the rest of their lives? And moreover, why did he have to do it at all? So secretly and so unexpectedly, never giving her the chance to help him—or had she been deaf to his cry for help? Veronica didn't know and didn't think she would ever know the answer to these questions. On a good day she knew them to be unanswerable and therefore best not considered, but this wasn't a good day.

The phone rang, and she leaped on it, hoping one of her three sons had called back. She had spoken to them in the late afternoon, but it would be just like Brad, her sixteen-year-old, to want to make certain she was still all right.

"Hello?"

"Good evening. This is Jay Jennings. Do I have the Mike Dubcek residence?"

The name was vaguely familiar to her and the sound of his voice rich enough to impress itself upon her deadened awareness of such things. "Yes, this is Veronica Dubcek."

"Hi," he said with a slow Texas accent. "I'm an old friend of Mike's. I made your husband a promise seventeen years ago in Da Nang to look him up if I was ever in Southern California. I never thought it would take so long, but here I am. May I speak to Mike, please?"

Mike had been gone for two years now, and she hadn't received such a request in over a year. On a better day Veronica could have handled it, but not now. A floodgate of pent-up tears burst open, and she found herself weeping into a phone with a man she had never met on the other end. He said something else, but she was too distraught to make sense of the words.

"Hello? Are we still connected?" Jennings asked when she didn't respond. By the time he recognized the gulping sounds as a woman's sobs, she had already slammed down the receiver in his ear.

His teenage son walked into the room to get a Santa Claus cookie from the plate on the coffee table and caught the expression on his father's face. "What's the matter, Dad? You look really spaced out." If J.J. ever had to decide what he hated the most in the world, it would have to be seeing his father unhappy.

Jennings shook his head, looking as baffled and discontent as he would have had his boy suddenly sprouted wings. "She hung up on me," he said in a tone that wasn't conversational, almost as though he were speaking to himself.

"Struck out again? Poor Dad. Try calling another one," he consoled awkwardly. His father could either lash out at him or laugh right now.

"Shut up, J.J.," the man said more harshly than he meant, amending his words with a smile when he saw the stricken look on his boy's face.

"Sorry, Dad."

"It's all right."

J.J. grinned and sat down next to his father. "Thanks, Dad," he began cautiously, gauging his father's mood by the way he rubbed his hands together and how tightly the lines on his forehead were drawn. He concluded it was permissible to continue. "Do you mind if I ask who hung up on you? Was it that lawyer lady from Boston who's been chasing you around since last summer?"

"Rita? No, I can't imagine her hanging up on any-one. It was the wife of an old army buddy of mine. She hung up when I asked to speak to him." They must be divorced or something like that, Jennings decided, hav-ing had time to overcome the initial shock of a receiver jarring his eardrums after he had heard the woman weep so uncontrollably. Jay Jennings couldn't stand the sound of a woman crying, or of anyone else sob-bing, especially like that, as though she had lost her best friend. *Oh, God,* he thought, slamming his palms together in a gesture that let his son know it was time to be quiet until his father spoke again. What if Mike was dead? What if Mike had recently died, and he had just gone ahead and upset his widow by asking for him on the phone? It was something he wouldn't want to do to anyone, much less Vee Dubcek.

Jennings had cherished her memory for years, carry-ing the poignant eroticism with him like a miser's fa-vored jewel, buried deeply and treasured in rare private moments. God, he couldn't bear the thought of hurt-ing Vee, sender of boxes of salami, saltine crackers, and homemade cookies that her husband had shared with the rest of the guys; Vee, the author of long letters her teenage husband had also shared, taking a lascivi-ous delight in reading aloud her intimate thoughts, and that used to make Jay Jennings want to put his fist through Mike's mouth as much as he loved the guy; and Vee, the subject of most of his erotic fantasies be-cause of some of the things she wrote and all the pho-tos she sent to that miserable godforsaken hellhole. Those pictures had shown her to be just about the pret-tiest teenage girl he had ever seen in his life, tall and slender like some kind of fancy lavender flower his mother used to grow at home in Texas, and twice as lovely.

Jay Jennings had seen many women in his life in various forms of undress, and when he thought about them, the images were undefined in his mind, as impossible to focus on as a ship off in the distant mist. But when he recalled one particular photograph of Vee Dubcek, the erotic impact was still there, potent and as full of life as the first crocus bursting through the snow. It was a picture Mike should never have showed to anyone, and no one should ever have seen, but he did and they all looked, the five of them who were the closest.

Vee's girl friend had taken the picture at Mike's persistent request. She was lying down on a bed wearing a pair of lacy baby doll pajamas, with a smile on her face that used to drive Jennings crazy, a come-hither look he would have given his very soul to know. The outfit was actually quite tame compared to the way a woman might dress now on a public beach, but then it had fueled the furnace of his fantasies, the dark-haired girl on the pink bedspread, the hair flowing like brown satin over a pillow case with a Raggedy Ann and Andy cover and the semisheer fabric thinly veiling her breasts.

Mike had hung the photo on a locker in their barrack, and it stayed there for a week or so until Jennings couldn't stand to see this woman's privacy invaded any further. He stole it and lusted over her when he was alone, praying to the Lord for forgiveness of his neglect of the ninth commandment should he be blown up tomorrow.

"I wonder what's going on," Jennings said at length.

"Maybe they got a divorce, Dad, and she's still upset about it," J.J. suggested.

"Yeah, I had the same thought, but I'm worried something worse happened. She started to cry."

"She cried? Maybe he just walked out on her on Christmas Eve."

"Could be. I have to find out what happened. I'm going to try to track down John Silvers. Last time I heard, he worked with Mike at DataBank. As I recall, John was a principal investor in that company."

"Is he that black guy with one leg who stayed with us in Paris for a while?"

"Yeah, he was in Nam with me and Mike. Do you remember where he said he lived? As I recall it was Burbank."

"I think that's right. There'll probably be a million John Silvers in Burbank, Dad. Do you know his middle name or initial?"

Jennings had already found the number in the phone book. "Here it is. The name of this street rings a bell. I would prefer to be alone for a few minutes, son. Do you mind going into the next room for a while?"

"No, I was going to make a sandwich anyway. Want one?"

"Yeah, but leave it on the kitchen table, okay?"

"Turkey or ham?"

"A little of each." Jennings thanked his son and dialed the number, tremendously relieved when his friend answered in the rich Virginia accent he'd recognize anywhere. "John, this is Jay Jennings. How are you, buddy?"

"Jennings! Merry Christmas! I'm fine, how are you, man?"

"Okay, look, I need to know something. What's happening with Mike Dubcek and his wife?" Briefly he explained his reasons for asking. Jennings felt a cold panic in the pit of his guts when Silvers expelled a prolonged sigh.

"You haven't heard? Where in the hell have you been for the last two years, Jay?"

"Out of the country. I was working on a security

project in the Mideast and took J.J. with me. We just flew into California a few days ago."

"California! Where are you?"

"Glendale."

"Glendale! That's a hop and a skip away. We have to get together, Jay. Come over now if you want."

"Maybe I will a little later. Is Mike alive?" he asked, unable to ask if he were dead.

"No, he died two years ago. Funny you should ask now. He died on Christmas Eve."

Jennings slammed his fist onto the coffee table. "Oh, my God, no. That poor woman. I should have called you first before I phoned her. I hadn't heard anything about Mike since I talked to you three years ago."

"You had no way of knowing, man. Don't feel bad," Silvers consoled.

"What happened?"

"He committed suicide."

"Oh, no. Not Mike. What happened? When I saw you in Paris, you said the computer firm you and he were with was doing quite well. Mike was a partner in the firm, wasn't he?"

"Yes, he was. A lot of us, the guys from the company, were in on DataBank. We were at the top of the field for a while, and now we're just getting back on our feet. We nearly went belly up two years ago," he explained.

"Two years ago?" Jennings asked in a terse tone. "When Mike killed himself?"

"That's right."

"Are you saying he may have done it because the business was failing? That doesn't sound like the man I knew."

"Apparently he wasn't the man any of us thought we knew, Jay."

Jennings had the definite impression Silvers was holding back something. "Stop stalling, John, and tell me what happened, or what you think happened, will you?"

"You'll have to come over. Some of this is confidential, and I have a lot of people from the computer industry in my house right now. I wouldn't want anyone to either overhear me or pick up the extension phone. Are you familiar with the L.A. area?"

"Some. Tell me the best way to get there," he asked.

"Can you find the Golden State Freeway?"

"Yeah."

"Go northbound until you hit the Olive Avenue turnoff. You can't miss it. It'll take you right into Burbank. You'd better write the rest down, my place is hard to find after that. Got a pencil?" Silvers gave his friend more explicit instructions when he returned to the phone.

"I'll be there as soon as I can. I hope this isn't too much of an intrusion on your family and yourself, John. I realize its Christmas Eve, but I'm not going to be able to sleep at all until I know more about Dubcek," he offered by way of apology.

"It's all right, Jay. We're having a party here tonight anyway. I certainly would have invited you had I known you were in town. What are you doing here?"

"I'll tell you later," he said, anxious to be on his way.

"Good enough. How's your son? Do you think you would be able to pull him away from a computer terminal long enough to get him over here?" he asked affectionately.

Jennings chuckled. "I'll do my best. See you soon, buddy." He went into the kitchen and asked his son if he wanted to drive to Burbank with him.

J.J. saw the way his father's hands were shaking and offered to drive the car.

Jennings handed him the keys as they got into the car. "Remember the way there, son. I have a very strong premonition you're going to be driving me home, too."

"Are you and Long John going to get drunk?"

"There's a high probability of that, J.J."

"Then maybe you had better take the sandwich and eat it in the car."

"I'm not hungry anymore. Let's go, and be sure to remember not to call Dr. Silvers, Long John. He only allows the guys who served under him in Nam to do that." He reached out and clasped the boy's right shoulder. "Just remember to call him Dr. Silvers unless he gives you permission to do otherwise."

"Yes, sir. What did he get his degree in? Physics, wasn't it?"

"No, electrical engineering. Where's that map of Los Angeles? We'd better bring it in case we get lost. I've never seen so damn many freeways in my life." He passed the directions to his friend's Burbank home on to J.J.

"Yeah, me neither. It's neat. I'm glad we decided to settle down here, Dad. Wanna go to Universal Studios with me sometime next week and see the tour they advertised on TV last night?" J.J. glanced at his father as they headed for the freeway and wondered why he was bothering to say anything at all. His father seemed a million miles away. Obviously the news about his friend hadn't been good, and he assumed Dubcek had died in the three years since John Silvers visited them in Paris and spoke with enthusiasm about the new software company the two men had started up in downtown Los Angeles.

"What did you say, J.J.?" Jennings still couldn't believe it. Mike Dubcek was gone. Mike would have been thirty-seven now, the same age he was. They had talked a lot about death and dying seventeen years ago, but never would he have thought Dubcek would go by his own hand. It didn't make any sense. Jennings had seen many senseless things in his life, and outside of the pathos of war this topped them all. Mike Dubcek had been one of the most vital, forceful individuals he had ever known, hopelessly unfaithful to his wife back then, but undyingly loyal to his comrades, a man who would have jumped on a grenade thrown into the midst of their camp without a second thought if he could save someone. In short, Dubcek was the most courageous man he had ever met, and Jennings couldn't understand why he had taken the coward's exit from life, how he could have done that to his wife and family, how he could have done it to all of them.

J.J. looked at his father and saw it would be futile to repeat his request. His father's hazel eyes glistened with unusual brightness in the dimly lit vehicle, and J.J.'s throat went dry when he realized those were tears. He had never seen his father cry before, not even when his favorite aunt died. "Are you okay, Dad?"

"What makes you think I wouldn't be?" Jennings said gruffly, turning his face toward the window and folding his arms across his chest.

"Nothing. You're just awfully quiet. That's all."

"I'm thinking about something. Where did you say you wanted to go next week?"

"Universal Studios. Here's the turnoff we want."

"I'll go with you." He lapsed into silence again, speaking only to navigate the car up into the wooded region of Burbank into foothills of the Verdugo Mountains.

"Hell, where am I going to park?" J.J. asked when he saw all the cars surrounding the large bungalow-style home.

"How about over there?" his father suggested.

"Where?"

"Next to the Mercedes, and whatever you do, don't hit it. That's a vintage model. It must be worth a fortune."

"God, she's beautiful!" He eased their diesel Rabbit into the slot between the Mercedes and a Porsche. "Old Long John must have some rich friends," he commented on the way into the house.

"I beg your pardon?" Jennings said sharply.

"Sorry. It would appear as though several wealthy individuals frequent the unhumble abode of the distinguished Dr. John Silvers."

"Don't be smart, J.J."

They were met on a porch ablaze with red lights by the owner of the house. Silvers took Jennings into his arms. "Jay, it's good to see you! I can't believe it's been three years!"

"I can," he said glumly. "A lot of things have happened."

"Yeah, Jay, I know. Come inside and have a drink." He extended his hand to the young man. "And how's the only thing worth keeping we brought back from Vietnam?"

"Fine, thank you, sir." The hand that clasped his own was so powerful J.J. nearly winced. "And how are you and Mrs. Silvers?"

"Very well, thanks, son. Why don't you go inside and say hello. Tell Rebecca I'll be in the computer room with your father."

"Yes, sir. Dr. Silvers, I read your article on the Goldberg system in *Byte* magazine last month. You wouldn't happen to have one of those computers around the house, would you?"

John laughed. "As a matter of fact, I do. It's set up in a small alcove off of the laundry room. You wouldn't be interested in playing with it by any chance now, would you?"

"Yes, sir. I would."

"Need any help getting started?"

"No, sir."

"She's all yours, then. Help yourself," he said graciously while the boy's father stared impatiently on.

"Thank you, sir."

The doorbell rang and Jennings propelled Silvers away from it when he pivoted. "Let someone else get it. We have to talk about Dubcek."

"Bad news can wait, Jay."

"I've waited long enough. Where's your computer room?"

"Over here. That's a nice boy you have there, Jay. What is he now? About sixteen?"

"He just turned seventeen."

"Goodness, it's hard to believe it's been that long since we were there, huh?" Silvers unlocked the door to the room and then relocked it on the opposite side. There was a bottle of brandy on the table next to the printer. He poured a glass for Jennings and directed him to sit down at the chair near his desk.

"Do you always keep this place locked up?" Jennings inquired.

"I do when I have a houseful of drunken computer freaks. How are you, J.J.?"

No one had called him that for a long time. The name seemed to belong to his son now. "I'm still in a daze over Dubcek, Long John. I just can't believe it, and I feel like a total fool making Vee cry like that on the phone," he confided without a moment's hesitancy. He hadn't seen his friend for three years, but the rapport had been reestablished the second Silvers answered the phone.

Silvers smiled. "You always did have a thing for Dubcek's old lady, didn't you?"

"Oh, hell," he denied. "Of course not. I never even met the woman. Every time I saw Mike over the years it was away from California and she was at home with the three boys. You're crazy, John."

"Bull. You took that picture of her in bed off the locker so no one could see it except yourself."

"It wasn't me," he said, disowning the deed. "I always figured that sex-starved marine who used to come around did it."

His former sergeant let out with a hearty laugh. "The hell you did, J.J. I was standing three feet behind you when you took it down."

"I don't believe that. You would have said something, Long John."

"No, I figured why not let a frustrated boy get his jollies. She was pretty, wasn't she?"

Jennings didn't bother denying the theft again. He downed the brandy and poured another one. "Tell me everything you know about Dubcek's death."

"All right," he said somberly. "How much do you know about the company?"

"Basically what you told me three years ago, and I've read a little about it since. You guys designed software for security systems, right? You came up with the Safe-Loc system some of the automatic bank tellers use, didn't you?"

"Yes, that's right. J.J., Dubcek took programs that cost the company several million dollars and nearly a year to develop and sold them to a British operation.

We found out about it when they began to market pirated disks just weeks before ours were to go on the market. We were going to ask nine hundred dollars for each program, and the outfit in the UK was selling them for fifty bucks apiece. There was no way we could compete. We confronted Dubcek with the facts, once we were certain he had done it, and the next day they found him dead in one of the lavatories at the plant." He spoke slowly, knowing full well how J.J. would take the news.

Of all his men, Dubcek and Jennings were the closest, the same age, from the same background, both halfway in love with Vee though one man was married to her and the other had yet to meet her, and both sleeping with the same village girl as though they were twin brothers and she were the family sports car. It didn't matter who drove her, as long as the other guy didn't have to go any place. And like brothers, they had their differences of opinion. More than once Silvers had been forced to intercede between the two when the nights were long and tempers high, and like true brothers, neither man held a grudge the following day.

Jennings was momentarily silent, and then he exploded like a tank of gasoline with a bullet inside, violent and incinerating until nothing was left. "Silvers, you're a cold son of a bitch!" The glass he had held in his hand hit the opposite wall.

John Silvers didn't move a muscle. He'd anticipated the action and knew it wasn't as entirely spontaneous as it seemed. J.J.'s aim was meticulous. Had he tossed the glass any place else, highly expensive computer equipment would have been rendered useless. "Why do you say that, Jay?" he asked quietly, all too aware of the answer. "Feel free to throw my glass if it'll make you feel better," he offered, holding it out to him.

Jennings accepted, opting instead to down the contents. He stood briefly and then whirled toward Silver with murder in his eyes. "Because you of all people should know Mike would never do what you're accusing him of. Hell, if it weren't for him, you'd be sitting there with a lot more than a leg missing. He risked his life to rescue you after you got hit, and you know it."

Silvers stood and placed his hand on the other man's shoulder, only to drop it when Jennings jerked away. "Son, I hear what you're saying, and I know what you're going through. Believe me, I went through the same thing."

"Don't son me, Silvers, this isn't Nam and you're not my superior officer." Jennings slammed his glass onto the desk. "I just don't believe it! There's no way I will. Dubcek's worse fault was being an incurable skirt chaser. He'd never sell any company out, much less one that employed so many veterans, and one you owned part of. Dubcek wouldn't do it," he insisted.

Silvers returned to his chair with a little limp that was discernible only to someone who knew it was there. "Jay, I pretty much expected your reaction. As a matter of fact, I would have been disappointed in your loyalty to your friend had it been otherwise. Look, I've pulled all the tapes pertaining to the theft of our data. You can mount them on the UNIX system over there," he said, pointing his finger to the left corner of the room, "and there's nothing I'd like more on this earth right now than for you to come up with something to exonerate Dubcek, because God only knows how we tried, and always came up with the same answer. Finding out Dubcek never did it would be the best Christmas present I could ever have, the best a lot of us could have, especially Vee."

Jennings's head jerked up. "Vee knows what Mike was accused of?"

"I'm afraid so. We tried to cover it up, but she's a smart lady and figured everything out within a few days."

"And what about the kids and the public?"

"No, we kept it away from them." Silvers stood. "I'm going to join my other guests now, Jay. Call for me if you have any questions. Right now I think the best thing for you to do is to review the data and convince yourself of...of the facts," he concluded hesitantly. "There's a lot of it—I doubt that you'll be able to get much out of it tonight."

"We'll see. Just how confidential is this stuff, John?"

"In terms of revealing data, not at all. The British have had it on the market for two years. We're keeping how the data was stolen confidential to protect the family."

"Good, I'm glad the company saw fit to do that. I assume this is a multiuser system?" he asked, glancing at the elaborate display of technology around him.

"Sure. What are you getting at? Do you want me to stay and help? I really can't, J.J. My wife is always down on me for spending too much time in here. I can't leave her alone at our own party, especially on Christmas Eve," he said with an apologetic grin.

"No, Sarge." The old name slipped out. "My boy knows his way around this system almost as well as I do. Mind if I have him check out the coding system? I assume you encoded any data transmitted over the wires?"

"Can he be trusted to keep his mouth shut, J.J.? Mike left three young boys who know nothing about this."

"Yes, he can be trusted. Mind fetching him for me?"

"Not at all, and the encoding system is detailed on one of the tapes I set aside," he said, rising to leave the efficiently designed room with computers lining all four walls and a central work area for printers and his desk.

"Thanks. Hold on for a minute, John," Jennings said when he was at the door. "We have to do something about the woman. She shouldn't be alone, not on Christmas Eve, not after what I said to her. Where did you say her family was?"

Silvers returned to his seat. On certain days his leg bothered him, and it was a safe bet his friend would have more than one question on the subject of Vee Dubcek. He rubbed his leg. "The kids went to Nevada to stay with her folks."

"Why didn't she go?" Jennings tried to downplay his interest in the woman by fiddling with a stack of floppy disks while he listened to Silvers.

"She wanted to catch up on her studies, Jay. She's taking some kind of correspondence law school course and working almost full-time as a secretary at Cal Tech. I think she told Rebecca she's preparing for exams right now," he said, still massaging his leg about the knee.

"That thing still bother you, Long John?" he asked sympathetically.

"Occasionally. It's not bad."

"Hum." He turned on the power source to the terminal. "What in the hell is correspondence law school? I've never heard of any such thing. Is it one of these places where you buy a degree?"

"No, not at all. Right now California is the only state in the union to permit individuals who haven't attended an accredited law school to take the bar exams. I think one can start the courses with just a few years of college credits, and they let anyone in. Vee didn't want to commute every day to a regular campus, and had to keep her job."

"There wasn't much money left?"

"No. Like I said, the company nearly went bankrupt after the software came out in the UK."

"There wasn't anything you could do to collect for damages?"

"No, that's difficult enough to do here, much less there, J.J. The British Parliament might as well subsidize the pirates." Silvers could tell Jennings was more anxious to discuss their friend's widow than the problem of theft in the computer industry.

Jennings mounted the disk. "Vee's still a secretary? Remember, she used to do that when we were in Nam," he said when John Silvers nodded. "Did she work all these years?"

"No, Mike was doing pretty good for a while. She quit working right before the first baby was born and didn't return until two years ago."

"It sounds like she hasn't had an easy time of it," he commented. "John, I'd like to call her to offer my condolences and apologize, but I feel rather awkward about doing it right away."

"So wait a few days," he advised.

"I don't like the idea of her staying home alone on Christmas Eve under the circumstances, Long John. She's obviously not going to get any studying done, not after what I went and did. Do you know Vee well enough to give her a call and invite her over to this party?" he asked hopefully.

"Vee Dubcek is one tough lady, J.J. If she wants to stay home, it's what she'll do. We did invite her to the party and she declined. Here, let me give you a hand scanning through that file. I know right where you would want to begin." He left the desk and sat down at one of the terminals.

"Can't you call her again? You should have heard the way she cried, John," he repeated.

Silvers smiled, watching the index of data flit down the green tinted screen. "You don't give up, do you, J.J.?"

"Not easily. Call her, please."

"To tell you the truth, I don't really know her that well. Mike was pretty much a workaholic, and we rarely socialized outside of the job. I wouldn't feel comfortable phoning her, but Rebecca knows Vee a lot better than I do. I'll ask her to give Vee a call."

Jennings tried to hide his pleasure. "Good. If Rebecca is the woman I remember, she can charm the birds out of a tree. Thanks, Long John."

"Or an attractive widow right into the arms of a waiting spider," he laughed. "There you go," he said when the data appeared on the screen. "I'll get the boy and talk to my wife."

Jennings glanced over the comprehensive index. "This is going to take a while. You don't suppose..." he began.

Silvers cut him off. "The guest room is already set up. Stay as long as you like. Hey, that reminds me, we never did discuss what brought you to L.A."

"I've resigned my job with DOD."

"Really? I thought you and the Department of Defense were mated for life," Silvers commented with a baffled expression.

"I couldn't take the traveling anymore. J.J. was accepted by Cal Tech on an advanced placement program, and I decided to move here with him."

"Do you have any job prospects?"

"A few, but we'll talk about them later. I have to get into this. And don't forget about calling Vee," he reminded Silvers as he left the room.

John Silvers paused with one hand on the knob. "Man, I don't think you'll let me do that. It will be interesting to see which project absorbs more of your time, J.J. Exonerating your best friend or getting his widow into your bed."

Chapter Two

In the hour or so it took Jay Jennings to get from Glendale to Burbank and have time to talk to John Silvers, Veronica Dubcek had rebounded from her depressed state and was getting ready to attend a party given by another secretary where she worked. Part of the turnabout in her emotional state was due to the man who had sent her plummeting into a tailspin with his request to speak to Mike. It had been months since she'd allowed herself the indulgence of a good cry, and when it was all over, Veronica found herself mortified by what she had done to the poor man, bursting into tears in his ear, and then slamming down the receiver.

As she had continued to weep, the identity of the caller came back to her, and she remembered Jay Jennings to be one of Mike's old army buddies, one of a close-knit group of five. Veronica had met all of them over the years except Jennings, who seemed to be constantly on the move from country to country, involved in some kind of government security work. She knew of his son and admired him for his devotion to the boy, probably a young man by now. Sometimes the years passed so quickly she didn't know what happened to them, and there were other times when they crept by, interminably long. The last two had been the slowest of all.

Veronica counted out the boy's age on her fingers as she pulled up her panty hose. She knew J.J. had brought the boy home the same year he and Mike were discharged, so that would put the boy at sixteen or seventeen. As far as she knew, Jennings had married when the boy was five or six, and according to Mike, who had touched bases with the family a few times over the years, Jennings's wife had adopted the boy and was as devoted to him as was the father. Veronica frowned to herself as she brushed out her hair in front of the bathroom mirror, thinking the Jennings family would be certain to conclude before very long that she was an hysterical fool for reacting as she had after Mike was gone two years. Somehow, she would have to track them down if they didn't call back, and explain.

Veronica was standing in front of her closet debating whether to wear a red silk dress or a blue jump suit when the phone rang. As awkward as it was sure to be, she halfway hoped it was Jennings calling back with the thought he may have had the wrong number at first.

"Vee? Hi, this is Becky Silvers. Merry Christmas and Happy New Year, and so forth and so on. How are you, honey?" she asked.

Veronica and Becky weren't the closest of friends. They rarely saw each other more than a few times a year, but each was fond of the other, and Becky had been very supportive two years ago after Mike's death. "I'm fine, Becky," she dissembled. It wasn't her way to complain when she was down, and she did feel much better now than an hour ago. "And Merry Christmas to you. Wish your family a happy holiday season from me, will you?"

"Vee, better yet, why don't you come over here and

do it yourself? The party is in full swing, and the caterers are just starting to set up the dinner buffet. We cleared away the pool table in the game room for dancing, and my son and some kids he jams with are going to play. I know you'd have fun," she said.

Veronica was pretty good at putting two and two together and coming up with four. As much as she and Becky liked one another, it wasn't highly probable she would call to invite her to the same party twice. Since John Silvers had served in the same unit as Jay Jennings and her husband, it was a safe bet Jennings had phoned Silvers when she hung up on him. "Becky, have you been in touch with Jay Jennings?" she asked quietly.

"Yep, you've got it, kid. He's here right now," she admitted.

"Did he ask you to call me?" she wanted to know.

"No, John did, but I highly suspect Jay put him up to it. You know John, his mind is always in that computer room of his. It's not like him to go out of his way to invite someone to a party, especially one already in progress. What happened, Vee?" she said.

Veronica was surprised Becky didn't have more details. "He didn't tell you anything?"

"Uh-unh. You know how closemouthed John is when it comes to talking about his old army buddies. All I know is that John told me Jay and his son were coming over. I didn't even get a chance to see Jay. John met him on the porch and hustled him off to the computer room. A while after that my husband came out and suggested I give you a call. What happened, Vee?"

"Basically I was feeling down for a while and Jay called and asked to speak to Mike. No one's done that for a long time, and I really overreacted," she confessed. "I feel like a complete fool."

"Oh, don't, you poor baby! I can imagine how something like that would shake you up," she consoled, tactfully refraining from asking Veronica exactly what she said or did. "I don't think John and Jay have been in touch for three years, Vee. He probably knew nothing about it," she said by way of purveying the obvious.

"I know. It just shook me up. Becky, I think I'd better apologize to Jay. May I speak to him, please?"

"Certainly, and Vee, I meant it about you coming over to the party. Your studies can wait for a few days. It is Christmas Eve, you know, and you shouldn't be by yourself."

"Becky, thank you for your concern. I really appreciate it. To tell you the truth, I was just getting ready to go to a party one of the girls from work is giving," she informed her, touched by Rebecca's thoughtfulness and relieved to have an opportunity to apologize to Jay.

"Come to our party instead, or go to both of them, then, Vee."

"Maybe I'll do that."

"Please do, honey. Hang on, I'll get Jay for you." Rebecca left the phone and ran into her husband on the way to the computer room. "Where are you going, John?"

"To tell Jay about something. Did you call Vee, sweetheart?"

"Yes, she's on the phone right now and wants to talk to Jay," she told him. "John Silvers, I warn you, if you get tied up with those damn machines of yours and leave our guests on the only big party we give each year, you can move a cot in there and spend the rest of the year next to your beloved computers, got it?"

He took her into his arms and kissed the side of her face. "Don't worry, Becky, I'll only be a minute. I'll tell Jay that Vee is on the line, and get right back to you. How did she sound, by the way?"

"Very good. She said she was getting dressed to go to another party but might come here," Rebecca replied, walking away to return to her guests. "John, it's almost time for dinner. Be sure you and Jay are there," she called over her shoulder.

"Okay." He unlocked the door. Jennings was hard at work in front of one of the terminals, reviewing the encryption method that was used to transmit data over the telephone wires. "You have a phone call, Jay."

"Not now, I'm busy. Tell who ever it is I'm not here or something, will you, John?" he asked without looking away from the screen.

"It's Vee Dubcek." He watched Jennings's shoulders jerk up from their hunched position over the video display. "Still want me to tell the caller you're not here?"

"No, I'm on my way. Where's the phone?"

"Right in front of you. If it was a snake, J.J., it would have bit you," Silvers said with a broad grin. "Try to talk Vee into coming over. I always did like that lady." He excused himself and returned to his wife and the guests.

Jennings tried to think of an opener before picking up the receiver and couldn't. "Hello, Mrs. Dubcek?"

"Yes. Hi. Mr. Jennings, I'd like to apologize for what happened earlier in the evening. I . . . ah, I wasn't myself. I'm terribly embarrassed about the whole thing." There. Her heart was pounding and her palms started to sweat, but she'd said it.

"No, please. You have nothing to apologize for, Mrs. Dubcek. I was entirely at fault, and I would like you to accept my apologies. I would also like to offer my condolences about Mike. He was one of the best friends

I've ever had in my life. We were as close as brothers once. We more or less went our separate directions over the years, but a part of him has always stayed with me, and will continue to do so." His voice was tight with emotion and Jennings knew he couldn't go on. "I'm so sorry, Mrs. Dubcek," he managed after a pause.

She heard his grief and her sympathy went out to this stranger whom her husband had loved so much. "Thank you, Mr. Jennings. Thank you very much."

He wanted to tell her they were all wrong about Mike Dubcek, that he never would have sold out anyone, much less a company that employed so many vets and was partially owned by John Silvers, but Jennings couldn't say it. Somehow telling her now seemed inappropriate at best and insincere at worst. "Call me Jay, please. How are the children?"

"Fine. They went to Nevada to visit my parents. How are your wife and son doing?"

"My son is doing quite well. He's here with me now. My wife and I were divorced a few years back. As far as I know, she's doing well. I haven't talked to her for several months."

"Oh! I'm sorry to hear that!"

"I'm not. I haven't enjoyed talking to that woman for a long time," he remarked in his slow Texas drawl. "Mrs. Dubcek, we've never met. All of your Care packages made some of the most unbearable days of my life just a little more tolerable, and that little bit more was a lot then. I'd love to finally meet you face to face. Why don't you come over here? I would be delighted to pick you up if you'd like, Mrs. Dubcek."

"Vee."

The way she said her name quickened his pulse. "Vee. I understand you were on your way to another party. What can I do to persuade you to come to this one?"

There hadn't been anyone since Mike. Veronica had woven a coat of many emotions—grief, guilt, anger, fear of loving and losing again—and never removed it. The demands of her three jobs, one as a law student, one as a secretary, and the most important as single parent were enough to keep the coat from becoming too heavy to bear, and she didn't feel the absence of a man in her life. "I don't know," she said slowly. "I really don't get out much."

"I thought you just said you were on your way out, Vee," he replied, knowing what she was driving at. Vee was telling him she wasn't ready to date yet, and he sought a means of reassuring her she was safe with him. "I won't have much time for socializing myself tonight. I expect to be tied up in John's computer room most of the evening, but maybe we could get together long enough to say hello. I'd like you to meet my son."

"I would love to meet him. His name is Jay, isn't it?"

"Yeah, that was a bit of egocentrism on my part I couldn't resist. We call him J.J."

Vee unfolded her indecision and examined it. Jay Jennings very obviously wasn't asking her for a date. He came to her as a dear friend of her late husband's, one who had probably never given her a passing thought beyond a kind appreciation for all the food she sent to Vietnam. She had always wanted to meet him and the boy, but her duties at home with the children prevented her from traveling much with Mike. "I'll be there in about half an hour, Jay. I look forward to meeting you and your son. I'd like to have both of you out to dinner when my children return, if you're still in town."

"We will be. We're settling down, for a while at least. My son's enrolling at Cal Tech in January."

"Cal Tech! I work there! Maybe I'll see him around." They spoke a few minutes longer until Veronica excused herself to finish dressing.

"Are you sure I can't offer you a ride?" he repeated.

"No, I might decide to leave soon and go to the other party."

"I understand. Drive carefully." He hung up and returned to the terminal. By now Jennings had realized the software theft problem was far too complex to even begin to analyze in a single evening. Old Long John had undoubtedly gathered the data and suggested he tackle it more as a cooling-down exercise than anything else. It worked. Just thirty minutes of pounding on the keyboard and watching information race down the screen had assuaged his anger with John and the rest of them for accusing Mike of something that may have contributed to his death. Jennings knew them all to be reasonable men. Either his friend had changed far more than he knew, or someone smarter than all of them had framed him. Perhaps Mike had even let a key piece of data slip out accidentally one night, and it was all some computer whiz needed to decipher the encoded telephone transmissions. Jennings was well aware that after Nam Dubcek pursued drinking and bragging about his professional accomplishments with the same zeal he had used to chase local women in the war. That was a dangerous combination in a highly competitive industry where research became outdated overnight, and carefully guarded trade secrets were only as good as sealed lips that were all too apt to come unglued.

Jennings logged off and went to find his son. He had excused the boy from helping him after a more careful look at the data, and J.J. had returned to the other computer. He was sitting at the terminal playing a sophisticated game of chess when his father walked into the alcove. "Hi, son. How is this thing?"

"Wow! Check it out, Dad! Do you think Dr. Silvers would let me copy these programs?"

"I think John has a very dim view of software piracy, J.J. His company nearly went out of business because some outfit in the UK got a hold of their work and mass-produced the tapes. I don't want you doing it anyway. If you want the program, save your money and buy a legal copy, all right?"

His father spoke in a tone that wasn't to be argued with. "Yes, sir. Maybe I will buy this one."

"J.J., have you been in here since we arrived?" he asked.

"Yeah, I have."

"I really think you should go and join the other guests. There's someone in particular I want you to meet."

"Who?"

"Mrs. Dubcek. She'll be here soon. I just talked to her on the phone. Log off now, will you?"

"Okay. Dad," he began cautiously, debating about asking the question and rapidly ascertaining that his father's spirits were considerably elevated from the time they had left home. "What did you find out about your friend from Nam?" Jennings frowned and the boy wished he hadn't brought up the subject. Not that his father seemed angry because of it, but because he looked so sad. J.J. had a far greater tolerance for his father's disapproval and occasional bursts of anger than for his sorrow.

Jennings placed his hand on his son's shoulder as they exited the room. "He died a few years back. On Christmas Eve in fact," he said somberly.

"Geez, that's grim. The poor lady. It's too bad that he had to die during the holiday season, huh?"

"Yes, but people seldom consciously choose the time of their deaths." Jennings shook his head and released a long sigh of frustration. "Son, I feel like such a fool for calling up his wife and asking to speak to him."

"Oh, Dad, it wasn't your fault. What were you supposed to do? Call up Dr. Silvers and ask if Dubcek kicked the bucket since you last heard of him? We were out of the country for a long time, you know."

"You didn't phrase things in the best possible manner, J.J., but basically I guess you're right," he conceded. "Still, I wish it could have been avoided."

J.J. basked in the warm glow of his father's approval before saying anything else. "I know you do, but I'm sure the lady understands. Is she the one you said was real pretty and used to send food to all the guys in your unit?"

"Yeah, but not to the whole unit, just the guys who were closest together, and I never saw her in person, but from her photographs she was the prettiest girl I ever saw in my life. I sure as hell used to wish I was going home to her instead of Dubcek," he confided to the boy.

"Did you ever have fantasies about her?"

Jennings laughed. "I'm not telling. Why, do you ever have fantasies about girls?"

"I'm not telling if you don't tell. Well, I bet you won't be having any more fantasies about her, Dad. She'd be pretty old by now. She's probably fat and ugly. She must be what? Thirty-five or forty?"

J.J. shook his head and chuckled. "You make it sound like a hundred and five. Vee's a few years younger than I am. Do you think of me as over the hill?"

"Naw, it's different with men."

"You have a lot to learn, J.J. Remember, they say that beauty is in the mind, and Vee could never be ugly in my book," he said. "Come on, now, I want you to mingle a little. You spend too damn much time with those computers. You can't marry one, you know."

"That would be a whole hell of a lot better than what you married, Dad. At least the computer's faithful to me." He said it without thinking and regretted the words in the split second before the sound waves hit his father's eardrums.

"What did you say?" Jennings demanded sharply.

"Nothing," the boy said meekly.

"You're damn right it was nothing." Jennings relented when he saw the look in his son's eyes. "Look, J.J., I have a lot of things on my mind right now, and I can't talk to you the way I want to or should. I just found out my best friend from a long time ago is dead, and it really got to me. Be patient with me for a while, and we'll talk soon, okay, son?" he asked gently.

"Yeah, all right," J.J. agreed, wondering in his heart what bothered his father the most, the fact that Dubcek was dead or the way he died. Though his father had yet to allude to how the man died, some intuition that was seldom wrong dictated to him the means were either dishonorable or mysterious, perhaps both judging from his father's reaction. J.J. couldn't say just how his father tipped the cards, but he would bet the best piece of electronics he owned on the fact something was going on beyond the ken of his father's conversation about Dubcek's death. As certainly as he knew that, he also knew it was time to keep his mouth shut and that his dad definitely seemed to have some kind of hang-up on his friend's wife. His father rarely had anything pleasant to say about Vietnam over the years, but whenever he did it had something to do with Mrs. Dubcek.

"Good boy," Jennings said. "Be real nice to Mrs. Dubcek, and don't mention her husband, okay?" he asked, adding "What's the matter?" when J.J. groaned. "And don't say 'nothing'."

"It's the way you speak to me like I'm an insensitive five-year-old sometimes. What kind of a fool do you take me for? Do you actually think I'm going to run up to this lady whose husband died and ask about him when I don't know anything about her or the circumstances of his death? Really, Dad. Gimme a break."

"I'm sorry, J.J."

"Apology accepted," J.J. replied in the deepest voice he could muster.

"Yes, sir!" Jennings quipped, nearly running into Silvers's wife as they rejoined the group. "Rebecca, it's been a long time," he said, kissing both her cheeks with respectful pecks.

"Too long, Jay. How are you?" she asked. "I've heard you've finally decided to join the human race and settle down for once."

"Yes, I figure it's about time, Becky. Every time they sent me out on location for the last five years it was in the Mideast, and you know what it's like there."

"Not too pleasant from what I hear, Jay," she said, looking around for her fourteen-year-old daughter, who had been gone too long for her comfort with a young teenage boy.

"And that's an understatement, Rebecca. How's the medical practice going? Are you still in pediatrics?" Jennings asked, anxiously glancing from the elegant black woman to the almost as elegant French Provincial clock on the fireplace mantel.

Rebecca laughed and ran a nervous hand over her short curly waves. She didn't know Jay Jennings well, but she knew him well enough to know he was tense as hell, and it wasn't very difficult for her to imagine how bad she would feel if she had done what he had so inadvertently done to Vee. "Of course I'm still in pediatrics, Jay. Physicians don't just switch from a specialty. Some do, I know, but not me. Only nowadays we call it pediatrics and adolescent medicine. So many of our thirteen-year-olds think they're too sophisticated to sit around an office with pink kangaroos on the walls and coloring books on the tables."

Jennings smiled and looked at his son. "Tell me, Rebecca, do you take on seventeen-year-olds?"

"Certainly."

"Good. My son doesn't have a local pediatrician," he said with a wink.

J.J. was too dignified to do anything more than cast his father a disparaging glance. "If you'll excuse me, I think I'll check out the food now, Dr. Silvers."

"Be my guest, J.J.," she replied graciously. "That was a low blow, Jay."

"It was only father–son talk and my boy understands. I couldn't resist the opportunity to needle him a little, Rebecca." His eyes strayed again to the clock. If she came when she said she would, she should be there any minute.

Rebecca Silvers linked her arm through Jennings's and escorted him into the dining room, where a buffet Christmas Eve dinner of turkey, ham, and various side dishes had been set up by the caterers. They joined the line of guests who had formed near the table. "Jay," she said, "I'm terribly sorry you learned about Mike so late and in such an unfortunate way. It came as quite a shock to all of us at the time."

"I still can't get over it, Becky. How have his wife and children been coping? You know, I've never met Vee or the youngest boy." Jennings noticed a few strands of silvery tinsel in her graying black hair and smiled. He removed one and held it up for her inspection. "Is this part of some avant garde style?"

She laughed. "No. That must have happened when we were decorating the branches over the mantel. Jay," she began in a more serious tone. "Vee and the three boys are doing as well as anyone could be expected to under the circumstances. Christmas is a bad time for her. Everyone who knows her tried to persuade her from staying home alone tonight, but she's managed to delude herself into thinking the holidays are just plain old days to catch up on her studying. I'm so glad she finally agreed to come over."

He accepted a generous portion of turkey and stuffing from the caterer. "So am I. Maybe I can do something to atone for what I said to her earlier."

"That wasn't your fault, Jay. She was pretty down before you called and has snapped back already."

Jennings nodded and looked around for his son. "Becky, have you seen J.J.?"

"Yes, he was ahead of us in line and just left the room. My guess is he's going back to play with the computers. Is he always like that?"

"Always." J.J. returned to the room to get butter for his dinner roll, and Jennings motioned him to his side. "Where were you going?" he asked.

"Back to the small computer room, Dad. Old Long—I mean Dr. Silvers—said it was okay."

"I realize that, J.J., but it's not generally considered socially acceptable to hole yourself up at a party. There's a lot of young people here. Why don't you get to know some of them? Maybe you can find out a little about the L.A. area," he suggested. Rebecca saw some of her colleagues from the hospital enter the room and excused herself to greet them. "Catch you later, Becky, and thanks again for inviting us to your party. It's lovely.''

"I'd be happier with the computers, Dad, really," J.J. said after bidding good-bye to Rebecca. "This is the first opportunity I've had to get my hands on a Goldberg system.''

"I know, J.J. But there'll be other days to come here, and if you're a good and obedient boy, Santa Claus might bring you something like that computer for Christmas," he said with a wink.

"Dad! Really? You're kidding! Wow, that'd be great!" J.J. was about to pressure his father for more details about the computer system he'd purchased when a very strange look passed over Jennings's face. The caterer had to ask him three times what type of salad he preferred as his father stood there staring toward the door as though a ghost from his past had just entered the room. "He'll take the green salad with French dressing," J.J. said to the impatient young man. "Dad, step aside, other people are in line." He ushered his father away from the table and followed the line of his vision.

Jennings was staring at Veronica Dubcek, and she at him, each having recognized the other from old photographs they had seen. Her hair was redder and curlier than before, and fell to her shoulders in chestnut layered waves that he suspected were the results of ammonia solutions and tints, and she was heavier now, maybe fifteen or twenty pounds overweight, her breasts and hips much fuller than in the old photos. She had on some kind of scoop-neck dress, and his eyes strayed to the rise of her bust. She was lightly freckled there, and the spots were as tantalizing as the little ones on her nose.

"She's not bad for an older woman, Dad," J.J. commented, munching on his drumstick. "Nice cleavage.

That's the one thing I like about fat ladies. They always bulge out of their dresses in the right places."

"J.J., if you don't stop looking at her like that, my foot—"

"The way *I'm* looking at her? I merely stated a piece of empirical data, Dad. From the way you're looking at her, I'd say it's a safe bet you'll be stopping by a motel tonight instead of coming home to Grandmother's house with me."

"No way. She's not the kind of lady I'd ever bring to a motel," he disagreed, his eyes still fixated on the woman standing near the door.

"What kind of lady is she?"

"The kind you court with red roses and a great deal of patience," he explained impatiently.

"You're going to ask her out and give her flowers?"

"No, I'm going to send her flowers and then ask her out."

"I'd never waste my money on flowers for a girl I don't even have a date with," J.J. scoffed. "What if she says no?"

"You have a lot to learn, J.J. Stay here."

The panic in Veronica's stomach rose like champagne bubbles flowing out of a glass as he approached her. She had finally settled on the red silk, though it showed a little too much cleavage for her personal comfort. She'd steadily put on a pound or two a month for the last few years, and was rapidly approaching the time to either diet or add to her expanding wardrobe once more. Jennings's intense stare from across the room had unnerved her to no small degree, and she credited it to his amazement in the way she had aged over the years. She forced a self-conscious smile to her lips when he stopped a few feet from her.

"Vee." He extended a warm hand and she clasped it.

"I'm Jay Jennings and I'd know you anywhere from your photos. Thank you for coming." He found himself drawn to her at once, as much now in the flesh as he'd been all those years in his dreams. Jennings wanted to take her into his arms and ride off into the night with her, get away from all these damn noisy party makers and just be alone with her until dawn, to absorb her anguish and share his own with her, but he knew it was a fanciful thought so he stood there awkwardly smiling down at her. He was several inches taller than she, and could see straight down the silk dress, and felt like an adolescent fool when his pulse quickened at the sight of the flesh-colored lacy slip she had on and a glimpse of her pale peach brassiere.

"I'm surprised anyone would ever recognize me from those photos. I don't even recognize myself when I look at them," she said with a little laugh. "I recognized you from yours, too." His hair was much longer now than in the old army pictures, and she found the thick dark brown waves that tumbled past his collar and over his ears infinitely more appealing than his GI crew cut of seventeen years back. Then the hair had been so closely cropped to the skull that one didn't really notice the richness of the sable shade. Now in the brightly lit room it reminded Vee of the color of highly polished walnut burl, with a variegated pattern of brown and deep chestnuts, the shades altering somewhat with the play of light across the sheen. She knew his eyebrows were thick, so much that they appeared grizzled in the old photos, but up close for the first time in person Veronica saw the wiry effect was due more to the way some of the hair was a blond shade while the underlying hair was darker. And she had never known his eyes were hazel, that unusual golden brown color, flecked with green, gray, and the pure blue of a spring iris. Yellow glimmered there with the other shades like golden sunlight filtering into a shaded forest glen.

Veronica returned his friendly handshake. A light-headed sensation besieged her senses as the impact of his presence made itself known to her fatigued brain. For the first time in two years she was attracted to a man, and what should have been a joyous thing struck her instead as an act of disloyalty to her deceased husband, for Mike had forbade Jay to her. The two men had been best friends once upon a time, and Mike had asked her repeatedly over the years not to get involved with any of his close friends should something happen to their marriage. Veronica had assumed she and Mike would be together forever and never paid any attention to his request until now.

Jennings looked into her eyes and saw the anxiety there. "Vee, are you all right?" He assumed she hadn't been to many parties lately, and all the merriment and confusion were too much for her. "This place seems to be overrun with teenagers. Why don't you get a plate of food and we'll go on the deck and eat? For the end of December it's a balmy night out there."

"Oh, no! I couldn't!" If she were unable to control her attraction to him in the midst of that loud crowd of happy people, what would happen were they to be alone on a mild winter evening, the black night resplendent with glowing heavenly bodies? Vee had noticed how clear the sky was on her drive over, how brightly the stars shone up there, and how the scent of winter blooms hung in the air. "I mean I have to talk to Becky and John a little, and say hello to the children."

"Of course you do," he said cordially, the vehemence of her refusal to eat alone with him still hammering in his ears. "But first I'd like you to meet someone. Come here."

"That's your son, isn't it?" she asked with a smile as he led her to the boy. "He's a fine-looking young man." The only resemblance between father and son seemed to be their height. Both were around six feet tall, give or take an inch. Vee wasn't surprised. Most Eurasian children she had met seemed to favor the Oriental side, and in J.J.'s case the mixed racial inheritance was a truly remarkable one. The boy was strikingly handsome with very dark almond-shaped eyes and equally dark hair, far darker than his father's, and similarly darker complected.

"I know," Jennings said proudly.

J.J. jumped to his feet as soon as he saw his father with the woman. "I'm pleased to meet you, ma'am," he said politely when they were introduced.

"I'm happy to meet you too, J.J., and please don't call me ma'am. It makes me feel older than I am."

"I'm sorry, Mrs. Dubcek," he apologized with a grin that reminded Veronica of the way her two oldest sons smiled, a restrained gesture that seemed to withhold more than what it offered.

"That's not much better! How about calling me Vee?"

"With your permission." J.J. struggled for something else to say and couldn't really think of anything. "Can I get you a drink, Vee?" he finally tried since it was one of the things he had heard his father say to a lady he'd just met.

She grinned at his awkwardness. "Yes, J.J. I'd love a glass of fruit punch. You've raised a fine young man," she told Jennings after he left. "I can't imagine one of my sons offering a woman a drink, under these circumstances at any rate."

"Well, it's been just me and him for most of the time. I have observed many of his mannerisms are a little different than the average kid, but overall I think I've done a good job with him."

"I'm sure that's an understatement, Jay. I understand you didn't marry until the boy was six or seven. Tell me, what does a GI barely twenty do with an infant son? He was just a baby when you brought him home, wasn't he?" she asked.

"Yes. The medics in our unit delivered him, and he was immediately handed over to me."

"I understand you more or less smuggled him out of the country."

"Yeah, there wasn't time to do it any other way. The nation was in a state of chaos and we were all pulling out. I gave him to some Red Cross workers who took him to Cambodia and then to Paris, where the American Embassy helped me get him a passport and bring him back to the States as a citizen."

"Where did you go from Paris?"

"Straight home to my mother! I lived with my parents while I went to college. That was outside Dallas."

Veronica giggled while she scanned the room for familiar faces. "Well, that must have made your parents happy. How many mothers send one son off to war and get two back?"

"Yeah, my mother was wonderful with him. My father too, after they accepted the fact that their own baby boy had lost his virginity," he said wryly.

J.J. returned with the punch. Veronica thanked him, and excused herself when she caught sight of Rebecca and John.

"Becky!" The two women embraced, kissing one another on the cheek. "And John. How are you?"

"Wonderful, Vee," John replied. "I see you've had a chance to meet our pair of wayfaring strangers over there."

"Yes, I have. They certainly seem to be a delightful pair, don't they?"

"They sure are, Vee. They're settling down here in Southern California, you know," Becky said. "Why don't you get some dinner, honey?"

"Thank you, but I had something before I came over and I'm trying to lose a few pounds," Veronica explained.

"Oh, don't worry about dieting during the holiday season!" Becky admonished with a laugh. "I never do!"

"That's because you don't have to, Becky. Where are the kids? I'd like to say hello to them."

"They're setting up the band in the game room, Vee." John took the glass from her hand and sniffed it. "This was the punch we made for the kids. Come here, I'll get you some finer brew."

"Thank you," Vee said when he returned in a few minutes with a glass of champagne punch. "I'm going to say hello to your kids now." Veronica sipped the drink slowly, all too aware of the effects of alcohol on a near-empty stomach. She found the three Silver children, Steve, nineteen, Grace, seventeen, and Paula, fourteen, in the adjoining room. The oldest was setting up a small PA system, and the girls were flirting with his friends who played in the four-man band. She spoke to them until it was time to begin, and couples of varying ages began to dance to the fast-beat rock music. Veronica sat down by herself on a chair abutting the wall.

Jennings wandered into the room half an hour later, after having decided he'd left Veronica alone long enough not to appear in active pursuit of her. His son had found a few kindred souls, a teenage boy and his sister, both computer freaks, and had obtained John

Silvers's permission to use the terminals in his main work room. Jay took in the loud sounds of the music and frowned. Whatever it was, it wasn't conducive to romance. He approached the band and stood to one side until he had Steve Silvers's attention. "Nice sound you have here, Steve."

"Thank you, Mr. Jennings. We have an audition next week at United Artists. They might use some music we wrote as the sound track for a new movie," he said, putting the bass guitar down and reaching for a glass of water.

"Congratulations, that's some coup. Does your group do any other kind of music?"

"Sure, you name it and we can do it."

"I want something slow and romantic, if you get my drift."

Steve laughed. "Who's the lucky lady?"

"You'll see. Look, wait until I have her on the floor and then start, okay?"

"Yeah, wilco." He returned to his band and gave them the instructions.

"Hello, there," he said to Veronica. "May I have the next dance?"

She smiled up at him. "I'll have to check and see if I have any slots left on my card."

"Please do so."

"All clear." She took his hand and rose. "But I have to warn you, I'm not much of a dancer."

"Neither am I. We'll just have to do what everyone else is doing, I suppose." When they were in the center of the floor, Jennings looked up and nodded at Steve. The raucous number suddenly became a slow one. Couples stopped and then wrapped their arms around each other. "Shall we?" Jennings asked. "It doesn't look very complicated."

Veronica had watched Jay as he approached the band but hadn't expected this. She glanced around and saw the couples dancing to the slow tune wrapped in each other's arms, something that didn't surprise her because most of them were young, and she had chaperoned at several high school dances over the last few years. She stared down at his brown leather loafers, the panic rising in her stomach, setting poorly on the glass of champagne punch.

Jennings was certain he had blown it by moving in what was undoubtedly perceived as too quickly in her eyes, when to him he was going in halftime—less than halftime, more like a snail's pace because she was worth it and he wanted to hold her so badly. "Is it all right, Vee?" he asked, resisting the temptation to tilt her face upward. "We don't have to do this, if you'd prefer not to."

She looked up and was lost in a pair of rainbow eyes and the most tender smile she had ever seen in her life. "I want to."

She raised her arms to encircle his neck the way the younger women were doing with their partners and was surprised when he took one hand, holding it out to the side in the more traditional style of slow dancing. She rested her other hand on his shoulder while his dropped to the small of her back.

"We can talk better this way," he explained, wanting nothing more than to crush her to his body and hold her there, to feel the thrust of her full breasts next to his heart, the outline of her female hips juxtaposed to the leanness of his.

Veronica saw right through the pretense of his gesture and it endeared him to her. "Yes, we can, Jay. Tell me more about what brings you to Southern California. I would have guessed when the time came for you to settle down you would have chosen Dallas since it's your hometown.''

Her fingers were soft and warm in his hand and he dared to brush his thumb back and forth across her inner wrist. ''That's what I always thought at one time. But you see, my parents moved here a few years back, and then J.J. independently decided to attend Cal Tech. This seemed as good a place as any for me to live when things got too hot in the Mideast.''

''You took him on assignment with you?''

''Only for the last two and a half years. We weren't in Beirut all the time, just toward the end. After my wife and I were divorced, J.J. didn't want to live with her anymore. Sally was good to him and legally adopted J.J. when he was eight, but he never really identified with her as a mother because of his attachment to my mother. He enrolled in a boarding school in Massachusetts for a while, and then wanted to be with me,'' he told her, trying to keep his eyes from lingering longer than politely acceptable on the swell of her breasts in the scoop-neck dress. They were dancing at a greater distance than any other couple in the room, and he wanted to ease in just a bit so the tips of her breasts would graze his lightweight cotton shirt, but he couldn't allow himself that luxury, not now.

''How long were you married?'' she asked, trying to match her steps to his and too distracted by the feel of his hand in hers and those polychromous eyes that twinkled in the most bedazzling of ways when he smiled down at her.

''Seven years.''

''Any other children?''

''No, just J.J.''

''What happened?'' she asked cautiously, encouraged by his openness to ask a question she may not normally have posed to a man she barely knew.

Jennings shrugged and the motion drew her closer to him. The song was over, and Steve and the group immediately went into another of the same type. He smiled his appreciation to the group, and gave in to the impulse to fold her hand over and rest it on his chest. "Oh, a lot of things. I suppose most of it was my fault for being more involved with my career and my son than Sally. She went back to school to finish her degree about five years after we were married, got in with a new group of people, and just changed."

As a reentry woman herself, Jennings had hit upon a sensitive point with Veronica. "She changed? What do you mean, Jay? That she stepped outside of the living room and realized there was a whole world out there? Maybe one she didn't know much about and was beginning to discover?"

"Yes, I suppose Sally did change in that respect, but there was more," he said hesitantly, wishing she hadn't brought up the subject.

"Oh? Just how did she change that made marriage to her impossible?" Veronica demanded with a frown.

"Vee, if you really must know, she became an advocate of open marriage and wanted to see other men while we were together. I may be behind the times on the subject, but to me marriage is a commitment between two people," he said with some difficulty. "Does that answer your question?"

Veronica buried her head on his chest in embarrassment for having provoked Jay to discuss a subject that obviously made him uncomfortable. "Oh, Jay. I'm sorry. I had no right to pry like that. I guess I really put my foot in my mouth that time, didn't I?"

"We all do at times, little darlin'," he said, the endearment rising to his lips before his brain could censure it. He spoke in a rich Texas drawl, dropping the final letters of each word, and stressing different syllables than someone from the North would have done.

A man hadn't so addressed her for years. Her husband wasn't the most demonstrative of men and had omitted such words from his vocabulary long before his death. Veronica stopped fighting Jay and surrendered herself to the magic of the moment, their bodies so close together, his palm at the base of her back, and their hands on his chest, fingers entwined. She felt the strong even cadence of his heartbeat under her ear. "You're very kind, Jay. It was foolish of me to push you like that, much less ask why the marriage ended in the first place."

"It's okay," he whispered into her ear. Jay drew her in a bit more, resting his chin on the top of her head. The sweet feminine scent of her, the cosmetics and perfume, invaded his senses. He inhaled deeply of her, his breath ruffling the layered curls. "I remember when your hair was long and black," he said to change the subject from his ex-wife. The sound of Veronica's laughter against his chest, fanning upward and warming his neck, persuaded him to ease back some lest his desire become too inappropriate for the time and place.

"So do I. My girl friends and I used to iron it on the ironing board and wash it in all the jet-black hair dye we could afford. It was quite a fad for a while, before blondes came in," she confessed.

"Really? It wasn't natural? I thought this wasn't," he said, tugging on one of the auburn waves.

"That's the real me."

"It's lovely," he commented.

"Why, thank you. And did anyone ever tell you you

have the most beautiful eyes?'' she asked, knowing legions of women must have.

"My mom used to tell me all the time," he said, making no reference to other admirers. Keeping her at a safe distance for both of them, Jennings whirled her around so that the clock came within her line of vision. He couldn't see the timepiece, but he watched the blue eyes dim with an incredible sense of helplessness in his heart. He did the first thing that came into his head, clasping her back to his chest.

Veronica admitted a little gasp of pain and disengaged herself from his embrace, fleeing the room and heading out into the patio beyond.

Chapter Three

Not going to Veronica at once required more restraint than Jay had found necessary to exert for as long as he could remember. His hands were frozen immobile fists, the knuckles white with impotent frustration. Thin-lipped and cursing himself for upsetting her, he went to find John, the genesis of an explanation for her behavior forming in his mind. Jennings may have been lured by the siren song of her allure into holding her more intimately than his intellect dictated, but he was certain he hadn't violated her privacy unduly. Had he done so, Vee wouldn't have just run from him like that. No, she would have retreated more subtly, given him some barely discernible sign to back off, not left the way she did. Or was he viewing the incident in the best light from his own perspective? he wondered, barging from room to room until he found John Silvers in the kitchen talking to the caterers.

"I'll get back to you in a minute," Silvers said when he saw Jennings, looking thoroughly miserable with both hands slammed into his pockets and a scowl darkening his features. "Jay, come here." He led him into the unoccupied laundry room off the kitchen. "What happened?"

"John, Mike died on Christmas Eve, didn't he?" he asked tightly.

"Yeah, man," Silvers said slowly. "Why do you ask? I thought I told you that before."

"Yes, you did. What time was it, John?"

John Silvers shook his head and frowned. "Oh, Jay. What difference does all that make now? It's Christmas Eve. Relax and enjoy the party. I don't want to think about that now. Please."

"I don't either, John, but I may have to. I was dancing with Vee, and she just bolted out the room like the place was on fire. I think she was looking at the clock right before she ran," he explained hurriedly, grinding his teeth together in a sound that gave Silvers goose bumps on his spine. It reminded him of the year when Jennings was a young man and had slept on a cot near his, making the same godawful sound for hour upon hour, a subconscious response to the unbearable stress they were all forced to endure.

Silvers checked his watch. "Oh, damn. It's nearly eight. Dubcek left his farewell note on one of the computers in the company office, his personal one. Naturally the time of the message was recorded."

"And it was eight P.M.?" he asked, suppressing a quick wave of nausea. "What did it say?" Jennings asked when his former sergeant nodded unhappily.

"Nothing special. It was your usual apology, telling his friends and family he was sorry for causing everyone so much pain, but he couldn't go on anymore, you know that kind of stuff. There was nothing specific about the program thefts, nothing about his work at all."

"Oh, damn, John, why didn't you erase it before Vee saw it?"

"I thought about it, and didn't know if I had the moral right, J.J. You want me to go talk to her with you? I could get Rebecca to help. Being a doctor and all she's better at this kind of thing than I am," he suggested, resting one large hand on his friend's shoulder.

Jennings shook his head. "No, I want to take care of her."

"You always did," Silvers said in an undertone as Jennings rushed off like a madman in search of the Holy Grail.

He found Veronica after a frantic search of the wooded area beyond the redwood deck. She was leaning into a solitary digger pine that jutted from a dry stretch of the winter chaparral land like a jeweled sword thrust into stone, unbearably majestic and alone. There were tears running down her face. In a second great act of self-discipline Jennings didn't rush to her side and throw his arms around Veronica.

"Vee," he said softly, in almost a whisper, stopping five or so feet short of where she reclined into the tree. That crazy image of riding off into the darkened slopes of the San Gabriels came to haunt his mind again, but Jennings knew it was like snowflakes falling into a furnace. It simply couldn't be.

Veronica had heard his footsteps in the darkened glen, and she knew who it was before he said her name, drawing it out into a multisyllabic sound, a product of both his native accent and the high emotion in his voice. She debated with decorum and the turmoil in her heart and darted into his arms.

Jennings caught her, hugged her, and held on to her for dear life, like a drowning man just thrown the last life jacket. "Oh, darlin' Vee, I think I know why you had to leave." He swayed her ever so gently, holding her close to his body, making the soft consoling sounds one might utter to a distraught child. "It must have been so difficult for you. So senseless, so unnecessary, and there was nothing you could do."

The more he consoled her the more she sobbed, but

he went on until she rested, spent and drained from the surfeit of tears with her head on his shoulder, making little gulping noises that ripped into his guts. The pathos of it all was getting to be too much for him to bear the way he had to, so tenderly and without displaying physical want of her. Jennings wanted to kiss away those tears, taste the salt of them on his lips, make her forget the grief in a way he knew he could and would, but that time wasn't now.

She lifted her head from his chest with a self-conscious grin, chastising herself for breaking down not once but twice when he was witness to her weakness, that annual paralysis of the soul that had held her in its clutches for three consecutive holiday seasons. "Oh, Jay. I don't know what got into me. I'm not always like this. You must think I've cornered the market on tears in the entire Los Angeles county."

"No, little darlin', I know you didn't. And that's a fact, because I shed a few of my own today." He brushed a thumb across her cheek, taking a few tears with him.

"You?" she asked, raising her head from his face in disbelief. "Because... ?"

He nodded, searching her face for another tear he could remove and wiping his forefinger over the area below her left eye.

"Well, I bet you at least had the self-restraint to do it in private." Her eyes were beginning to burn from the mascara and liner that had smeared into them. Her purse was in the house, and when Veronica attempted to rub her eyes with her hands, she exacerbated the problem.

Jennings looked in his pocket for a handkerchief and couldn't find one. Finally he pulled out his shirttail and dabbed at her eyes. "No, darlin', it happened on the way over here. J.J. was driving because my hands were shaking so much I couldn't. Between upsetting you the way I did and finding out about Mike, I wasn't much good for anything."

"You sure were good for me," she said spontaneously. "Jay, you don't have to soil your shirt. Eye makeup can really stain."

He continued his ministrations. "That's okay. It's on the tail. I always wondered why they made these things so damn long. Vee, you'd better do this. I don't want to rub anything else into your eyes." He tilted her face toward the moonlight. "There's some black stuff near your iris. Would I do more harm than good if I tried to dab it out?" Her eyes, the color of a dark blue primrose, almost violet, were luminous in the untamed acreage behind the formal garden, and all the smudge around them and running down her face did nothing to detract from her beauty to him.

"I think it would be best to let it tear out," she said. Veronica did the best job she could without a mirror to repair her disheveled appearance, swabbing at her face with his shirttail. "You really should bring this by the house and let me wash it for you," she offered, examining the grime on the off-white cotton cloth.

"Don't be silly, Vee," he dismissed. "It's nothing." Jennings couldn't have cared less if the stains and scents of her cosmetics stayed there forever, a fragile monument of the first time she had let him enter her life, become closer to her. Her despair tortured him down to the depths, but she had run to his arms and there was no place he would rather have Veronica be when she needed someone.

"Jay, you are so sweet." An exposed male abdomen came into view as she continued to dab her face. The man and his body were heart-stoppingly beautiful in her eyes, that flat abdomen with a deep navel encircled by wiry dark hair that looked so resilient it seemed to spring back as she stared at him there; the sensation of him brought a hot flush to her cheeks and she thanked the night that hid her high color from Jay. Veronica sighed, closed her eyes to wash the grit away, and marveled that desire for one man and grief over another could coexist in the same soul.

"That's me, sweet Jay," he quipped. "Shucks, ma'am, if you don't mind me saying so, you're awfully sweet yourself. I never did see a pecan pie that was your equal," he drawled, exaggerating his southern accent. "If I ever do, I'll bring it by when I come a-courting you."

She laughed, her eyes still closed. "Don't, Jay. A pecan pie is the last thing I need. Look at me."

Jennings smiled, wondering how far down the freckles visible on her upper chest went, bedazzled by the light reddish shade. "Vee, I haven't stopped looking at you since you walked into the room, and I like what I see. Yes, I like it very much. I want permission to phone you, to take you out. What do you say?"

Her eyes fluttered open. "I, ah, it's so soon..." she began.

"Vee, it's been two years. I went through a period of grief after Sally and I split, and it wasn't a fraction that long. Of course, I know it wasn't the same," he hastened to add. "We weren't together as long as you and Mike, and everything else was different about the situation, I suppose. I really don't know too much about what you're going through, but it seems to me two years is long enough to begin seeing other people. I don't propose to rush you into anything. We'll take it nice and easy," he promised, wondering how in the hell he could when she stood there holding onto his

shirttail and looking so vulnerable to the world. He
could protect her, he knew it, and he knew he could
help her regain some of what she lost, if only she would
permit him.

"I guess it is time, but I'm not sure if you're the
right person." She heard the peculiar little way he expelled his breath. "Oh, Jay, I didn't mean it the way it
sounded."

"How did you mean it, Vee?" he asked tenderly,
untangling one of her hands from the ball she'd made
of his shirt and holding it.

In just a few hours they had shared too much for her
to deceive him now. "Well, I'd feel strange because
you were one of my husband's best friends. He used to
write home about you all the time. When he came back
he said . . . said you were a ladies man and he'd better
never catch me near you."

The improbability of Dubcek catching her near him
occurred to Jennings, but he didn't tell Veronica.
"Vee, he's gone now and life goes on. It has to."

"I know, but still, Mike used to make me promise
never to get involved with any of his buddies if we ever
separated," she went on, embarrassed by her admission but not knowing how to tell Jay anything less than
the truth.

Jennings cursed to himself. Dubcek had always been
a possessive man in his book, but as his best friend
once he'd overlooked the fault. Until now. Dubcek
used to worry day and night over his wife's faithfulness
back home while they were in Nam, all the time making more women than Jennings could count. Other
men he knew did the same back then, but Dubcek
seemed to do it to the point of obsession. He could
easily imagine the man extracting such a strange promise from his wife after Vietnam. He was surprised he

just hadn't asked her to sign a pledge of eternal celibacy while he was at it.

"Vee, his request was unreasonable. No one has the right to bind another individual to a promise like that," he said, not phrasing himself nearly as strongly as he wanted.

Veronica saw the logic in his words. She knew Jay was right, but Mike had left her with guilt and confusion as his primary legacies, and trapped in the vise grip of the two she felt honor bound to obey his wishes. "I know it's not reasonable, but that's the way I feel, Jay. It's hard enough for me to imagine making love to any man, much less Mike's best friend whom he never wanted me to be with."

"Oh, Vee," he sighed. "I'm not asking you to make love to me. All I want is a chance to get to know you, for you to know me, and we'll take it from there. Please?"

She opened her mouth to speak and nothing came out. Something she couldn't articulate, something as nebulous as the night mist in a temperate area, dictated to her befuddled brain that of all human beings on earth, this gentle, patient man before her was the one who could assist in freeing herself of the bonds that kept her tethered to the earth; somehow he could release her, and Veronica was frightened. Maybe there were some bonds a woman had to throw off for herself, and there were so many things on her mind.

Jennings waited for her to speak as long as he could and then held his finger over her lips, the sensation of them maddening though he touched her with so little pressure. "Vee, please, don't say anything right now. I chose the worst of all possible times to speak to you about these things. Let's wait until after the first of the year, shall we?"

Veronica nodded a mute agreement and that was good enough for him. "How do I look?" she asked hesitantly.

"Beautiful, but there's just a speck of silverish stuff on your cheek," he replied.

Veronica toyed with the eye shadow and managed to spread it along her cheekbones until Jay licked his forefinger and wiped her face. The intimacy of his gesture diminished the strength of her reservations against him like the hot morning sun vaporizing rain on a red clay rooftop. She rested her head on his chest and asked him a question she had never dared to ask any of them, any of the people from DataBank.

"Jay, do you think Mike really did all those things?"

"Not on my life. I'd stake my professional reputation on it, Vee," he said without a moment's hesitation. The courage of his convictions had the effect of an intoxicant in loosening the guards he had to maintain around her. His arms tightened around her waist as he spoke. "I knew Mike Dubcek, Vee. Time was when I knew him better than you, although that was a long time ago, but certain things don't change, not about certain men anyway. He had his faults just like the rest of us." The fondness of the memories made him smile and forget whom he was speaking to. "Dubcek's worst fault was chasing skirt, but never, never... Oh, don't pay any attention to me, Vee. I was talking about before he met you," he extemporized, recalling all the nights Mike spoke of the women he knew before his marriage, and how no one believed a fraction of what he said. Jennings found her as delightfully unpredictable as the long shot in a horse race when she laughed, the sound throaty against his chest.

"You are a jewel, Jay Jennings. You don't have to cover up for Mike's infidelities in Vietnam. I know all about them," she replied. For a teenage wife Veronica had had a remarkable insight into the man she married, and moreover she forgave him. Lord only knew what she would have done, subjected to the unthinkable aspects of existence as he had been. She supposed she may have grabbed what little pleasure she could in a pleasureless land, and when you were there, home must have seemed as far away as did the moon to the ancient Greeks. "Here, tuck your shirt in so you'll look respectable when we rejoin the party," she advised.

Jay muttered something incoherent and said, "Excuse me," before he turned to unsnap his brown corduroy slacks and undo the zipper. There was nothing he could say to her about Dubcek without compounding his slip of the tongue, so he let the matter be.

She watched Jay tuck in his shirt. They were standing on a slope in the wooded glen, and his position a few feet away and above Veronica exaggerated the six-inch difference in their heights. The early winter moon, full but low in the sky, silhouetted his body, making her all too aware of the male lines of it, the lanky arms busy at work rearranging his clothing, the wide shoulders and the taut buttocks.

"Do I look respectable?" he asked when he turned toward her. The red rims around her eyes continued to cut through him like a pair of skis in new white powder, clean and piercing.

She nodded. "Probably far more than I do." Veronica's nose started to run in the aftermath of all that sobbing and she was mortified to realize she had nothing to wipe it with. If Jay offered her his shirttail again, she was certain she'd die from embarrassment on the spot.

He quickly surmised her predicament, and an indulgent smile passed his lips. "Wait here, Vee. I'll be back in a second." He darted across the yard and was relieved to see John Silvers and another man on the redwood deck.

"Did you find Vee?" John asked, noting his friend seemed in considerably better spirits than he had when he saw him last.

"Yes."

"How is she?"

"Much better."

"Were you right about why she ran off?"

Jennings nodded his head in the affirmative and asked Silvers if he had a handkerchief on him.

John chuckled. "A handkerchief? What in the hell are you going to do with it? Drop the damn thing and see if Vee picks it up?" He found one in his shirt pocket and handed it to Jennings. "A bit quaint, isn't it?"

"Thanks. A man has to start somewhere, John."

Veronica walked to Jay when she heard him approach. She was beginning to wish by now that they had met on some other day, sometime when she was less emotional, and he could see her as she really was. If Jay Jennings was drawn to weak and highly emotional women, he was going to be disappointed before too long. She accepted the piece of white cloth. "Jay, thank you. You have been so kind to me today."

He smiled and suggested they return to the party when he wanted nothing more than to remain with her out there in the fragrant chaparral growth. "Tell me about your studies. John said you were in law school."

"I suppose you can call it law school if one wants to be generous," she said, laughing. "I'm taking a correspondence course. I'm just about finished with my second year."

"Why didn't you enroll in a regular law school?" he wondered.

"Several reasons. The only one I could get into without a bachelor's degree is way over on the other side of the county, the courses are taught from seven to ten at night, every day but Friday, and since I have to work I would have been away from the kids too much. Besides that, I hate commuting on the freeways, and the tuition is far less expensive at the correspondence school," she explained.

"How does it work? I mean with exams and that sort of thing."

The sounds of music and happy people became louder as they neared the house on the hillside, and Veronica found herself engulfed by a sudden wave of relief. Just two short years ago she had been as certain as she had ever been of anything that never, never again would she be able to listen to the sounds of Christmas without feeling death in her heart. Her mood had swung back to gaiety, and she wondered how much was due to the healing balm of time itself and how much to the man at her side who so tenderly offered his comfort, his acceptance, and his friendship. And all the while he seemed to promise the part of her soul that ignored the confused dictates of her intellect, that which had been forbidden to her for so long, the reawakening of her sensuous self.

When she didn't answer his question, Jennings glanced at Veronica sideways and was delighted to see the little smile on her lips. "Feeling better?"

"Yes, and it's largely due to you. About the exams, Jay, one has to find a sponsor to proctor the tests, and mail them in to be scored. Mine is a retired judge who lives in South Pasadena. He's wonderful. If I need special help, I can speak to the staff at the school over the phone or visit them if there's any problem. And when I'm all done, I have to take the state bar exam like everyone else. If I pass it, I have the same license to practice law as people who graduate from a more traditional school. Of course, the type of practice I go into will be limited. I won't be able to just walk into the most prestigious law firm in town and ask to be a partner. Large firms and corporations pay attention to where the degree came from, but that's no problem. I don't want to work at any of those places anyway."

"Do you know what you would like to do when you're finished?" he asked as they passed the deck and entered the game room. Apparently the notion of old-fashioned slow dancing had gone over well with the rock generation; the young couples were still locked in each other's arms. "Vee, they're playing our song. Dance with me."

"Jay, you must certainly like to dance. Mike hated it. You know I haven't danced this much in years and years?" she asked, offering him one hand and placing the other on his shoulder.

"No, actually, I've always hated it. I haven't danced for years and years either," he confessed with a disarming grin.

"Oh? Then why now?"

"Because I needed a respectable way to get you in my arms. Why else?"

She laughed, not in the least surprised by his admission. "Next you're going to tell me you paid off Steve's band!"

"No, little darlin'. They did it for nothing, but I would have bribed them if I had to." He tucked her head under his chin and folded her hand that was locked in his onto his chest, lost once more in the perfumes of her body. Jay clamped his other hand firmly on her lower back to prevent it from drifting where he wanted it to go, down to the soft slope of her derriere.

"You're really something else, Jay," she remarked, her own nostrils full of the scent of him as she swayed with her head on his chest. Veronica detected moisture beneath her cheek. They were her tears on his shirt, and she brushed her hand across the wet spot.

"Is that good or bad?" he said flirtatiously.

"Good, very good, Jay." Veronica glanced at the damp area, about five inches in diameter, amazed she had wept so profusely on his chest. "Jay, I'm really sorry about this."

He looked down and couldn't see anything but her hand stroking his upper body, and the sight delighted him. "About petting me? Don't, Vee. I love it. Pet away."

"You impossible flirt! That's not what I meant. I'm referring to the wet spot here," she told him, pointing it out.

"Oh, I'm too warm to feel it," he remarked lightly. "So tell me about the kind of law practice you're interested in," he asked to quell the mounting desire, but it was no good.

Veronica lifted her head from his chest and stepped back. "The protection of intellectual property is what they call it."

"Yes, I'm familiar with the field. As in the protection of computer programs?" he ventured tentatively.

"That's right. I had a strong interest in the field before... before everything happened."

He interrupted immediately with a question about her professional interests to redirect her thoughts. "Vee, did you hear about the cases involving algorithms? They can't be patented anymore."

"Yes, fascinating decision, wasn't it? I think we're

going to see major changes in the patent laws pertaining to intellectual property in the next five years," she speculated. They had danced themselves to the exit of the room, and both were surprised to run into John Silvers glowering in the doorway.

Veronica and Jay said hello, only to have their salutations ignored.

"Would you look at this?" Silvers demanded of his wife, who stood behind him.

"Look at what, dear?" she asked patiently.

"At this teenage orgy, that's what. Look at that Johnson boy over there. He's practically phagocytosing my daughter. I thought these kids didn't even touch when they danced nowadays," he complained.

Rebecca Silvers laughed. "Oh, John, you're so out of it. If you weren't too tied up with your computers all the time to chaperon a few dances at the school, you'd see this is the way people slow dance now. Leave them be."

"No, Becky, enough is enough. This isn't the kind of music Steve and the group rehearsed earlier in the week. Who's responsible for this?" he demanded, taking one look at Vee Dubcek, who had drifted away with her head on Jennings's shoulder. "I think I know, Becky."

"Know what, dear?" she asked, scanning the small room for her other daughter.

"Who the musical director around here is. Look at Jay."

"Oh, John, isn't that wonderful? Vee hasn't had anyone since Mike died. It's about time, don't you think?"

"Yeah," he conceded, "I just wish he would make time someplace else, Becky."

She extended her arms to her husband. "Dance with me, Johnny."

"Oh, Becky, you know I'm not good at that sort of thing," he demurred.

"It's easy. All you have to do is stand there, move around a little, and hold me tightly," she cajoled.

He couldn't resist her pleading velvet brown eyes. "Okay, sweetheart, just once, and then that son of mine is going to liven the tempo a great deal around here."

"Having problems, Long John?" Jennings quipped when his friend danced by with an immense frown on his bearded face.

"Nothing I can't handle. Where's your boy?"

"Off in computerland somewhere, probably. He likes them better than girls," he explained, snuggling Veronica against his body.

Silvers smiled and danced away with his wife.

"Oh, Jay!" Veronica exclaimed, burying her head on his chest. "Get me out of here!"

His arms tightened around her as they moved to the door. "Vee, honey, are you all right?"

"I'm fine, but I just remembered about my makeup! I meant to go directly to Becky's bedroom where I left my purse and clean up a little before joining the party, and I completely forgot as soon as we started dancing," she explained hurriedly, breaking free of his embrace when they were out the door.

"Oh, Vee, is that all? You look fine," he said with a relieved sigh. "You really had me worried for a while."

She flashed a pixie grin, the effect exaggerated by the freckles on her nose. "Afraid I was going to burst into tears again?"

"Something like that, yes."

Veronica opened the bedroom door and Jay followed her into the room. "And where do you think you're going, Mr. Jay Jennings?" she asked.

"With you," he said hopefully. "I was just going to watch."

"Jay, I really think I can manage to wash my face by myself. I'll see you later, okay?" she said. Veronica was standing with one hand behind her back, holding the knob and leaning into the door.

Jay placed his palm on the wall over her head and tilted her chin up with his free hand. "Is that a promise?" he asked softly.

She nodded, aware his question extended beyond the immediate future. "Yes, sort of one on the installment plan, to be delivered bit by bit."

"Fine, I'll take my first installment now." He grazed her lips with his mouth, ever so gently and briefly, and was down the hall before the impact of his action had time to register on her senses.

Veronica stood there in the doorway for a few minutes and then touched her forefinger to her lips. They felt as though they had been kissed by sunlight, as warm as clean baked earth that would retain the heat for a long time, and maybe that light and heat would be the catalyst for new growth someday. She had the premonition her life had altered ineffaceably that evening, and the irony of two such significant turns in her life happening on the day before Christmas dimmed the fire in her eyes.

Veronica wasn't a woman to run, but she just couldn't handle so much at once. Of all men, why did it have to be one Mike made her promise never to love?

She gathered her things and left through the back door after scribbling a hasty apology to Rebecca, safe in the knowledge that the very kind and gracious woman would understand. She wasn't sure if Jay would, but there wasn't time to worry about that now.

Chapter Four

A messenger came to Veronica's door on the first day of the year, one none too friendly and undoubtedly in the throes of a New Year's Eve hangover, standing there pasty faced and with trembling fingers, holding a long box in one hand and a miniature potted tree in the other. He managed a lukewarm smile when she tipped him generously.

The identity of the gift giver had been apparent to her the second she looked through the peephole and saw the man. No one she knew, or had ever known for that matter, would send such things on no special occasion just to let her know she was in his thoughts.

Veronica closed the door with a contented smile, peeked in the box, and inhaled of the heady rose perfume. All week long, since that party at the Silvers', she had prayed Jay would not call on her in any form, but now, as she opened the box, she knew she would never have forgiven him had he kept away. Her feelings about that pledge to Mike remained unresolved in her mind, but somehow the emergence of a new year like welcome spring after a hard winter, verdant and vibrant with life after colorless days far shorter than the nights that came before and after, Veronica knew of a reawakening of the spirit that gave rise to a more positive attitude than she had known in a long time.

She undid the narrow silver ribbon, and when the boxtop was removed Veronica saw there was a single white flower in the center of the arrangement, and that it would be unnecessary to search in her kitchen for a long unused vase. The sender had provided one, a delicately carved piece in dark blue glass, so fragile and light Veronica hadn't even noticed the box weighed more than flowers alone would have. The miniature tree, less than eight inches in height and planted in an oval ceramic bowl decorated with painted birds, was a pine, a type common to Northern California, so perfectly proportioned in spite of the diminutive size one would have undoubtedly assumed it to be a hundred feet tall and ten times that old in the right photograph. Veronica placed Jay's gifts on the oak sideboard that had belonged to her grandmother and stepped back to admire the effect. With the exception of small offerings of color crayon art and plaster hand prints and other such things from her children over the years, they were undoubtedly the most special and endearing gifts she had yet to receive from anyone.

The obvious cost of the items began to bother her after a while, though. She hardly knew this man, and common sense told her to be wary of gift givers of the masculine persuasion. They always wanted something in return, and it was usually the same thing. She ran her fingertip over a high-gloss blue peacock on the ceramic bowl and wondered if she were guilty of unfairly accusing Jay of motives of which he was innocent. After all, what did she really know about men and dating nowadays?

Veronica was thirty-five, and hadn't had a date since high school, and the only boy she dated then was Mike Dubcek. Somehow between her second and third year of high school she became labeled Dubcek's girl, and any boy with whom she shared a passing fancy would never have pursued Veronica Jankovich because she was Mike's, big man on campus, and no one flirted with his girl. Mike and those high school dates, an awkward courtship carried out in drive-in movie theaters, unlit porches, and the backseat of a '54 Chevy, were the extent of her working knowledge of men, and Veronica supposed she had no right to assume the retribution Jay would demand for his gifts would be something she didn't have to give him, not now.

She searched the box for a card and found a simple note. "Dear Vee, Many years ago I wanted to thank you for everything you sent us, but there wasn't time for thanks then. There is now. My best wishes for a happy New Year for you and the boys, and best of luck with your law studies, Jay Jennings."

A more romantic note would have made her uneasy, but the impersonal tenor of this one left Veronica vaguely dissatisfied and in need of more, but more of what she couldn't say. She sat idly tapping the postcard-size piece of stiff paper on the tabletop until it accidentally fell to the floor, calling her attention to a second message on the reverse side. "Vee—J.J. and I will be at Cal Tech next week to tour the campus. Give me a call if you're free for lunch, will you?" He signed his name again, this time with Jay, and left his phone number.

Veronica shook her head and laughed out loud. He wasn't going to stop at anything to persuade her to date him, including making a chaperon of his teenage son in an offer that would be difficult to refuse.

"What's so funny, Mom?" her twelve-year-old, Keith, asked when he came into the living room.

"Oh, nothing. What are your brothers up to?" she asked routinely, preoccupied by Jay and his tactics. The man was as sly as a fox in a henhouse, but not quite so subtle. She saw right through him and liked what she saw.

"Brad is in the garage tuning up your car and I'm not sure where Greg went. He was riding bikes with Paul the last time I saw him. Hey, Mom, where did you get the little tree? That's neat. Are you going to put it in the backyard so it'll grow?"

"It's not supposed to grow much, Keith. That's called a bonsai tree and was wired or pruned or something like that to shape it like a big tree."

"Where did it come from?" he wondered, rotating the bowl on the oak surface of the sideboard.

"A friend gave it to me. Keith, be careful, you're going to scratch the wood," she requested patiently.

"Who?"

"An old friend of your father's, someone I met at the Silvers' house on Christmas Eve," she explained.

"Did he give you this too?" When Keith reached out to touch the vase, he knocked it over, shattering the delicate glass into numerous fragments beyond repair.

Veronica leaped from her seat. "Keith! Dammit! Can't you ever be careful?" she said sharply, hastening to wipe up the water with the nearest available piece of cloth before it damaged the wood. "Get me some paper towels and a bag from the kitchen."

"Okay, sorry, Mom. I'll get you another one," he said contritely.

Veronica regretted the loss of her temper almost as much as the loss of the lovely blue vase. "Don't worry about it, Keith. Hurry up and get what I want, and then try to find something else to put the flowers in."

The flowers wound up in a pair of mason jars because they couldn't find any vases. Veronica had put them away some place after Mike's death because flowers were too closely linked to funerals in her mind, since everyone had sent so many at the time. Jay's arrangement of red roses with the single white one in the center held no such connotation for her, and when she prepared for bed later that night after a holiday dinner with another single parent from work and both their families, her three boys and Sara's son and daughter, Veronica took a red flower and the white one and placed them in a glass of water on her nightstand.

She took the card to her room also, rereading and rereading the words until she saw them when her eyes were closed, sweeping bold strokes written with a black felt tip pen on an ivory colored card with a dark trim. Like the man himself, the note was as simple and elegant as a lone oak tree on a green and gold spring hillside.

Veronica lay in bed with the note resting on her abdomen, images of Christmas Eve returning, gentle impressions of a tender man who had held her as she wept on his chest replacing the sad thoughts that were so apt to haunt her when she thought of the holidays. And as she lay there, the wanderings of her mind traveled from Jay's innate sensitivity to his inherent sensuality, to the feel of his hand in hers as they danced, the other hand on her back, her head on his shoulder, the texture of his shirt soft beneath her cheek and the scent of him strong in her nostrils. And that kiss, the ephemeral glory of it driving her out into the night only to want to race back to his arms once she returned to the sanctuary of her home. Veronica picked up the telephone receiver. Jay deserved an apology for her abrupt departure, a thank you for his lovely gifts, and she deserved the pleasure of his company at lunch.

Jennings was in the shower when she called, and his son answered the phone.

"Don't disturb him, then. This is Veronica Dubcek. Will you tell him I called, please?" she asked, nervously twiddling with the beige telephone cord, winding it first around one finger and then another.

J.J.'s ears perked up at the mention of her name. It hadn't required a great deal of perceptiveness on his behalf to know this woman meant something to his father. A week ago, at the Silvers' party, his dad had walked around the house and grounds looking for her until he realized her car was gone, and then spent the rest of the evening as disconsolate as a little boy who wakes up to a bag of coal in his Christmas sock. Since then he had been either working on the stolen software problem or grumbling and moping about the house, sometimes both at once. "Wait a minute, hold on, Mrs. Dubcek," he said, forgetting she had given him permission to use her first name, "I think I hear him getting out."

Jennings was standing at the sink naked and shaving his chin when J.J. opened the door. "Dad, telephone."

"Do you know who it is?"

"Yeah, Veronica Dubcek."

He dropped the razor into the sink and went into the adjoining bedroom. "Is there anything I can do for you?" he asked his son when he lingered near the closed door.

J.J. grinned. "I take it this is a private conversation, Dad?"

"Get the hell out of here," he ordered in a pleasant enough tone, his hand held tightly over the receiver. "Hi, Vee," Jennings said when the boy was gone.

"Hi, Jay. I'd like to thank you for the lovely gifts. You really didn't have to thank me for something I did seventeen years ago, you know," she said, well aware his motivations had been otherwise in part, but so phrased to make the presents impossible to refuse.

"Well, I wanted to, Vee, and I must confess that wasn't the only reason I sent the flowers," he admitted slowly. "You see, I expect something in return."

Jay was flirting with her and Veronica wasn't sure if she knew how to flirt back. "Oh, you do, do you? And what might that be, Mr. Jennings?"

"Whatever I can get, Vee. I'm not very particular at this point."

"I see. How about if I pick up the check when you and J.J. come to Cal for lunch?" she offered.

"How about if I pick you up?" he countered.

"How so? There are pickups and then there are pickups, you know."

Jennings chuckled. "Vee, you're too quick for me, but let's just say I'll pick you up anyway you want. When would be a good day for lunch?"

"Is the day after tomorrow okay?" she asked, since it was closer to the present than any other day of the week when the campus would be reopened following the holidays.

"It's okay with me. Hang on while I check with J.J.," he asked, wishing now he hadn't used the boy as an inducement for Vee to accept his date and reluctant to change the game plan at the last minute. Jennings put the receiver down and slipped into a velour kimono-style bathrobe.

He found J.J. in the kitchen, helping his grandmother repair a torn hinge on the cabinet under the sink. "Hi, Mom," Jennings said. "Mind if I take your carpenter away for a while?"

"As long as you send him back, Jay," she replied. "I'm having trouble with screwdrivers because of my arthritis, and I can't get your father to do a damn thing around the house."

"He'll be right back, Mom," Jennings promised,

ushering his son into the next room. "J.J., do you have any plans for the day after tomorrow? Say around noon?"

"Nothing specific. I'll probably play with the computer you gave me for Christmas. I'm trying to come up with a program to analyze the encryption method Dubcek used on the pirated data, Dad. I know you think he's innocent, and just out of curiosity I'd like to see how someone could have cracked that code without getting the key from him. It's an interesting problem. Why, what did you want me to do?" he asked, eager to please his father, and just as interested in exonerating Dubcek because his father wanted it as he was in the intellectual challenge.

"I want you to go to lunch with me and Vee at Cal Tech."

J.J. laughed. "Dad, since when did you need a chaperon? Don't you want to be alone with Vee? I thought you really liked her."

"I do, I do, but I'm not certain if she's ready to be alone with me yet. I'll expect you to be ready to leave for lunch at eleven thirty, unless she wants us there at some other time."

"Yes, sir."

"Now go help your grandmother." He took the stairs three at a time to hurry back to Veronica. "Hi, Vee. Sorry that took so long. I had to check with J.J. and see when he wanted to tour the campus. The day after tomorrow is fine. What time?" He took off his robe and climbed into bed. Jennings had been working day and night on the software problem and had decided to turn in early, before ten.

"I get off for lunch at noon. Are you familiar with the campus?"

"No."

"I work in the administration building."

"I'll find it, Vee. How have you been?" he asked abruptly.

"Fine. Much better than in a long time," she elaborated since her initial response seemed so inadequate.

"I missed you when you left the party," he said cautiously. "Vee, I seriously considered going after you. I got your address from Rebecca Silvers. I had the key in the ignition to leave, and then decided maybe you needed your privacy at that time. Did I do the right thing?"

"Yes, you did exactly the right thing for me, Jay. Thank you, and I'm sorry I left without saying goodbye. That was the least I could have done," she replied, moved by his sensitivity and very definitely aroused by the melodic timbre of his Texas accent, so rich in texture that ordinary words became extraordinary when Jay said them.

"I understand." There was a pause. "Vee, mind if I ask you something?"

"No," she said at once, knowing the question would be a carefully chosen one, or so phrased as not to hurt her.

"Vee, was it my kiss that frightened you?"

"Hum, sort of."

He made a sound of frustration. "I'm sorry. I should have shown better judgment," he told her, secretly wondering how he could have when Vee stood there outside the Silvers' bedroom door in the darkened hallway with her eyes still moist and luminous from teardrops he had wanted so desperately to kiss away, and him standing above her unable to keep from staring at the fawn-colored freckles on the soft rise of flesh that he supposed was where her chest ended and her breasts began. "Vee, I won't do that next time," he said in reference only to the immediate future, and hoping she would understand.

"Jay, if you don't, there may not be a next time," she said in a husky, almost breathless tone that made Jennings shift restlessly under his bedding.

"Little darlin', if I hear you right, you're saying I can kiss you?" he asked, wondering what had become of Dubcek's ghost. Jennings had a few ghosts of his own born of the pathos of war, and he knew such specters weren't easily banished to the places where they belonged. Vee was coming to him, of that he was certain, but he knew retreat was still a possibility. He would have to tread easily with her, keep his head stronger than the stirrings in his body, those primal urges that spread quicker than smoke on a brisk breeze whenever he looked at her, heard the music of her voice.

Veronica didn't answer at once, a bit overcome by Jay's inflection when he spoke. The swaggering, sweet gentle flirtation was gone, replaced by an awe that bordered on reverence and she marveled that a kiss from her lips could mean so much to a man like Jay Jennings, who epitomized everything most women would want in a man and probably what most men would like to see in themselves. "Yes, Jay. That's what I said."

"Thank you, Vee. I want to kiss you. I... Did you like the flowers?"

"I loved them. I left most of them in the living room and took a few to my bedroom. I can smell them right now."

"The ones in the living room or the ones in the bedroom?"

"In the bedroom. I'm in bed."

Jennings groaned and resisted the temptation to say he wished he were there. Whatever had prompted him to want to know where she was? It was enough to drive a man insane, him there in bed desiring her the way he did, and she at home in her bed, smelling his flowers. He had to get out of bed. Jay stood and began to pace the room, locking the door so J.J. wouldn't barge in at an awkward moment that would embarrass the two of them. "Oh. Did you like the vase? They had a red one just like it, but I decided on the blue."

"I liked what I saw of it, Jay. I only had it for about ten minutes." Veronica hoped he wouldn't construe her statement as a plea to have the gift replaced.

"What happened? Did you think it was the disposable kind?"

Veronica giggled into the receiver. "No way. One of my kids accidentally knocked it over."

"The next time I'll get you a silver one," he said, making a note to replace the other. Jennings glanced at his watch when he paced past his dresser. It was late, but maybe he could find something open, buy another vase, and use it as an excuse to go to her right now. No, he concluded. Nothing would be open on New Year's Day, and Vee needed more time. He couldn't run to her like a boar in pursuit of a female in heat less than five minutes after she gave him permission to kiss her.

"Oh, Jay, you've given me enough gifts today to last a lifetime! Don't you dare! That little tree is so precious! Whatever made you decide on that?"

"Impulse, and I had to promise the florist I'd make it worth his while to open up for me this morning. They were closed for the holidays. I'm glad you like it. I bought another very similar to the little pine you have."

"You kept one for yourself?"

"Hell, Vee, what would I do with a little tree in a bowl? No, I gave it to someone else."

"Ah, I'm disappointed, Jay," she teased. "I thought I was the only woman in Pasadena you gave trees to on New Year's Day."

He chuckled into her ear, the resonant sound warming her blood. "Just you and good old mom," he assured Veronica, going on to answer her questions about his family and the type of employment he hoped to find in the Los Angeles area.

After an hour the conversation drifted to the subject of his former wife, and Veronica skirted the issue until she realized Jennings no longer seemed as reticent as he had the last time she broached the subject.

"Maybe it would have worked had I been less involved in my career and with my son, I don't know. Looking back, I never really had any energy for Sally. Everything was J.J. and my work," he concluded after. a while, silently reflecting how different it could be for him and Veronica.

"Well, it is normal for single parents to overcompensate sometimes and devote too much of their efforts to children, and you were single for a long time before you met her, weren't you?" she asked. She heard her two oldest boys go out into the driveway to play basketball on a hoop mounted over the garage door and excused herself briefly.

"Brad, honey, keep it quiet and don't stay out late, okay?" she asked.

"We won't, Mom. I want to show Greg a new shot I learned," he yelled up to the window.

Veronica returned to the phone. "Sorry about the interruption, Jay. I wanted my boys to keep it down. Some old man across the street was complaining the other day. Where were we?"

"You asked how long I'd been a single father before Sally. It was seven years. J.J. and I were very close." Jennings had been pacing the room for a long time by now, and returned to bed because he was cold.

"You still are, I can see that. I think it's lovely."

"Thank you. I think you're lovely."

Veronica couldn't handle the compliment, not over the phone anyway, and thanked him briefly before inquiring about Sally once more. "Do you ever see her?"

"We did at first, but she moved to Canada with her lover about a year and a half ago. J.J. might go up there and visit her next summer."

"Would you go?"

"Me, no. He'll be eighteen and perfectly capable of traveling alone—he already is—and I can't think of many men who make a habit of spending their vacations with their ex-wives, can you?" he asked logically.

"No, I can't."

"In fact I can't even think of a man who would lie here in bed discussing his ex-wife to a woman he wants as much as I want you, Vee," he acknowledged quietly in his quicksilver accent, rich and slowly easing.

Veronica remained silent on the other end of the line. A fragrant breeze filtered through her open bedroom window, redolent with the scent of blossoms that flourished in the Mediterranean climate of Southern California, and cool to her flushed skin. There had been no one for her since Mike, and her enfamished sensuality was daring to think of how little there had been when her husband was there, occupying the empty half of the double bed.

Jennings cursed himself once more for letting his emotions dominate when he knew she needed space. "Vee, honey, I'm sorry. I shouldn't have said that. I keep telling myself to slow down, and then I go ahead and say something like that," he apologized.

"Did you mean it?" she asked quietly.

"God, yes, I meant it, but a person can't just go around blurting out everything that comes into his head now, can he? I tell that to my son all the time."

"You really want me?" she asked in an awed tone.

"Yes, I really want you," he repeated with an inflection that conveyed just how sincere he was.

"Then say it again," she pleaded urgently.

"Vee, I want you more than I've ever wanted any woman in my life and that's the god's honest truth. I wanted you even when I had no right to want you."

"I don't understand."

"Perhaps you will someday."

"You can't tell me now?"

"No, darlin', I'd rather not. I'll only say that as much as I wanted you before, I want you a thousand times more now."

"Hum, that sounds nice," she said in a drowsy tone that reminded Jennings of a lovely solo ballerina in some kind of a surreal dream scene.

"Just you wait, darlin'. When the time comes, it's going to be so good. I know."

Veronica shared his sentiment. "I know." She looked at her bedside clock radio. "Jay, do you realize we've been on the phone for nearly two hours?"

"No, I knew we'd been chatting for a spell, but I didn't know how long. What time do you have to be at work tomorrow?"

"I'm off, but I have to get up early and study."

"I better let you go, then," he suggested.

"I suppose so, but I think I'm too excited to sleep right away."

"Excited in what way?" he ventured.

"Every way that's good."

"Stay that way," he requested. "I'll see you around noon day after tomorrow, Vee."

"Good, and thank you once more for the gifts, Jay."

It took them nearly half an hour to say good night.

Chapter Five

"I can't believe that creep, Vee," Sara Philips complained. "He comes in here no less than fifteen minutes before lunch and tells me to have all of this collated by one! Have you seen how long it is? He knows I get off at twelve, and man, I am starving!"

Veronica shook her head in sympathy for her friend, another secretary in the admissions office. "I know what you mean, Sara. They're having a big problem with budgeting right now, and everything is screwy. How long is the grant they want you to put together?"

"I don't know for sure. I fainted when I saw it. I think it's around two million pages long, give or take one and a half paragraphs," she said grimly, sitting down at her typewriter to finish something else. "Vee, if you ever get to be a rich lawyer, will you take me away from all of this?"

Veronica laughed. The thought of being an employer and perhaps hiring someone she had worked with had never occurred to her before, and it was an interesting one. "First of all, I doubt that someone with my prospective credentials will ever be very rich, Sara, and secondly, I wonder if a friend would want to work for me."

Sara ran a hand through her short blond hair and

considered the question. "Would you pay me decently?"

"I don't think I'd ever hire a person I couldn't afford to pay well," Veronica told her.

"Would you ever yell at me when I called in sick because my kids were ill and I couldn't come to work?" she pursued.

"Definitely not."

"Would you get mad if one of your colleagues flirted with me and I didn't flirt back?"

"Never in ten million milleniums, Sara!"

"Good, I'll take the job! And please, accept my congratulations for your future successes!"

"Wonderful, but I don't have anything to offer yet," Vee reminded Sara with a bright smile.

"Ah, but you will, Vee, I know it!"

Veronica hugged her friend. "Your confidence, my dear, is highly encouraging, but I think it would be better right now if we worked on immediate problems at hand instead of prematurely congratulating me. I'll help you. Between the two of us we can get this out in half an hour."

"Oh, no, thanks, Vee. I can manage, and besides, didn't you have a date for lunch? The man you met at the Silvers'?" she asked.

"It's okay. He can wait a few minutes. Let's collate, shall we?"

"No, really. You haven't had a date since Mike—" Sara put her hand over her mouth. "I'm sorry, Vee," she apolgized.

"Dont be, it's okay. It's been a long time since all that happened, and I think I'm just beginning to join the ranks of the living," she said wistfully, her thoughts on a holiday season that began with reminiscences of the recent ones and ended with the promise of spiritual regeneration afloat in the air.

"I'm so glad. But look. It's good to see you socializing a little with someone besides me and the gals in the building. Don't make your other friend have to wait, okay? Dr. Beerstein," she said in reference to the two women's superior in the office, Dr. Beirnstein, a rather obese individual with a protruding abdomen, "can shove it. I'm not going to starve for him. I'll work until noon, leave, and that's it."

"Sara, the employee evaluations are coming up soon. Can you risk annoying Beerstein now?" Veronica asked.

Sara snapped her fingers together and swore. "That's right! I'll run down to the machines and eat while I work."

"No, really, I insist on helping you. Collating these papers is so boring. Let's get started now."

Sara protested a few more times but was unable to persuade Veronica to change her mind and prepare to leave with her luncheon date. "So, tell me about this man. We really didn't get much of a chance to talk at dinner the other day. By the way, let me thank you again for making all the desserts. It was such a help. You should have taken the cheesecake home with you."

"I didn't want to. None of my kids like cheesecake, and one of my New Year's resolutions was to lose weight. I'd like to take off ten pounds a month, but I don't know if I can," she said, collating the papers quicker than a Reno blackjack dealer throwing out cards.

"Ten pounds a month, Vee? You'll be dead by summer!"

Veronica laughed, unlike previous times when any joke or reference to death sent her emotions in a tail-spin. "I'm not planning on a six-month diet! Just two or three dedicated months would do it for me."

"Does this new man have anything to do with your decision to go on the diet?"

"No, I've been going off and on diets for the last few years. You know that."

"What does he look like?" Sara wanted to know.

Veronica sighed like a woman falling in love. "He is gorgeous! Absolutely the most attractive man I've seen in a long time. He's around six feet tall, with a great body and the most beautiful pair of hazel eyes you'd ever want to see! Do you remember last year when that man was visiting from Wales? Dr. Krebs, I believe?"

"Certainly. How could I forget him? He looked just like Richard Burton did when he was younger. Why, does Jay look like that?"

"Very much so. He's coming here to pick me up," Veronica said with a giggle as she recalled her last conversation with Jay, "so you'll get to meet him."

"Good, I'd like to. May I help you, sir?" Sara asked when she looked up and saw a man in the doorway.

"Yes, I'm here to see Veronica Dubcek," Jennings said, looking around the office for her.

Veronica was behind a filing cabinet, out of his line of vision. She stepped in front. "Jay, hi! I see you found the administration building okay. Where's your son?"

"He wanted to get something at the bookstore. He'll meet us in a bit."

Veronica made introductions and explained to Jennings she would be a little late for lunch.

"I see. Need an extra hand?" he offered graciously.

Sara wouldn't hear of it. "Goodness, no! You run along and I'll have Vee out of here in fifteen minutes."

They agreed upon a meeting place and Jennings excused himself.

"Well, what do you think, Sara?" Veronica asked when he was gone. "Handsome, isn't he?"

Sara seemed a bit uneasy. "No, I really don't think so," she said honestly. "I mean he's not unattractive, that's for sure, but I wouldn't call him handsome. He does look a little like Richard Burton, but he's not nearly as good looking in my opinion."

Veronica was flabbergasted by her friend's assessment of Jay. "Sara Philips! He most certainly is good looking! Did you notice his eyes? His body? That cleft on his chin?"

"Yeah, but they were just regular hazel eyes, and as to his body, the man could use a few sessions at the local gym," Sara had decided. "But he was very nice, Vee. Not many men would offer to help us in here."

"Sessions at the gym! All right, Sara, he's not Adonis," Veronica conceded, "but he's damn attractive."

Sara grinned. "Obviously to you, and that's all that matters. I mean you wouldn't want me to think he's too devastating, now, would you?"

If Veronica didn't know Sara as well as she did, she would have assumed the other woman was jealous of Jay. "No, I suppose not," she admitted with a wistful smile.

"Vee, we're almost done," Sara said fifteen minutes later, "run along and let me bring these to Beerstein," she offered.

"Thank you." The temperature was on the cold side for a California winter in the south of the state, and Veronica reached for a warm sweater. "Sara, why don't you join us for lunch? We're eating on campus."

"No, but thanks. Have fun."

Veronica found Jay sitting on a bench in front of the

building after jerking her head in that direction in response to a wolf whistle. "I usually hit men for that,"
she warned him with a smile.

"Good, I like my women rough." He eased himself
from the bench and handed her a box. "This is for
you."

She knew from the size it was a replacement vase for
the one her son had broken. "Oh, Jay, I wish you
hadn't done that."

"Why?"

"Because you're just giving me too many things. It's
not right."

"Yes, it is, and I could never give you too many
things. Please accept it, Vee," he cajoled with a grin she
couldn't refuse.

"I will. Thank you, but no more for a while, promise?"

"No, darlin', I'm not in the habit of making promises I know I can't keep for more than a few days." His
hand found hers as they strolled along, and he held it
with fingers entwined and his thumb stroking her inner
wrist.

"Can you keep it simple, then, please?"

"I can't afford to send a Mercedes by," he remarked, raising her hand to his mouth. He kissed the
back.

"That's very consoling. I knew I could count on you
to be practical," she replied, a bit unnerved by his display of public affection. Veronica frowned, unaware of
how her hand stiffened in his, and Jennings released it
with a great deal of reluctance.

They found his son waiting for them at a table near
the door. J.J. stood and waved, and remained standing
until his father pulled out Veronica's seat. "My, my,"
she commented. "The two of you are so polite. You're

going to have to come by the house sometime and give my three sons lessons!''

"We'd love to," Jennings said quickly. "J.J. and I are experts in teaching the fine art of etiquette to young men, and you'll find our rates are quite reasonable.''

"Dad means he'll do it for a free meal," J.J. said pleasantly.

"Sold," Veronica agreed. "But not this week. I have exams coming up. Maybe early next week."

"I won't let you forget, darlin'," Jennings promised. "Let's get something to eat, shall we?" he suggested, glancing over to the long line at the cafeteria counter. "Vee, you don't have to wait in line. I'll get whatever you want."

"Dad, I went ahead and had something while you were waiting for Mrs. Dubcek. May I be excused to return to the bookstore? I couldn't find the book on Pascal I was looking for before," J.J. asked.

"All right, son. I'll meet you there, probably in an hour."

Veronica stood. "I think I'd rather wait in line with you than sit here by myself."

He pulled back the chair. "Good. How did your work go this morning?"

Veronica began to answer his question, stopping abruptly when she saw a frantic Sara Philips race into the cafeteria. "Jay, there's Sara, I wonder if she's looking for either of us. I'd better check." She waved and called the woman over.

"Vee, I'm so glad I found you! The high school just called. Both of your boys have been suspended and they want you to take them home and talk to the dean," she explained, breathless from her run to the cafeteria.

Veronica was stunned. Her two boys had never been

suspended from school, and fighting on campus was the only thing she could think of that would result in immediate suspension. "Oh, no. I don't believe this. Did they say why, Sara?"

"No, though I asked. They don't like to give information to anyone but the parents in most cases. My oldest son got suspended for a day once for telling the gym teacher to go to hell."

Veronica shook her head and frowned. "I can't imagine either Brad or Greg swearing at a teacher, much less both of them on the same day. I'd better call the school and get right over there. Sara, I'm sorry to stick you with extra work, but I may not get back this afternoon. The boys and I have a lot of talking to do. Tell Beerstein what happened for me, will you?" she asked, looking in her purse for a dime. "Can I borrow your car, Sara? Brad severed some wire the other day when he tried to tune mine up."

"Let me drive you over, Vee. I don't have any plans for the rest of the day," Jennings said before Sara could respond.

"Thank you. I'm so angry right now I'd probably think all the green lights were red and never get there."

Jennings patted her shoulder and gave her a dime. "There's a phone booth over there." He stood and chatted with Sara while she made the call. "So who's Beerstein?" he asked. "Your boss?"

Sara giggled. "Yeah, that's what we call him. He looks like he's ready to deliver any minute."

Jennings chuckled, his eyes fixated on Veronica. He saw the slight tremble in her hand as she pushed the buttons to dial, and his heart went out to her. "I knew a guy like that in Dallas. We used to tease him and say if it were stuffed with dollar bills, he'd be a millionaire."

Sara smiled, warming to Jennings. She still didn't

think he was much to look at, but it was easy to see how he would appeal to most anyone. "I won't tell you what we think Beerstein is stuffed with!" She saw Veronica slam down the receiver and rushed to her side, followed by Jennings. "Vee, what happened?"

Veronica was thin-lipped with anger and spoke in a clipped tone. "The two of them beat up another boy in the locker room. Two against one! I can't believe they would do something like that at all, much less the two of them against one boy!"

"Neither can I. I've known your boys since they were babies. I'm shocked. Is there any chance the school could be wrong?" Sara inquired, noticing the way Jennings took Vee's hand and glad her friend had someone to hold her that way.

"No. There were several witnesses, and three kids are in the nurse's office right this minute patching up their cuts. Two of them are mine. I have to go now, Sara. I'll call you tonight."

Jennings rested his hand on her elbow as they walked. "I'm parked over here," he directed. "Are any of the kids hurt badly?"

"No, nothing serious," she said grimly.

"Well, that's something," Jennings stated. "Don't let this get to you, Vee. These things happen with boys."

"Not with mine, they don't," she disagreed sharply, her anger not directed toward him. "I swear, I'm going to ground them until summer for this, maybe even for the entire year."

"There has to be an explanation. Kids who don't get into fights don't just go after someone without a pretty persuasive reason," he argued. "The red Datsun over there is mine." He held open the door for her. "Would you mind wearing the seat belt? These freeways make me nervous."

"No, not at all," she said, reaching on the floor behind her and then looking overhead when she couldn't find the belt. "Where is it?"

"In the center," he told her, passing it to her with one hand on the steering wheel. Jennings felt like he had been jolted by a thousand volts of electricity when his hand accidentally came into contact with the fullness of her breast. "I'm sorry, Vee," he apologized, unnecessarily because she had been too upset to notice the inadvertent gesture.

"Sorry, why?" she asked vaguely, rubbing her hands together in her lap.

"Never mind, honey. It was nothing. J.J. got into a fight once," he said as he backed out of the slot.

That galvanized her attention and she turned to him in the seat. "Really? How old was he?"

"Thirteen. How old are your kids?"

"The ones in trouble are fifteen and sixteen. I have a twelve-year-old in another school. Why did J.J. get in a fight?"

"Oh, we went on a fishing trip once to some jerkwater place down in Georgia. My car needed some minor work, and J.J. wandered down the street to get something to eat while I was dealing with the mechanic," he began. "Darlin', I need to know where the high school is," Jennings said when they were out of the parking area.

She had completely forgotten about giving him directions, and did so. "Tell me how you handled your son. I'm completely lacking in experience in this area."

"I don't have much myself, thank God. It was the only fight he ever got into."

"What happened?" she asked again.

"Well, like I said, J.J. wandered down to a hamburger stand where all the local kids apparently hung out. They made a few racist remarks. He's half Vietnamese, you know."

Veronica smiled. "Yes, Jay, I know the story."

"I guess you do. Anyway, these kids kept teasing him. You know how cruel children can be sometimes. J.J. ignored it for about five minutes, and then one of them asked how much his mother charged the American soldiers for her services. He blew up and jumped on the nearest guy."

"The poor boy. I can understand why he did what he did," she said sympathetically. "Was he badly hurt?"

"He still has a scar from the stitches on his forehead."

"I didn't notice."

"His hair covers it. Vee, I'm sure your boys will have a good explanation for what they did."

"I doubt it," she said sadly. "Blue-eyed boys with blond hair in Pasadena schools are rarely the targets of racism, and I can't think of many other things that would justify their behavior. Besides, the two-against-one thing really bothers me. If Greg had to fight, he should have done it fair and square, one on one, instead of running down the hall and getting his older brother to help him, don't you agree?"

Jennings nodded. "I suppose, but maybe other people were involved and the kids didn't plan for things to turn out the way they did."

"What did you tell J.J. when this incident occurred?" she asked, wondering herself about the boy's mother.

"Before or after I told him to never insult seven men when he's carrying a six shooter?" he asked with a sideways smile that was almost enough to charm Veronica from her dismal mood.

"There were seven of them?"

"You know, it all happened so fast we were never exactly sure, but there were a lot of them. This is where I turn, right?" He placed his hand on her shoulder when they came to a Stop sign.

"Yes. It's a miracle J.J. wasn't hurt any more if there were that many of them. He must have been a brave boy."

"No, he was a stupid boy and lucky to escape with just the cut on his forehead. A passing police officer broke up the fight right after it started, fortunately. Here we are," he said when the school came into view.

"What did you tell J.J. afterward?" she asked. Veronica reached for the door handle out of habit.

"I'll get the door for you, Vee," he said, rushing from his side to assist her. Jennings opened it and held out his hand to help her up.

"Jay, I may be fat, but I think I can manage to get out of the car on my own," she snapped in an uncharacteristic manner, her nerves overwrought with tension.

Jennings frowned and dropped his hand. "You're not fat, and I would have done the same thing for any lady. What kind of men are you used to dating?"

"None. I don't date. I'm sorry. That was a bitchy thing to say."

He locked the door. "It's all right. You have every right to be bitchy today."

"I suppose, but I should be taking it out on the boys, not you," she said with a long sigh. "What did you tell J.J.?"

"I said I would have done the same thing," he admitted, "but I added that didn't make it right. We talked about alternative ways to deal with the situation, and concluded walking away was the best one."

"Did he ever have to walk away from something like that again?"

"A few times, yes. I hope you don't mind my tagging along like this. I haven't seen your boys since the year Mike brought them to a computer fair in Manhattan. When was that?"

"Four years ago," she answered. "I was going to go too, but my youngest, Keith, came down with a severe case of tonsillitis. Jay, the school is within walking distance of my house. I think it would be better for me to deal with this situation on my own. Thank you so much for the ride, and I'm sorry I had to ruin your lunch."

"You didn't ruin anything. Are you sure there's nothing I can do?" he insisted.

"I don't think so. The boys have refused to tell the gym teacher and the dean why they fought with the other boy. They don't know you very well, and I think it may inhibit them more to have a stranger around," she speculated. "Oh, damn!"

"What, honey?"

"I left that vase you gave me on campus."

"Don't worry about that now. May I call you later this evening and see how you and the kids are?" he requested.

"I'd like that."

He kissed her cheek. "Okay, I'll call you around nine. Hang in there, kid."

"I intend to," she replied over her shoulder as he headed back to his car. Veronica wasn't certain if she should go to the nurse's office or to see the dean first, and finally decided to talk to the dean. Since the boys' injuries were minor, it was likely they had already finished with the nurse.

The dean was waiting for her in the outer office and jumped to his feet when she identified herself. "Mrs. Dubcek, yes, I thought so, I saw you pull up. It's too bad Mr. Dubcek couldn't stay. I'm not getting any-where with your sons."

Veronica's blood felt like it had just been exploded from a volcano and she struggled to maintain her composure. By some form of egocentric logic she had always assumed everyone at the school knew Mike was no longer with them. "Yes, it's too bad Mr. Dubcek couldn't stay," she said somberly, regretting the sarcastic inflection when she recalled Mr. Gibson was hired shortly after Mike's death. "Where are my sons, Mr. Gibson?"

"In my office. Shall we join them?"

"Not right away. I want to know what you've been told about this incident first, if you don't mind," she asked tightly.

"Please be seated," he instructed, indicating two vacant chairs in the corner of the room.

"Thank you," Veronica said as she sat down. "How is the other boy doing?"

"Not too well. The nurse sent him to the hospital for X rays. He fell down and hit his head on a bench when Brad tackled him. There's a possibility of a minor concussion. We can't be sure here."

Veronica gasped. "My God, I didn't know it was that bad."

"I didn't have as much information when I talked to you on the phone as I do now," he elaborated.

"Do you know what started all of this?"

"No, I have no idea. Ted Lewis—that's the boy your sons attacked—was so upset the nurses and his mother wouldn't let anyone talk to him, and Brad and Greg are being most uncooperative. The coach tried to talk to them, I did, and we even called in the principal, Mrs. Matthews. Neither one of them are saying anything. As a matter of fact, both seem thoroughly unrepentant and rather proud of what they did, and totally uncaring about the consequences. I've increased the usual suspension time from three days to a week for a number of factors. First, it was two against one, secondly, they refuse to discuss the matter, and finally because of their attitude. And I'm going to ask the coach to suspend them from the track team for the remainder of the season."

Veronica knew the boys would take that hard but felt the dean's stringent punishment was warranted. "The track team means a lot to both of my sons, Mr. Gibson, but I think they deserve to be suspended from the team," she said glumly, still numb from shock over the event. "Are you certain there's nothing more you can tell me about this?"

"Not really. From what I've been able to gather, Ted Lewis said something to Greg while the boys were running laps around the track. Greg left the gym and went to Brad's math class and motioned for him to come out into the hall. Your sons waited until Ted was alone in the locker room after the physical education class ended and jumped on him. The person who teaches the next period heard the scuffle and broke it up. By the way, Brad hit Mr. Boyd, the fourth period PE teacher, while he was trying to restrain him. Normally striking a teacher carries a stiff penalty around here, expulsion from school, but Mr. Boyd is convinced the blow was accidental and doesn't want to pursue the matter so we're dropping that particular aspect," Mr. Gibson explained.

Veronica simply couldn't fathom the thought of her boys in a fight, much less getting suspended and coming so close to expulsion from high school. "I'll have to thank Mr. Boyd for that," she said in a small voice. "How is he? I hope Brad didn't hurt him." Both her sons were tall like their father, the oldest five ten and still growing and the younger nearly the same, and Veronica shuddered at the thought of the sturdy young man striking an adult, one who was probably close to his size if not smaller.

"No, Jack Boyd is a pretty tough guy. He used to play professional football with the Raiders. Shall we join your sons now? I'd like to make one more attempt to reason with the pair, and then I don't want to see either around here for five days."

"Yes, I understand. I'll do whatever I can to cooperate with you in this matter, Mr. Gibson." When he opened the door to his inner office, Veronica saw her sons huddled together and whispering to one another. They quieted down immediately. She found their attitude as disturbing as their recent behavior. The boys exuded raw anger and clearly showed no signs of regret.

"What is going on?" Veronica asked tersely, taking a seat near the boys.

"We got into a fight with Ted Lewis," Brad ground out after a few moments of silence.

"Why?" Veronica demanded.

Brad and Greg exchanged conspiratorial glances and didn't say anything. Veronica repeated the question. "We don't want to talk about it now, Mom," Greg finally said.

"Mrs. Dubcek, the coach and I have been round and round with the boys. They're determined not to say anything here. Why don't you take them home, try to reason with them, and we can talk in a week, after their suspension has ended. I must warn you, however, that future incidents of this nature will result in automatic expulsion from school."

Veronica rose from her seat. "Let's go home, you

two." She apologized to the dean once more for her sons' behavior and left the inner office. "Can I call you later this afternoon to inquire about the Lewis boy?" she asked.

"Yes, certainly. Hold on a minute and I'll ask the secretary if she's heard anything." He spoke to the woman briefly and told Veronica the boy had suffered no serious injuries and wouldn't need stitches.

"So, he doesn't have a concussion either?" she asked anxiously.

"No, not so far as they can tell at this point. I'll keep you posted, Mrs. Dubcek," he assured her. "But he seems to be fine."

"That's wonderful. I'm very pleased to hear that," Veronica said as she left the building.

Brad and Greg were walking a few feet ahead of her. "Next time, we'll have to hit him with brass knuckles," Brad told his brother.

"There had damn well better not be a next time," Veronica cut in sharply. They returned home in an angry silence, Veronica too upset to speak and all too aware how futile dialogue would be at the present anyway. When they arrived home, she sat them both down on the sofa, taking a wing chair opposite the boys. "Okay, talk."

"We don't have anything to say, Mom," Greg said very wearily. His bravado and anger seemed to have diminished during the fifteen-minute walk from the school, and Veronica welcomed his change in attitude.

"Yes, we do, Greg. What you did is wrong, son. Maybe you had a good reason for it, I don't know. But I can't evaluate anything unless you tell me what's going on. Please, Greg, talk to me," she pleaded gently.

Greg seemed on the verge of saying something until his brother's cautionary glance silenced him.

Veronica turned to Brad. "What do you have to say for yourself? You know, you're older than Greg, and I've always counted on you to steer him in the right direction when he goes wrong, not encourage him to fight or make a serious error in judgment. I'm very disappointed in you, Brad. I can't recall ever being more disappointed in the two of you."

"Mom, we had our reasons, and they were good ones," Brad relented, setting some of his righteous indignation aside.

"I have to know what they were," Veronica insisted. "Tell me."

Brad thought about the question while examining a cut on his hand. It started to bleed again, and Veronica went into the bathroom and returned with a first-aid kit.

"How did this happen?" she asked, a good guess in mind.

"When my hand had a run in with Lewis's front teeth."

Veronica flinched. "Oh, Brad, whatever the problem was, we could have dealt with it in some other way." She dabbed the wound with hydrogen peroxide and bandaged it. "Tell me what happened now," she insisted after studying the little cut on Greg's left cheek and deciding it didn't require any more attention than what the school nurse had already done by rinsing the wound and putting an antiseptic on the abrasion.

Greg was the first to speak. "Mom, we don't want to hurt you."

"This has something to do with me?"

"Yeah," Greg said. "If we promise not to fight again, can we just forget the whole thing?"

"No, I have to know why you did what you did. Don't feel you have to be protective of me, Greg. I think I can handle it. What happened?"

Greg looked at Brad and received tacit permission to continue. "Mom, it was about Dad. Lewis was shooting his mouth off about how Dad killed himself because of a scandal at work. They said he was selling trade secrets to foreign governments and got caught."

Veronica winced and pressed her folded arms into her abdomen. She had never told the boys the true circumstances surrounding their father's death. Except for John Silvers and a few other executives at the computer company everyone thought Mike had died from a heart attack while working late one night. The idea was actually originated by Dolph Goodmen, a partner in the firm who found Mike; Veronica and John were too numb with shock to think of anything at the time. It had always made sense to her. Why put the boys through any unnecessary suffering when they had already lost so much, and since the software thefts were to be kept undercover anyway, it seemed best all around to conceal the facts. Greg assumed his mother paled in inner agony because of what Lewis had said about their father, but as Brad watched her he began to wonder if his understanding of his father's death was accurate.

Brad left the sofa and sat on the arm of his mother's chair, resting his hand on her shoulder. "Mom, that's not true, is it?"

Veronica couldn't say anything, and he repeated his question.

"Oh, Mom, did Dad commit suicide?"

She knew they had to be told the truth. "Yes, Brad, he did. There seemed to be no reason to tell you children at the time. I was only trying to spare you from more suffering. If I was wrong in that decision, I'm very sorry. It was the best I could do at the time."

"I think I understand, Mom," Brad said quietly. "Greg, don't cry," he told his younger brother.

Greg swiped at a tear. "Who's crying? What about the rest of it? All that computer theft stuff? Did Dad do that too?"

Veronica had to hedge on that one. "It's never been conclusively proven, but yes, it looks like he may have. We just don't know."

"I don't believe it," Greg said resolutely in defense of his father. "Dad wouldn't do something like that. I know it."

"Maybe he didn't. If it's any consolation, one of your father's best friends from Vietnam is certain your father couldn't have stolen the programs," she assured him.

"Who? The guy you were dancing with at the Silvers' party?" Brad asked.

Veronica suddenly felt nauseated. "I take it the Lewis boy learned about your father from someone who was at the party? I didn't see him or his parents there."

"He was there, Mom. He overheard the guy you were with talking to Dr. Silvers," Brad explained. "That's another thing..." he began, trailing off. "Forget it."

"I don't want to forget it. Let's get all this out into the open, okay? What did the Lewis boy say about me and Jay Jennings? That's the name of your father's friend from Vietnam, by the way, in case I didn't tell you."

"Mom, really, Lewis is an idiot. I've always hated that guy."

"What did he say?"

Brad took a deep breath. "He said it was pretty lousy of you to be making it at a party with Dad's best friend."

The air came from her lungs in a prolonged sigh. "I'm not sure if I know exactly what making it means, but Jay and I shared a few dances and talked, that was all."

"You don't have to explain anything to me. Dad's been dead for two years now, and it's your business who you want to date. I really don't care," he got out slowly. "And you don't either, right, Greg?"

Greg shook his head. "I don't care. I just wish Dad could have talked to us about these things instead of doing what he did. Even if he pirated the programs, he could have said he was sorry and made it up to the company."

"I know, honey, I know," Veronica said with commiseration. She had asked herself the same question thousands of times. "Have either of you eaten lunch?"

"No. We got kicked out right before noon."

"I haven't eaten either, boys. Let's go in the kitchen, fix something, and talk about this incident that happened with Ted. I understand now why you fought with him, but it's still not right. Come along now." They followed her into the next room, where the remainder of the afternoon was spent discussing the events of the day and what had happened two years ago. Greg and his mother did their best not to cry. Of the three, Brad seemed most profoundly affected by the details about his father's death, yet he sat there dry-eyed and composed, infinitely sad.

Chapter Six

Veronica found herself emotionally and physically exhausted after a marathon session with her two oldest sons, one in which the youngest became a participant when he returned from school at three thirty. Keith didn't appear particularly upset to learn how his father had died, and Veronica was grateful for his reaction, hoping upon hope his superficial attitude clearly reflected his inner feelings, unlike those of the eldest's. Brad projected a grieving serenity, but some internal sense forewarned Veronica the boy's distress ran deep. She made a maternal gesture to reach out to her oldest, the one his father had always seemed to love most of all, but Brad was unreachable, choosing to let his dinner grow cold before he opted to watch the sun set over the mountains beyond their veranda.

Since there was nothing else to be done, Veronica made a cup of herbal tea and went to bathe, wondering as she sat in the hot water if she had betrayed her sons, for in their mutual grief her thoughts turned to yet another male. Jay Jennings was never far from her mind, never had been since the moment they met.

She was soaking in the tub when Brad knocked on her door. The sudden rap startled Veronica from a sweet reverie where the thoughts of Jay were as warm as the fragrant sudded water that enveloped her tired body.

"Mom?" he said quietly. "Would you be okay alone here tonight?"

"Certainly, Brad," she called out. "Why do you ask? Were you kids planning on going somewhere?"

"Yeah, I was wondering if I could borrow the car and take Keith and Greg down to a movie."

"It's a school night," she reminded him, reaching under the water for a bar of soap.

"Not for me and Greg, it isn't, and we won't stay past eleven. All right?"

"Brad, the car isn't running. When you tuned it up you did something wrong with a distributor wire. Why don't you go on the weekend instead?" she recommended.

"I fixed that this afternoon, Mom. It's running fine. Can we go?"

She figured they all needed a little fantasy at this point in their lives to distract them from reality. "Yes, you may. Take the money from my purse. It's downstairs on the sideboard," she instructed. She had already decided not to make good on her threat to restrict the boys' activities because of the fight. Whereas she certainly didn't condone their behavior, Veronica was convinced after their conversations that the fight was an isolated event, duly provoked though unfairly fought, and was not apt to be repeated.

"Thanks. Do you need anything at the store? I can stop at the all-night market if you do."

"No, honey, thanks for asking. Have fun at the movies, and don't stay for a second show. Keith has to be in bed around eleven at the latest." Veronica lingered in the tub until the water was lukewarm, stirring bubbles with her hands and thinking about Jay.

The sheer delight of those images played pitch penny against the powerful forces of her sense of duty and lost. Her tired brain felt like a six-cylinder engine running on eight pistons by the time she left the bath to dress, but she had come to a decision about the relationship with Jay.

She had so much to do and so little time to do it in, she rationalized, unwilling to admit her guilt and feelings of responsibility had dominated her sense of self. The correspondence law courses were demanding, exams were coming up soon, and the boys needed her, especially now that they had learned the truth.

Though the two youngest had taken it well on the surface, Veronica was beginning to think their outward reaction was in part a display of bravado for her sake, and the news could well prove to be disconcerting to them in the future. She didn't really know, and the fact that she was rationalizing the relationship with Jay out of her life became more obvious as she continued to mull over the situation. Some strong inner sense evolved for the purposes of self-preservation dictated that she was pulling herself too hard in too many directions at the present. Something had to go and Jay was the most dispensable, she concluded, while all the time Ted Lewis's comment about she and Mike's best friend ripped through her like a stone cast in a calm pond, sending the concentric circles in widening arcs to the edges of the water.

The phone rang and she knew it was him. Veronica let it ring, slowly drying herself off until the caller gave up, only to dial again a few minutes later.

Jennings tried once more that evening and was forced to conclude Veronica and the boys had gone out somewhere. The thought that she was intentionally avoiding him crossed his mind each time the phone went unanswered, a possibility that was proven correct when Jennings placed a call to her office the following morning. Sara answered and told him Veronica was available, only to return with a hasty apology that she had apparently just stepped out of the office, and the incident was repeated three days later. She failed to return the calls and left a very unhappy man pounding on a computer system borrowed from John Silvers at his parents' home in Glendale.

The source of his father's frustration was obvious to J.J., and the more he thought about it the less he liked Veronica Dubcek. She had been pleasant enough when they'd met at the Silvers' party and later at the university, but the boy didn't think she was anything special, clearly undeserving of the obsession his father seemed to have with her. J.J. had known so many other women, so much more attractive than the dumpy Dubcek widow, who had chased his father from one country to the next, and his Dad hadn't done much to any of them except take them to bed once in a while. Why then this big hang-up on her? he asked himself for the tenth time as his father sat brooding out on a chaise longue in the backyard.

"How's it going, Dad?" J.J. asked, sitting on the grass next to his chair.

"Can't complain," Jennings muttered. "How was your day?"

"Oh, all right. I went to Cal Tech and talked to my counselor."

Jennings's interest sparked. "Were you near the administration building?"

"Yeah, I had to file a paper there. I didn't see the Dubcek woman, if that's what you're getting at, and I consider it a blessing, to tell you the truth, Dad."

Jennings smiled indulgently. "You're lucky I'm too

tired to get up and slap you for a crack like that, J.J. You've been making snide comments about her all week. What did Vee ever do to you?"

"Nothing really. I just don't think she's worth the energy you're investing in her, that's all."

"Who says I'm investing any energy in her? I haven't talked to her in nearly a week."

"You've been in a lousy mood ever since you met her. She's just not worth it."

"I'll be the judge of that." Jennings stood and stretched. Vee wasn't going to get away with shutting him out of her life completely. If she wanted him to leave her alone, she was going to have to confront him face to face and tell him exactly why. "J.J., tell your grandparents I'm going out for a while, will you?"

"Yeah, sure," he said glumly, knowing his father was undoubtedly off to chase after the Dubcek woman. "Good luck, Dad."

Jennings drove his car to the front of her house, parked, and dialed up on his mobile phone unit.

"Vee, how are you doing?" he asked without saying hello.

"Fine," she replied automatically. "And yourself?"

The formal note in her voice chilled Jennings to the bone. "I'm fine, Vee. We haven't talked for a while. Tell me about your sons. What happened last week when they were suspended from school? You know, I have tried to get in touch with you."

"I'm sorry, I've been busy."

"So tell me about the boys."

"Oh, it was nothing. I really don't want to talk about it now."

"I didn't realize they suspended kids for nothing in high school these days," he said flatly. "Were they hurt?" he tried.

"No, just a few minor scrapes. The other boy was more seriously hurt, but he's okay too."

"How are the boys taking the suspension?"

"As well as can be expected."

"Are you making good on your promise to ground them until summer?"

"No, they went to the movies last week and now they're out again."

She was home alone and he wanted to go to her. "Vee, I returned to the college cafeteria last week and retrieved the vase for you. Let me come over now and give it to you."

"No! I really don't want it, Jay."

"What?"

She modified her statement. "I mean not tonight. It can wait. I'm tired and have a lot of reading to do."

Jennings thought for a while and decided to lay it on the line. "Vee, why is it that I feel you're not being totally honest with me? I know you're upset over the boys, but your attitude toward me seems remarkably different from what it's been. Talk to me, will you?"

Veronica welcomed his directness after overcoming the initial shock of his blunt statement. Now she could get it over once and for all with him. "Jay, I've been thinking. I'm not up to a relationship right now. I have two full-time jobs, the law courses and the one at Cal Tech, and a house and three kids to worry about. There just isn't any energy left for something else."

His hands tightened into an impotent fist of frustration. So Dubcek's ghost had reared its ugly head again. Jennings wasn't buying all of her story, not by a long shot. "I'm coming over, Vee. We have to discuss this personally, not over the damn telephone."

"Jay, no please. I'm tired."

"It's only seven o'clock. I'll be gone by eight," he promised.

"Eight! I don't want to talk about that for an hour!"

"Then give me half an hour, fifteen minutes, five. Hell, Vee, last week when you said I could kiss you, I didn't know you planned on kissing me off."

Veronica digested his remark, spoken in the most beguiling of tones, and laughed into the receiver. "No fair making me laugh when I'm trying to be serious. And if you say all's fair in love and war, I'm going to hang up."

"I won't. Let me come over and give you the vase and talk to you, please?" So much for your macho-man image, Jennings mused. He was literally begging this woman for a few minutes of her time and not in the least ashamed.

"All right. Do you know where I live?"

"Darlin', I'm talking from a mobile phone right in front of your house," he confessed.

"You don't give up, do you?"

"Not where you're concerned, no."

"I didn't see a phone in your car."

"It's concealed. Some of my security work with DOD used to be undercover."

"I see. Well, since you're in the neighborhood, drop in, but I can't promise you any undercover work here," she flirted, amazed at how little resolve she truly had when it came to Jay Jennings.

Jennings chuckled. "It's a deal. I'll be right in."

"Okay." Veronica remembered she was dressed only in a bathrobe and wanted to ask him to wait, but she could already hear the buzz of the disconnected phone in her ear. She ran a brush through her hair and stared at her rather disheveled image in the mirror. Oh, well, it didn't matter what she had on. Romance wasn't on her agenda for the evening anyway. She heard his knock on the front door as soon as she left her bedroom.

"Hi," Veronica said. She opened the door but failed to invite him in, too overcome by a certain charisma on his behalf that continued to eat away at the foundations of her resolve to avoid him. Jay had on a three-piece suit, of the type another man would wear to work if his job demanded such dress, but Veronica strongly suspected the formal attire was his notion of courting clothes. She found him dashing, the rainbow eyes smiling into her own with an expectant curve to his lips. She wondered just what he expected.

"Good evening, Vee," he replied, his every sense bombarded by the fresh afterbath scent of her, the little wet waves on her forehead, and the way the robe tied right under her breasts. Whatever she had on under that robe, it couldn't have been much, Jennings concluded. "May I come in?"

"Oh! Yes, I'm sorry. You look very nice tonight. Aren't we a pair?" she laughed, closing the door behind them.

Jennings agreed. "Yes, I suppose so. You're dressed for bed and I'm dressed for a night out on the town. Maybe we can wind up somewhere in between."

"That sounds like a cup of coffee in the living room," Veronica commented. "Would you like some?"

"Yes, please. Oh, here's the vase."

She noticed the weight when she accepted it. "I thought you said it was the same style?"

"No, I said it was a replacement. Open it."

Veronica laughed when she saw the sturdy unbreakable plastic container inside. "Thank you, Jay. There was a time last week when a vase such as this would have come in very handy. I could have tossed it at each of my oldest sons in turn and still had something for the flowers."

"I'm glad you like it," he answered. Jennings would gladly have given her one made of silver and gold, embedded with every jewel he could afford, beg, borrow, or steal, but at her request he'd kept it simple. "On second thought, I'd prefer a drink to a cup of coffee."

"Jay, I'm sorry. I rarely entertain and don't drink when I'm alone. Unless you can make do with some very rock-bottom quality sherry I use for cooking Chinese dishes, I don't have anything to offer you," she explained apologetically. Veronica placed the vase on the sideboard next to the tiny pine tree. The inexpensive dime store plastic was quite a contrast to the elegant dark blue glass that preceded it, but the sentiments they induced inside her were the same, a tingly sort of appreciation for the gift giver, a sense of wonderment at his kindness. The silly five and dime vase with its flamboyant pattern of pink and white flamingos had won a place in her heart forever, and Veronica couldn't imagine ever parting with it.

"Not to worry, little darlin'," he said in his slow drawl. "I figured as much. I have a bottle tucked away in my car."

Veronica laughed. "You do, huh? Just what kind of undercover work were you involved in? The seduction of female agents?"

"Me? Naw, I picked it up a few minutes ago. Back in a jiffy." He returned with a dry white Spanish wine.

"I'll get you a glass."

"Get two. I never drink alone either."

"Jay, I have to get back to my reading soon. I'm taking a course in criminal law right now. Some of that stuff is enough to put me to sleep when I'm stone sober." Veronica stooped and removed a long-stemmed glass from the lower cabinet of the sideboard.

Jennings dropped to his knees and removed another one. "Then just hold it so I don't feel like I'm in this alone," he replied, somewhat cryptically.

She allowed him to pour for her. The man was as disarming as wind on a neatly stacked pile of autumn leaves, taking order and casting it to free blowing confusion. Veronica marveled at her indecision where Jay Jennings was concerned. Her better judgment told her to retreat now before it was too late, but when she looked into those rainbow hazel eyes, she felt her chances of escape were about as probable as a downhill skier winning a race by taking a reverse route up the slopes. "Thank you," she said simply.

She led him into the living room and asked him to be seated. "I'm sorry if I sounded so rude on the phone a little while ago," she began, taking a seat across from him.

"Been a long week, darlin'?" he asked taking a sip of wine.

She nodded. The fact that they spent most of their time together discussing her problems had begun to impress itself upon Veronica during the week when they didn't speak to one another. She realized that other than a few details about his son and former marriage, she knew very little about Jay, and had perhaps been self-indulgent by crying on his shoulder as much as she had. "But everything worked out well. How was your day? What did you do?"

"Do you really want to know?" he asked over the rim of a glass that had belonged to her mother.

"You bet I do," she said sincerely.

"Okay. All morning I thought about you, desired you, wondered how you were doing…" Jennings paused, on the verge of telling her how he had spent two hours lying on a hammock he had strung up between a pair of secluded oak trees on his property, trying to gauge the depth of his feelings for her, speculating on the differences between falling in love and the actual state of being in love, and concluding it was all a matter of semantics. He was falling in love with her, or he already loved her, it made no difference how one labeled his emotions. All he knew for certain was that he cared deeply for Vee and had a very strong foreboding that his intensity would force her to retreat from him. He kept his love to himself.

Jennings cleared his throat and began once more. "And then I wondered how everything worked out with your boys, wondered why you wouldn't return my phone calls. Then I took J.J. out for lunch. We talked a little about the copied programs two years back, and went home and reviewed some tapes John Silvers gave us." He was about to elaborate on his afternoon thoughts of her when she interrupted.

"Did you come up with anything that could prove Mike innocent?" she asked, a bit flushed from his admissions. God, how she too had thought about him, desired him, wondered how he passed each moment of the days they had been apart.

Jennings shook his head. "No, I'm sorry. There's nothing yet. How much do you know about the way the data was encoded, Vee?" he asked, wishing he'd not mentioned Dubcek at all.

"I'm really not into computers, Jay. I don't know much. I do know the key to the code was the product of two long prime numbers, each about a hundred digits, right?"

"Yes, that's correct. It's called the RSA cryptosystem."

"Right, for Rivest, Shamir, and Adleman from MIT. That much I know. I also understand that even using a sophisticated computer to decipher the code it would take forever," she recalled. "Something like three point eight billion years for a two-hundred-digit key, right?"

"That's exactly correct. All of the stolen information was apparently tapped from the phone lines running from the company offices to your house. Supposedly no one except Mike had the decoding key, and no one could figure it out unless he passed it along, but there has to be a bug in that logic somewhere," he said, loosening his dark green silk tie. "Vee, it's much warmer than I thought. Would you mind if I removed my jacket?"

"Of course not. You're so formal," she remarked. "Does that come from working with the Department of Defense all these years?" She stood to take his coat. "I'll hang this in the hall closet for you."

"Thank you. Yes, I suppose a lot of it comes from that," he agreed, passing her the jacket.

Veronica hung it up and returned to the subject of her late husband. "And I understand that even John Silvers didn't have the key to data sent here?"

"That's right. Of course, they had access to the same data, but when the pirated disks came out it was obvious they were taken from the phone lines here."

"I know. They had some secret codes in there that didn't affect the way the program ran but identified the original source of data, as I remember," she said slowly. Veronica took her first sip of wine. "It seems to me Mike would have been smart enough to know the identification code was there and removed it before selling the information, unless, unless—" She left the sentence unfinished.

Jennings felt it would be good for Veronica to get her feelings out into the open. "Unless what?" he urged gently.

"Unless Mike just didn't give a damn who knew what he did and planned on taking off somewhere with whatever he expected to make on the pirated disks," she got out painfully.

"No, I can't accept that. There has to be another explanation. Mike didn't know how the data could be traced back to him. The identification codes were tagged on afterward by some guy like me," he explained. "As a matter of fact, I advised John Silvers on how to secure his data. I didn't do the job myself, I was on assignment in South America at the time."

Veronica frowned and took another sip of wine. "It sounds to me like John and the other partners didn't trust my husband very much. I mean, putting secret codes on the disk so they could trap him."

"Those are standard procedures in the business. They would have caught Silvers or anyone else who passed along information, or was thought to have done so. Mike knew measures were taken to protect the data, he just didn't know exactly what. That wasn't his job. Like I said, that's my line of business."

"I see. I never knew exactly what you did, other than that you were involved in security work for the government. I wish I was as convinced as you seem to be about Mike's innocence. Sometimes I am and other times I'm not," she admitted. Veronica tucked her legs underneath her and put her hand over the wineglass when Jennings made a motion to refill it. "I've had all I want, thank you."

"Vee, I don't believe Mike was guilty. I lived side by side with the man once, fought side by side with him. I knew him," he said emphatically.

"I lived and fought side by side with him, too," she replied with a rueful smile. "So, you think he did what he did," she continued, having difficulty with the word suicide, "because he couldn't stand to live with the dishonor of people believing he was guilty?"

"Yes, that's exactly what I think. I always found Mike to be a man with a very high sense of personal honor. My theory is that he may have inadvertently done something to give the code away and blamed himself for it. The company meant a lot to him, you know," Jennings related to her, thinking about the days in foxholes a long time before when Dubcek and Silvers and Olson and Dupont and the rest of them passed the hours of insanity by talking about how rich and successful they'd all be once they hit the States again and got out of that godawful place.

First, they were all going to get college degrees on the GI bill, and then they were going to pool their talent and other resources and go into business together. Each had his own idea of what the most lucrative business would be. He and Dubcek were for going into real estate and developing those huge new underground shopping malls that were springing up everywhere back home. Olson thought the way to go was with a chain of fast-food restaurants like McDonald's, only serving chicken and ribs instead of hamburgers. Dupont thought they could study the stock market and make it big there, but Silvers had steered them toward the computer industry because of what he had picked up on a furlough in Tokyo.

"I know the company meant a great deal to him. He used to write to me about it from Vietnam before there even was a company. You were going to be one of the original investors in the first business, weren't you?" she remembered.

"Yes, but I had J.J. and couldn't take any financial risks at the time they were getting started," he recollected.

Veronica shook her head and sighed. "It's just as well you didn't. They took a tremendous loss two years ago. I was certain they'd have to sell out what they had left, but John Silvers and Jerry Olson managed to get some new investors together and salvage what they had. Speaking of which, I ran into Rebecca the other day. She tells me you're thinking of joining the company after all these years."

"That's right. I have another offer to do security work at Universal Studios to consider before I make a decision on it though." Jennings refilled his glass and tried to think of a way to get Veronica from her chair to the sofa. She was driving him crazy with that soft fabric bathrobe that reminded him of a towel, and he was willing to bet from his observations she had nothing on underneath, with the possible exception of a pair of panties, from the way her full breasts molded to the material. Jennings was glad he'd phoned her from in front of the house, not giving her a chance to get dressed.

"I see. Is there a need for sophisticated security protection at the studios?"

"Yes, the systems aren't quite as sophisticated as most of what I've done in the past, but it sounds like interesting work and I'm inclined toward a few changes in my life right now. Speaking of change, Vee, we have to talk," he said after a significant pause that she knew heralded a switch in the topic of conversation.

"Funny thing, I thought we were," she said evasively.

Jennings chuckled and held out one hand to her. "Would you come sit by me? I'd come to you, but I don't think the two of us can fit in that chair."

"I'm lucky I can," she laughed. "If my latest attempt at dieting backfires I may not be able to fit in here much longer myself."

He put his forefinger over his lips. "Shush, Vee, I don't like it when you put yourself down like that. Come here now." Jennings left the sofa and offered her his hands.

She accepted them and stood, her gaze transfixed by a pair of the loveliest eyes she had ever seen in her life. The little yellow flecks around his pupils reminded her of honey held up to the sun or gold coins under clear water. It was a bright, dazzling color, and the blue there was the pure blue of a spring sky. "You have the prettiest eyes," she told him once more. Her hands were still in his and the pressure increased.

"Thank you, so do you. I like your freckles, too," he told her, staring down at the ample cleavage that was making his blood flow more swiftly through his veins. "How far down do they go?"

Veronica was aware of the angle of his glance and didn't mind, finding a delicious delight in being the object of his admiration. "Not far. They're from the sun." The circular pattern of his thumbs on her wrists drew out her breath in a fluttery sigh, and Jennings raised her palms to his mouth, kissing each in turn.

"Come sit down," he directed, deciding against kissing her lips then. Jennings eased Veronica downward and sat as close to her as he dared without making her uncomfortable. They were about a foot apart.

"Where were we?" Veronica asked, her palms on fire from two kisses unspeakably tender and sweet.

"We were going to talk," he reminded her. "If you don't mind discussing it, I'd like to know what happened with your boys at school. And there's something else on my mind." He shifted sideways, winding up with one arm extended out and resting behind Veronica's neck.

Her eyes had followed the movement of his arm. Veronica was upright in the sofa, but she knew where her head would be if she leaned back. "What's that?"

"I want to know why it was that my promised kiss sounded like it had turned into a kiss-off from the way you've been avoiding me all week," he said bluntly and with an inflorescent smile.

"Do you still feel that way?" Veronica asked in a tone somewhere between coy and serious.

Jennings laughed and ran his hand through his dark windblown hair. "No—how can I when you're looking at me like that?" The arm on the sofa came to rest on her shoulder. "Tell me what I did right to make you change your mind so I can do it again if you decide against this relationship at some other time in the future," he flirted, gently massaging the back of her neck with his open hand.

Veronica giggled. "I don't know. You're just so ... so nice."

"That's me, Mr. Nice Guy," he quipped. "What did I do earlier to make you forget that very self-evident fact? Accidentally bare my fangs?"

"No, nothing like that. It was tied into what happened at the school, and a comment some kid made to Brad about us," she said in a partial truth.

"The kid your boys fought with?"

"Yes."

"You'll have to tell me where he lives. J.J. and I are going to take him on next time if he says anything that can turn you away from me. I hope your boys won." He was stroking her earlobe now, and Veronica wondered what would happen when Jay finally kissed her.

It would be near ecstasy, she concluded when his

hand began to work its magic on the back of her head, tangling through her hair, damp from a bath. "I'll do that. Maybe the four of you can get together and take the Lewis boy on."

"So, what did this kid say about us? If he's at all psychic and can read my mind right now, he'd have a pretty erotic tale to tell." Her hair felt like wet gossamer in his hand, Jennings thought, whatever in the hell that felt like. But it had to be close to this, her hair so soft and fine he could touch her that way forever. The sweet scent of the shampoo she used drifted to his nostrils like jasmine on a good breeze, and Jennings had to get closer to her. He eliminated the twelve inches between them.

"He was at the Silvers' party. I didn't even see him."

"I wouldn't have noticed had I known the kid. I didn't see anyone but you that night. What did he have to say about us?" Jennings asked.

"He said it was lousy of me to be making it with one of Mike's best friends."

Based upon what he knew Jennings could easily understand how the remark would have upset her. "I'm sorry. How did your kids take it?"

"Take what? The comment or the fact we were together at the party?"

"Both."

"Basically they said it was my business who I see, and I'm sure the boy's remark was a factor in Greg and Brad's decision to go after him the way they did." Their thighs were touching, and Veronica could feel the warmth of him through the layers of material that separated their bare skin. She placed her hand on his leg, right above the knee, and Jay took it, leaving their hands where they were.

"What were other factors?"

"Jay, I never told the boys how their father died. They thought it was from a heart attack, and they didn't know anything about the software scandal either. I suppose I should have known someone would tell them sooner or later, but I sort of blocked all that out," she confided. Veronica petted the fine dark down on the back of his hand. The little hairs were resilient, and sprang up as she moved her fingertips around on his skin.

Jennings raised the hand that had been on her lap and kissed it. "I can understand why you didn't give them the full story, Vee," he said sympathetically. "There's a lot of things I'd never tell J.J. about his past either."

"I can imagine. Jay, were you in love with his mother?" He was holding both of her hands now, with one resting near his knee and the other across his chest. Veronica could feel the strong, even beat of his heart beneath her palm.

"In love with her? No, never. She slept with everyone and I had no respect for her. Over the years I've come to understand what drove her to take up such a life-style. The money she brought home supported a family of fifteen, and without her selling her body to the men they would have starved."

She'd never realized the boy's mother was actually a prostitute. "Then how do you know J.J. is yours?" Veronica realized that was the wrong question to ask. Jay lost his blissful, contented expression, the one that reminded her of a Buddhist monk who had just found Nirvana, and frowned. "Oh, Jay, honey, I'm sorry. That was a stupid, insensitive thing to say."

"No, it was a reasonable question, but I really don't want to get into all that now. Let's just say I had my ways of knowing whose boy he was, and J.J. is mine."

She found his pained expression unbearable. "Come here." Veronica took Jay's face in her hands.

"What are you going to do?" Jennings demanded softly, wrapping his arms around her waist.

"Kiss you."

"Off or on?"

"On."

"I'm already on."

She brushed her forefinger across his lips to silence him. "Be quiet."

Jennings had expected her first kiss to be timid. She, was, however, anything but shy in his arms, covering his mouth with a passion he felt must have been a long time in the making. Her tongue darted between his teeth at once, and he savored the sweetness of it in the receptacle of his open mouth, moving his around hers until he drew the husky sounds from her throat. The sound waves of her desire traveled to his ears and heightened his own need. Jennings pressed her closer to his chest.

Veronica dropped her hands to where his shirt was unbuttoned at the top and caressed the tiny pulse there, alive and throbbing beneath her fingertips while the kiss went on. When Jay moved his mouth to shower pitter-patter kisses on her eyelids and cheeks, she fondled the freshly shaven contours of his face, that crazy cleft on his chin that deepened with every smile, the fine cheekbones, the high forehead where she found a scar she hadn't noticed before because of the way his hair hung down. His mouth met hers again, and one hand found its way under her robe.

Jay eased her away just enough to grasp her right breast, the full underside in his palm while his fingers met the tumescense of the nipple. He felt her stiffen in his arms when he attempted to part her robe and lower it past her shoulders, but she sighed and seemed to re- lax once more, so he persisted in his lovemaking.

She felt as though two irreconcilable forces were tearing her apart. Not having Jay seemed too much to bear, having him impossible for the present. Guilt be- cause Mike had forbade this man to her surfaced in some distant region of her consciousness like a cruel and bitter storm that arises unseasonably and destroys the spring seedlings of what could have been the most bountiful harvest of all, but she fought the dark clouds. They faded away, but another battle waged within her. This sudden intimacy with a man she knew for so short a period of time confused her. It had been half a life- time ago since she reflected upon the rites of courtship, and in those days what they were doing now was pre- lude to the altar. Getting married was even more in- comprehensible to her than making love to Jay.

He increased the pressure on her breast, gently and with the result of pushing the flesh upward. "Vee, I want to kiss you here. I want to see how you look, dar- lin'. Let me take off this robe." The small sound of anguish that passed from her lips made him remove his hands from her body. Jennings readjusted the robe, catching a maddening glimpse of her breasts in the pro- cess. The nipples weren't the same color as the freck- les. They were darker, much darker, the color of clean earth, and he wanted to put his mouth there, feel the hardness of them between his lips.

Veronica turned her face away from him and he tilted it back. "I'm sorry, Jay. I wanted you so much, but there's never been anyone but Mike, not before or after, and it seemed so strange to have you touch me the way he did," she explained breathlessly. "I'm sorry. It must be extremely frustrating for you. I'm just so . . ."

"Go on, darlin'," he urged gently.

"Jay, I'm afraid I'm terribly old-fashioned about certain things. Every single woman I know has affairs, but I can't help but equate going to bed with love and marriage. I'm sorry."

"Don't you ever apologize for values like that. Tell me, are you still bothered by Mike's wishes for you to keep away from his friends?" Jennings clasped both of her hands between his and ran his forefinger over the ridge of her knuckles.

"Less and less with each passing day."

"Good enough, darlin'." He kissed her forehead. It was an undemanding kiss. "I think I understand. We'll take our time about all of this, okay?" His thumb traced over the rise of her cheekbones and to the freckles on the bridge of her nose.

"You're not mad, then?"

"Yes and no."

"I don't understand that."

"I'm mad *about* you, Vee, not mad *at* you," he explained.

"You're a very patient man," she said, with appreciation for all the things he was and all the kindness he had shown her.

"You're worth being patient for." He glanced at the clock. "Darlin', you're not going to believe this, but I promised my mother I'd be home by nine."

"You're right, I don't," she said with a laugh.

"It's the truth."

"Why?"

"Because today is my birthday and she wants me there with my father and J.J. to eat the cake she made."

"Oh, Jay, you should have told me before. I would have given you something."

"You already have," he said, kissing her cheek and rising from the sofa.

"I meant something else." Veronica linked her arm through his and walked him to the door. "What would you like? I can get it later."

"How about quitting your job, leaving your kids, and running off to a deserted island with me?" he teased, drawing her closer to his side.

"You're impossible!"

Jennings spun her around so that she faced him, and kissed the tip of her nose. "No, darlin', I'm possible, very possible, and don't you ever forget it," he said with the sudden optimism of a man in love. He would have her someday, he just knew it.

"I won't," she promised. "Good night, Jay."

Chapter Seven

The harsh chime of her alarm woke Veronica from a fragmented dream of Jay Jennings. She slammed in the buzzer and tried to recapture those midnight moments when she moved from sleep to a somnolent consciousness, images of Jay all pervasive, her body awash with languid heat, her loins bathed in the sensual warmth of a dream lover's intimate caress. But the fleeting images were gone, and she arose to get on with day. Coffee cup in hand, she opened a heavy tome on criminal law.

When she had grown weary of reading, Veronica drew the patio door drapes to watch a late rising winter sun climb from a distant valley beyond the San Gabriels. A solitary figure walking along the ravine that led to the foothills summoned an anguished gasp from deep in her throat. It was Brad. He looked so much like his father off in the early mist that she realized keenly just how alike the two were in both physical appearance and mental disposition. It was a disheartening thought in light of recent studies documenting the inheritance of certain personality traits, and Veronica's upbeat mood plunged downward. She went out on the redwood deck to be closer to him.

Brad saw her standing there after a while and waved a reluctant acknowledgment, as though his private meditations had been unduly violated. Veronica returned the gesture and let him be.

In a gradual insight she realized the recent revelation of his father's suicide had forced the boy to act out the process of grief all over again. As before, Brad would be disconsolate for a while and in time his sorrow would diminish. For now, there was little a mother's love could do for him, so Veronica began to consider what she might be able to accomplish for Brad and Greg. She found herself preoccupied with the incident at the school, and whereas she could accept the weeklong suspension, the expulsion from the track team didn't sit well with her. The team was far more important to either boy than they were willing to admit, and she knew Brad harbored hopes of winning a college sporting scholarship and participating in the Olympics someday.

Never a woman to ask special considerations for herself or her family, Veronica decided an exception was in order, and she called the high school as soon as her youngest was off to school. The office had just opened and Mr. Gibson answered the phone himself.

"Mr. Gibson, this is Veronica Dubcek."

"Yes, Mrs. Dubcek, how are you?" he asked cordially.

"Fine, thank you. Mr. Gibson, I was wondering if we could discuss my sons. We've had several long talks about the incident with the Lewis boy last week, and I certainly feel there was no just provocation for what they did. However, I do feel there were extenuating circumstances that may cause you to rescind the measures you had to take, at least partially."

"I see. Would you like to come to my office now? I don't have any appointments until midmorning."

"I would like to, but I'm very busy. I have to be at

work soon. Could we possibly discuss this over the phone?" she requested politely. With the receiver between her ear and shoulder Veronica poured another cup of coffee.

"Yes, of course, Mrs. Dubcek, I understand. So many of our mothers have jobs outside the house these days. Let me grab some coffee and go into my office," he said.

Veronica overheard him yell out to his secretary to bring coffee to his desk and shook her head. *Typical,* she thought, listening to him complain to the woman for buying whole milk instead of half and half.

"All right. I'm back. The main thing that bothered me in this incident in the locker room last week was your boys' attitudes. The coach and I were completely unable to get through to either of them. Were you?"

"Yes, I was, Mr. Gibson."

"Well, that's a step in the right direction," he acknowledged. "Did they tell you what this was all about."

Veronica supposed the best chances of winning her case to reinstate her sons on the track team lay in telling Mr. Gibson the truth. "The altercation ensued because of certain comments the Lewis boy made regarding my husband's death," she said evenly.

"I don't understand," he interjected when she paused. "By the way, please accept my apologies for assuming the gentleman who gave you a ride to the school last week was Mr. Dubcek. My secretary gave me hell for it after you left."

Good, I'm glad she can give you something besides coffee, Veronica thought to herself. "It's no problem. My husband didn't pass away from a heart attack the way the boys thought. That was something I made up to protect them. He committed suicide under—under possibly suspicious circumstances. The Lewis boy chanced upon this information over the holidays, and apparently teased Greg about it during the PE class. Naturally they were very upset," she summarized briefly.

His next words dispelled Veronica's image of him as an insensitive bureaucrat. "Of course they were," he said quietly. "My own father committed suicide when I was about their age. I'll never forget how I felt for the rest of my life. It must have been extremely difficult for Brad and Greg to find out in such a way."

"It was, and thank you so much for your understanding."

"You're very welcome, Mrs. Dubcek, but that's something I should hope anyone would understand. I think we should review the measures the coach and I felt were appropriate punishment last week. Whatever the cause, fighting is against our rules, but under the circumstances they can return to school tomorrow and forget the last day of formal suspension. And I'm certain the coach will allow them to return to the team now. Your boys are two of his finest runners, and he would have probably insisted on letting them rejoin the team before next fall anyway," he told her.

Veronica was grateful for his kindness, but she had different thoughts with regard to the suspension. "I can't thank you enough for reconsidering. My main concern was the track team. It means so much to both of them, but the two-against-one thing with the Lewis boy bothers me. I think they deserve to be out the full week."

"Whatever you say. Brad and Greg are straight A students so I don't expect their academic records to be affected. If you care to drop by the counseling office today or tomorrow, I can have someone give you their new assignments," he offered. "I would like to speak to the pair before they return to school, however. I promise not to give them a hard time, but I think Brad should apologize to the coach for accidentally striking him."

"You're perfectly correct; I'll send Brad to your office."

"Will you be by to get the assignments today?"

"Yes." Veronica thanked him and agreed to go to the school before five that afternoon. She heard the back door open. Brad walked through the kitchen without saying a word as she hung up the phone. She followed him into the room he shared with Greg, eager to tell them what she sincerely hoped would be received as good news. "May I come in?" she asked, knocking on the door.

"Yeah, Mom," Greg yelled out.

Veronica entered the darkened room and drew the drapes. "I have some good news for you two."

"What's that?" Brad asked quietly, yawning and propping himself up on one elbow. He had slipped off his pants and returned to bed after his walk through the foothills.

Veronica resisted the temptation to ask him how long he'd been in the mountains. "I just spoke to Mr. Gibson on the telephone. I explained what provoked the fight last week, and he's agreed—"

Brad groaned and cut her off. "Mom! You didn't! We don't want the entire student body to know about what our father did!"

"I'm sure Mr. Gibson will keep the information confidential. He seemed very understanding. Anyway, from what you've told me of Ted Lewis, he's probably already spread the story around," she speculated.

"No, he won't, because I told him if he says anything else, he won't walk away the next time," Brad ground out.

"Brad Dubcek!" Veronica exclaimed. "I thought we talked about fighting all week and you promised me not to do it again."

"It was only a threat. Don't get so upset."

"I don't like threats like that, Brad, not one bit," she admonished sharply, "but I'm due at work soon and don't have more time to discuss it with you. We'll talk at dinnertime."

Clad in a pair of pajama bottoms that rose above his ankles, Brad left the bed. "Oh, all right, Mom," he said almost contritely. "Is there anything I can do to help you with dinner tonight?"

"Yes, please. There's a roast defrosting on the kitchen counter. Would you put it and some baking potatoes in the oven around four?"

"Sure."

"Anything you want me to do?" Greg asked, also leaving his bed.

"It would be nice if you could do the laundry."

"Okay."

Veronica turned to leave. "Mr. Gibson has agreed to let both of you back on the track team," she said, a bit disappointed to have her statement met by Brad's bored shrug of the shoulders. "One thing though, boys. Before you're officially back on you have to go and talk to the coach and Mr. Gibson. The dean said any afternoon between one and three would be fine. Why don't you do it today and be done with it?" she suggested.

Greg looked at his older brother questioningly. Brad's face darkened. "No way," he said ominously.

Veronica saw the way his hand tightened around the brush he held and her abdominal muscles followed suit. "Why do you object to speaking to the dean and coach, Brad? It seems to me they are being very reasonable to reinstate the two of you on the team, especially after the way you hit Mr. Boyd."

Brad sighed impatiently. "That was an accident, Mom. I didn't know he was trying to grab my fist when I flung it back."

"I realize that, but still, you never apologized."

"I will, sometime when I get a chance during practice," he agreed.

"That's not good enough, Brad. Mr. Gibson wants you and Greg to go to his office and talk, and you have to do it," she insisted.

"No way. Gibson's a jerk. The guy's on an incredible power trip, and I'm not about to go along with it."

She was late for work and highly annoyed with her oldest son, but Veronica struggled for patience. "Brad, honey, to tell you the truth, I've never cared much for Mr. Gibson myself. He's always struck me as a pompous, regimental old fool who belongs in a second-rate military academy, but he was very understanding to me on the phone, and terribly sympathetic with you and Greg. You know, he said his own father committed suicide," she confided. "Just go in and talk to him for a few minutes."

"No, I can't stand the guy."

"Then do it for your teammates. I don't think they'll let you back on the track team until you officially talk to the dean and apologize to the coach," she said, trying to persuade him calmly.

"I don't care. I'd rather not be on the team than have to kiss up to Gibson's ego," he said grimly.

"Brad, where's your sense of loyalty to your teammates? You know they can't win this season without you and Greg, don't you?"

"Yeah," he conceded in a tone all too nonchalant for his mother.

"Well, then, don't you feel any loyalty to your team-mates?" Veronica repeated.

Brad slammed the brush down on the dresser and turned to face her. "Mom, if loyalty to one's team-mates is a genetic trait, then I guess I don't have any. Look at the way Dad screwed his friends and partners over."

Veronica lost the battle to control her tightly checked temper. It ignited, and before she could master her out-rage, her hand rose in the air and came down on Brad's cheek. "Don't you ever, and I mean ever, speak that way about your father again! None of us in this room or anywhere else knows what was going on in his head when he did what he did, and no one knows for sure if your father behaved unethically toward his colleagues! Why, even Jay Jennings, your dad's best friend from Vietnam, doesn't believe for a second your father is guilty!"

His mother had never struck him for so far as he could remember, and Brad's jaw went slack with shock. He knew it was time to shut up, but the sense of out-rage and betrayal over his father's actions were stronger than his better instincts. "Mom, did it ever occur to you that maybe Jennings is telling you what you want to hear for his own purposes?"

"Oh, and what might they be, Brad?" she asked tersely, ashamed for having hit her oldest son and try-ing hard not to repeat the act.

Brad backed down. He wanted to embrace her and apologize, but somehow, he was helpless to do what he wanted. "Nothing," he muttered under his breath be-fore disappearing into the bathroom.

Veronica looked over to the bed where Greg sat ner-vously rapping his fingers on his knees and staring down at the blue shag carpet. In many ways it seemed as though he had been closer to his older brother than she had been since his father's death. She saw the tension in his pursed lips when he glanced up, the unspoken apology in his eyes, but knew he wouldn't say anything to her until he had Brad's tacit consent. She crossed the room to his side and combed her hand through the sleep-tousled yellow hair. "It's all right, Greg, honey. It's going to be all right," she murmured.

A ragged little gulp came from his throat at the same time his shoulders shook in a convulsive shudder. Greg didn't say anything. Jerking from his mother's touch, he bolted to the bathroom to join his brother.

Don't shout, don't cry, don't break down, don't do anything. Go to work and when you come home everything will be fine ran through her brain in a ceaseless litany, the words permuted, twisted around each time until the order became meaningless. But the anguish remained the same, tearing away at her soul. Veronica didn't know how she'd ever get out of the house and through the day, but she knew she would. She had journeyed to hell and back in the last two years. There were circles in the inferno lower than this. She had been there and survived, had returned to the land of the living, had known of the promise of spiritual rebirth, had known of the pleasure of a man's intimate touch and yearned for much more in his arms. She had endured and known so much, and this too would pass. She knew it.

Chapter Eight

"I'm late, I know!" Veronica said breezily when she entered the office. "Is Beerstein around?" she added in a whisper.

Sara stopped typing at once and studied Veronica's expression. The women were close enough for her to know Veronica's bubbly demeanor on this particular morning was a smokescreen, and that surprised Sara, since her friend had seemed in such good spirits since the first of the year.

"No, he's in a meeting. Someone up there must like you. You couldn't have picked a better day to be late. Old Beer Belly is in a great mood," Sara replied, rising from her desk to get a cup of coffee at the automatic machine in the corner. She had decided not to inquire about Veronica's mood until later.

"Really? Wonderful! Any idea why?" Veronica helped herself to coffee.

"Uh-huh. Some alumni, a wealthy aerospace engineer, gave the university a huge donation, and Beerstein managed to get his greedy paws on a considerable portion. He's holding court right now, trying to work out a new budget."

"Fantastic! Maybe we can strike while the iron's hot and get a raise. What do you think?" she asked, stirring the coffee with a fork because it was all she could find.

"It's worth a try, I suppose, but I don't think he's in that good a mood. By the way, you have a few messages. Beerstein took one himself before he left, and he didn't even yell at the person for making personal calls to you at work."

"Will wonders never cease," Veronica commented. "Who phoned? I hardly ever get personal calls here except when the kids are sick. It wasn't the school, was it?"

"No, the call I took was from your son, Brad, and the one Beerstein got was from Jay Jennings. Did I get a chance to tell you how nice I think he is?" she asked.

The unexpected messages from Jay and her son were like waking up in the morning after a bad night to find her favorite wild bird perched on the tree near her bedroom window, singing a song. The world seemed a far more hospitable place than before. "Yes, as I recall you said Jay was homely but nice," she laughed. "When's Beerstein due back?"

"I didn't exactly say that, Vee! He's not a bad-looking man. Now that I think about it, he's well above average. It's just that I expected more from the way you kept ranting and raving about him. You made him sound like the best-looking man ever to step foot into the county of Los Angeles! Oh, well, they say love is blind."

Veronica giggled. "Maybe so, but I'm not in love, and I still think he's adorable. When did you say Beerstein is returning?"

"I didn't, but not for another hour. If his meeting extends into the noon hour, it wouldn't surprise me to see them go out to lunch and come back late in the afternoon."

"Good, I'm going to his office to make a few phone calls. Buzz me if he comes back early, will you?"

"Oh, so it's going to be a hot conversation, huh? If the wires start to smoke, I think I'll pick up the extension. I could use the vicarious thrill. Have fun."

She called her son first. Greg answered the phone and passed the receiver to his brother. "Brad, how are you, honey?"

"Uh, okay. Mom?"

"Yes?"

"I'm sorry about this morning, Mom," he croaked out. "I've just been really down about Dad. I had no right taking it out on you the way I did. I phoned Gibson and told him Greg and I will be in at one thirty. We couldn't go later because we have something special planned for dinner," he said. "It's for you, Mom."

"You do? Why, thank you, Brad. And, honey, I'm sorry about this morning too. I feel really bad about hitting you. I wish I hadn't done that."

"I deserved it. It's okay. What time will you be home?"

"Five thirty. How's Greg?"

"Fine. We had a talk about some things. I'll tell you later. Wait a minute, Greg is saying something." Brad spoke to his brother briefly. "Mom, Greg says he doesn't know what temperature to wash your red silkish dress on."

"Honey, that's real silk. It has to be dry-cleaned. Any other things I have that look like that can go on cold," she explained.

"Okay. Mom, Jay Jennings called for you right after you left. I gave him the work number. I hope that was all right with you."

"Yes, it was fine."

"Okay, Mom. I'll see you tonight."

"Good-bye, sweetheart."

She dialed Jay's number, and her spirits soared at the sound of his deep voice, that rich Texas accent an aphrodisiac to her ears. "Hello yourself," Veronica replied after he said hello.

"I hope you didn't mind my calling you at work. I tried to catch you at home, but it was too late," he said, shifting the cordless telephone onto his shoulder so he could log off the computer he'd been on since dawn.

"No, it's fine. Brad told me you called. How was the birthday cake?"

"Good. Wished you were there."

"At your birthday party?"

"No, afterward, when Mom and Dad took the kid out and I was alone in the house."

"Jay!" she laughed. "What am I going to do about you?"

"For starters, you can have lunch with me today. As I recall that was on our agenda last week until we were so rudely interrupted."

"I'd be delighted. Tell me something," she began coyly.

"When you speak like that, anything," he replied in a similar vein.

"Are you going to use your son as an excuse to be on campus?"

"Not unless I have to, darlin'."

"You don't."

"Then I won't. When shall I be there?"

"Noon."

"You wouldn't have time enough to mosey off campus, would you?"

"I just might. What did you have in mind?"

"How about a place with a twenty-course menu that takes three days to eat? Know of anything like that?

They used to have them in ancient Rome, I believe.''

She laughed into the receiver. "Not that I know of around here.''

"Damn. Then I guess that little French place a few blocks over will have to do, darlin'.''

"I guess so.'' The intercom buzzed, and Veronica jumped, knowing it was the one Sara would have used to signal her. "Jay, thank you and I'll see you at noon,'' she said hurriedly.

"Why the big rush?''

"Because I'm sitting in the boss's chair, that's why.''

"Well, all I can say is the boss had better not be in the chair with you,'' he remarked lightly.

"That will be the day. Good-bye, now.'' Veronica slammed down the receiver and jumped to her feet, the most delightful flush coloring her cheeks and bringing out the freckles on her nose.

"Good morning, Veronica,'' Beirnstein boomed loudly. "How's my favorite girl this fine day?''

"I don't know, Mr. Beirnstein. How is she?'' Veronica returned with a grin. "I do assume you're speaking about Mrs. Beirnstein, aren't you?''

He rubbed his bald head, stared at her blankly, and then burst into laughter. "Veronica, that's one thing I've always liked about you. Your sense of humor. I can always count on you for a good one!''

"Why, thank you, Mr. Beirnstein,'' she replied in a tone that would have made Sara howl but managed to flatter her employer. "I understand you've come up with some additional funding for the department. Congratulations.''

"Yes, we did, Veronica. I'm very pleased about it. I just came back for a second to get the projected salary reports. Do you know where they are?''

"Yes, over here. I'll get them for you," she said, taking the files from a cabinet near a window that overlooked one of the original campus buildings, a single-level structure built after the style of an early California mission.

"Great. Still taking those law courses, Veronica?" he asked while glancing through the papers.

"Sure am, Dr. Beirnstein. I have exams coming up in a few days."

"When?"

"Friday and Saturday." Since Veronica's course was a home correspondence one, there was a certain amount of flexibility as to when she took exams. She found it best, however, to maintain the same strict schedule a student in a traditional school would have.

"Hmm, today's Wednesday, isn't it?"

"Yes," Veronica replied, wondering what had been served at his morning meeting.

"Well, I tell you what, honey, take the rest of the week off."

She ignored the word she would have normally addressed with some gentle but firm reminder. "With pay?"

"Of course with pay!"

Were the workload in the office less demanding, Veronica would have seized upon the opportunity immediately, but she thought of Sara and questioned the offer. "Mr. Beirnstein, that's very kind of you, but there's been so much to do lately. I hate to burden Sara with everything."

"You won't be. Do you know Loring over in purchasing?"

"Yes, I've known him for years."

"Well, he had to let one of his girls go a few weeks back. She's a cute little blond thing, and I offered her a part-time job here this morning. It should remove some of the burden from you and Sara. She can start at once, even before personnel processes the papers," he explained.

Veronica frowned, but brightened before Beirnstein caught it. "We need some extra help around here," she said slowly, "and thank you so much for the time off. I can certainly use it, and this is very generous of you. When may I go?"

"Whenever you want, honey. I can get Patty over here at once. In fact, there's nothing I'd like better than to get Patty here at once," he said with a wink that disgusted Veronica.

"Thank you, but I think I'll stay until noon and give Sara a hand with something we started before the holidays."

"Fine. I have to get back to the meeting now, Veronica. Best of luck with your exams."

Veronica left his office as soon as he did, and told Sara about the new woman scheduled to work in the office and about the time off their employer had given her.

"That's great, Veronica. Since Beerstein's in such a good mood now, I'm going to hit him up about reclassifying me from secretary class three to administrative one. Do you think he'd do it?" Sara asked hopefully.

"Probably. You are, after all, a cute little thing." Veronica laughed. "I would suggest you bleach your hair blond before you broach the subject, though."

"That's a thought. How do you think this new kid will do with Beerstein? I think she's only nineteen or twenty. I hope she'll be able to handle the old goat," Sara expressed with concern.

"Well, if she can't, I'm sure we can teach her quick enough," Veronica predicted easily. "I called Jay back."

"Oh?"

"We're meeting for lunch." Veronica found the notes for a fact sheet about recharges Beirnstein wanted distributed to the staff and faculty and began to reorganize the information in a presentable form.

Sara grabbed the handwritten pages from Veronica. "What are you doing? When Beerstein gives you time off, don't sit around here, take it," she advised.

"Sara, it would take longer for you to explain this to Patty than for me to help you. We can finish it by noon, and then I'll be long gone."

Veronica began to work on the lengthy memo, silencing her friend's protests by ignoring them. When Sara realized she wasn't getting anywhere, she gave up and joined Veronica in the task, pausing thoughtfully from time to time to observe the dolorous pall that darkened her friend's face every so often, the one she had observed when she first walked into the office and later forgotten as Veronica seemed to brighten after her conversation with Jay. It was something Sara had seen many times during the course of her friend's mourning, but today it seemed unwarranted by the bright turn Vee's life had taken in the last several months.

"Let's break for coffee now," Sara suggested around eleven. "I want to hear how things are going with you and Jay."

Veronica told her over a fourth cup of coffee for the day, vowing not to drink any more before her luncheon date with Jay. Her fingers were likely enough to tremble when he traced a feather-light touch along her inner arm, her stomach all too apt to become the home for dancing butterflies when she became the willing captive of rainbow eyes.

"So, how's it going?"

"Oh, okay, I guess," Veronica said evasively. Not

only was she unskilled in the art of dating, she found it difficult to discuss relationships with women friends.

"Only okay?" Sara asked, after refilling the filter in the automatic coffeemaker. "Is that what has you kinda down?"

Veronica had no idea her emotions were so transparent, especially since she had all but overcome the dismal mood that had cast her into the abyss of despair briefly earlier in the day. Brad had called and apologized, she had spoken to Jay, and even her employer had bestowed an unexpected gift upon her. All these things had done much to dispel her depression, and Veronica was mildly surprised Sara had detected the residual gray clouds beneath her otherwise cheerful demeanor. Her only hope was that Jay would be less perceptive than Sara. Since their initial encounter over the phone on Christmas Eve, Veronica felt he had seen her at her worst, an image she wished to correct. "Sara, do I really seem down? Honest, I don't feel that bad. A few things are on my mind, yes, but nothing major."

"Oh, not really. I suppose it would only be obvious to someone who's known you for over eighteen years like I have."

"Has it been that long since we were in high school together?"

"Yeah, it sure has. You've done well. I'm so proud of you for finally getting out of here."

"I still have three more years of study before I can take the state bar, Sara. I'm not out yet," she said realistically.

"You will be. I know it. Tell me how the boys are coping now. Any better? I did try to call you a few times last night, but the line was busy."

Veronica set another chair in front of the one she sat in and stretched her legs out. "Jay calls almost every night," she said before going on to share her concerns about Brad. Sara was among the very few people who knew of the true circumstances surrounding Mike's death. Veronica had confided in her shortly after the event when Sara came to her home to help with the three children. At first Veronica had been able to go through the motions of cooking and caring for the boys, numbed into an insentient state by the unexpected event. But after a few days the cold reality of it all descended upon her deadened senses, and she couldn't do much more than lie in bed and cry. Sara and her ten-year-old daughter came into the house then, and were the ballast to a sad and confused family.

Sara placed her hand on Veronica's knee. "Oh, Vee. I'm so sorry to hear that about Brad, but don't worry. He's a survivor. He'll snap out of it soon enough."

"My sentiments precisely, Sara, but I must say it broke my heart to see him out there wandering in the hills this morning. He and Mike used to walk there at night," she said thoughtfully. "Did I tell you I phoned the dean this morning?" Veronica went on to relate the conversation to Sara.

"Wonderful! I'm glad Gibson was so understanding. I've never cared much for that man myself," she told Veronica.

Suddenly Sara placed a finger over her mouth. "Shush, Vee, I think I hear the footsteps of an amorous suitor," she whispered.

They both pivoted in their seats to see Jennings standing in the doorway. "Good morning, ladies. How are you?" he asked, smiling at the two of them but with eyes only for Veronica.

"I'm fine. How are you, Jay?" Sara returned with a pleasant smile, inspired, from the way the pair stared at one another, more by amusement, than from Jay's cheerful salutation.

"Can't complain," he drawled. "Are you ready to leave?" he asked, bending to Veronica's chair and resting his palms on her shoulders.

"Yes, let me get my jacket."

Jennings removed a lightweight purple blazer from the coatrack on the wall and held it behind Veronica.

"How did you know that was mine?" she asked, slipping into it.

"Deductive logic. Your dress is nearly the same color, Sara is wearing yellow slacks, and I doubt that Beerstein could fit into this."

"You're absolutely right!" Veronica congratulated him.

"I usually am," he told her, taking hold of the lapels of her jacket only to drop them when he remembered they weren't alone in the office.

Sara realized why he had released Veronica's clothing and laughed. "Oh, don't mind me, Jay. If you guys keep this up, I won't have to go down to the lounge to watch the noontime soap."

Jennings chuckled and clasped his hand over Sara's shoulder. "I think we'd better pause for a commercial break now. What time shall I have Vee back?"

"You can keep her until next Monday as far as the office is concerned. Old Beerstein was in a great mood because he got his hands on some big bucks and gave her three extra days off."

"Wow!" Jennings enthused, saying good-bye to Sara and dragging Veronica from the room. "Can I really have you until Monday?" He took her hand and kissed the palm, releasing it reluctantly when Veronica flinched. "Vee, I'm sorry. I should have remembered public affection bothers you. It does, doesn't it?"

"Yes, especially where people know me. I've always thought of myself as Mike Dubcek's wife, and then his widow around here," she said unhappily, displeased with herself for her inability to be more receptive toward him at times.

"I understand, Vee," Jennings replied, but he didn't. In his mind it was high time Dubcek's ghost was put to rest, banished from everywhere, from where she worked, wherever people might know her, and most of all from her heart. "But all that's going to be changing soon, Vee. You're going to start thinking of yourself as Jay Jennings's woman before too long," he predicted.

"I would prefer to think of myself as my own woman."

Jennings frowned, hoping he wasn't going to have to tap-dance his way around some feminist rhetoric about the male–female relationship. Not right now, anyway, and not with her. They had enough problems to overcome without adding a soft-shoe shuffle he didn't need. God only knew how often he had gone through all that in the last few years since his divorce, and it bothered him because he had always thought of himself as a fair and sensitive individual. Yet, his attitudes and patterns of speech had been challenged more than once. "My intentions are not to strip away your sense of autonomy," he returned more gruffly than intended. "That simply isn't what I'm trying to do at all."

Her head spun toward him. This was a side of Jay Jennings she'd never seen before, the suggestion of a tempestuous nature. "I never said you were. But since you mention it, what are you trying to do?" she asked with interest, assuaging a loaded question with a grin.

Jennings shrugged, unused to point-blank questions of that nature. "I want to be your friend."

"Oh?" she asked skeptically. They had reached a near-deserted parking lot and Veronica linked her arm through his.

Jennings placed his hand over hers, right below his elbow. "Yes, your very intimate friend, if you follow me," he said lightly, knowing there was no way she truly could, since he was unable to speak of the blossoming love in his heart for fear of pressuring her. Let her think of him as the carefree flirt for now, Jennings thought, since it was what she seemed comfortable with. Their time would come.

"I believe I do," she laughed, won over once more by his charm. She stood to one side and watched Jay unlock the door before he held it open for her.

Jennings made an exaggerated pretense of searching the area for other people. "Coast is clear," he murmured, seeing no one and stooping to kiss her forehead before sliding into the driver's seat.

The strong scent of an after-shave she had never noticed on Jay in the past lingered in her nostrils after he kissed her, and the same fragrance permeated the air in his car. He didn't strike her as the type of man who would use such an overstated scent, and Veronica questioned Jay about it. "What do you have on?"

"Clothes, Vee. What am I supposed to have on?" he said, placing his hand on her knee and backing out of the slot with one hand on the steering wheel.

"No, I meant the cologne or after-shave, whatever it is," she corrected with a smile.

"Oh, that. I meant to apologize for it. It's awful, huh?"

"No, I wouldn't say that. Just rather strong. Why did you put it on if you don't like the stuff yourself?"

"Because it was one of the things my son gave me for Christmas. My original intentions were to stash it in a drawer and forget about it, but J.J. assures me the scent is guaranteed to drive women mad with desire. Feel anything yet?" Jennings ran his hand down the side of her face, tugged an earlobe, and squeezed the back of her neck, right below the hairline.

"Oh, yes indeed," she murmured dreamily as the magical caresses went on, orchestrating the chorus of delightful sensations afloat in her body.

"Yeah?" he questioned in a provocative tone that had the power to provoke only one emotion within the woman to whom he spoke. "Then maybe I'd better just pour the whole bottle on my head next time."

"Jay, you can pour the whole bottle down the sink next time and it wouldn't make any difference in how I feel," she replied in a fluttery whisper, too enchanted to say less than the absolute truth.

Jennings made a sound of contentment and removed his hand from behind her head. "Darlin', slide over closer to me, I need both hands to drive now."

Veronica moved in as close as possible, their thighs juxtaposed, her hand making a timid foray of the taut muscles in his leg that responded to her touch by alternately flexing and relaxing. "How was your morning, Jay?"

"Fine. I've decided to take the job with DataBank. Right now I'm trying to find a house to buy. My parents are great people, but they're starting to get to J.J. and me a bit."

"What will you be doing for DataBank?" They came to a Stop sign, and Jay covered her hand with his.

"Basically the same things I did with DOD. Security work." Her hand jerked and he held it tighter. "Hey, what's this?" he asked softly.

Veronica bit her lower lip. "Oh, nothing. It just seems ironic that Mike's death was so closely tied into security at DataBank, and now you're working there to prevent things like that from happening again," she commented somberly.

Jennings hated to let her hand go when the light turned green and he had to get onto the freeway. "That was something I considered very seriously before accepting the position."

He looked so pensive now, almost forlorn, that she had to trace the back of her fingers up and down the side of his face. "Why's that?"

"Because of you. I didn't want to do anything to upset you, I mean in terms of our long-term relationship. I didn't want to come to you with what might have been a constant reminder of what you'd rather forget. But the more I thought about it, I realized that with the best security system conceivable maybe data wouldn't leak out with the unfortunate result of having an innocent man accused," he explained quietly.

His thoughtfulness humbled her, silenced the irritation that had caused her to reflect unfavorably upon Jay's employment at DataBank. "I harbor no ill feelings toward the people at the company, Jay. I mean I did at first; I hated John Silvers and the rest of them for falsely accusing Mike, but as more information became available to me, and I reached a point where I could review it objectively, I realized I would have thought the same thing they did. Maybe I do now, I just don't know." She spoke with her hand on his shoulder and Jay closed his left hand over his chest to hold it when they came upon a straight section of the road and he felt comfortable driving with one hand on the wheel.

"I'm glad you're working there, Jay. It's a good company with a lot of good people. They kept the details of Mike's death private when they could have gone public and sued the estate, taken our home away from us. I'm eternally grateful to them for all they did, especially John Silvers and Jerry Olson."

"I'm glad you feel that way, Vee. It means a lot to me," he said simply. Jennings pulled off the freeway and drove toward an area of picturesque shops and restaurants in downtown Los Angeles on Olavera Street. "I hope you don't mind, but since you have a little extra time, I thought we'd come here. Do you like Mexican food?"

"Yes, very much so. I haven't been here for years. Thanks. I understand they've added a great deal to the area," she remarked as Jay parked the car and hastened around to open her door.

"That's what I've heard too. Vee," he began with a playful smile that tugged at Veronica's heart, bending over her before she rose, his pungent cologne almost enough to make her sneeze, "you haven't been here for years? May I take that to mean you don't know anyone in this neck of the woods?"

She saw what he was driving at and laughed. "Yes, you may." When she accepted his hand to rise, Jay didn't let go until she sat down at an al fresco restaurant bordering a cobblestone street and surrounded by colorful open air stalls.

"How are the two juvenile delinquents?" he asked, taking her hand once more after pushing in the heavy wood and black wrought iron chair.

"Forgiven but not forgotten," she sighed as his fingers tapped a lazy rhythm on her wrist. The sensual beat coursed through her blood and wound up somewhere near her heart.

"Yeah, teenage boys can be pretty hard to ignore at times," he sympathized, smiling his approval as Veronica related the story of how they came to be reinstated on the track team, omitting the ensuing encounter that resulted in her striking Brad.

"Good for you, Vee. I'm glad you decided to call and talk to the dean. Sports are good for a kid. I've always tried to interest J.J. in something, but he's never been able to get his nose very far away from the computer or his chessboards to do anything more than take a long walk with me once in a blue moon," he said, glancing over the menu that had just been given to him. "Most of these selections are unfamiliar to me. Can you recommend anything?"

It had been years and years since Veronica visited a real Mexican restaurant. Her restaurant experience with the type of food was limited to tacos and enchiladas served in fast-food restaurants and eaten with her boys. "No, I rarely eat out. I'm only familiar with the same dishes you probably are."

Jennings rotated the menu and found an explanation of each dish in English, since the establishment catered mainly to tourists. "Aha. Look, Vee, here we go. This *menudo* sounds good. I could use a nice bowl of soup."

"It does sound good. I think I'll try the *pozole*." They ordered the different dishes and shared them, eating from each other's plate. "I didn't know J.J. played chess," she commented after Jennings spoonfed her more of his soup. "Do you?" She put her fork into his mouth and gave him a piece of pork from her plate.

"Thank you," he said, swallowing the meat. "I play some, not very well. I taught him what I knew when he was six or seven, and he's long since outstripped me. As I recall, Mike and your kids used to play."

"Yes, but the kids haven't played since Mike died. Maybe J.J. and Brad could play sometime. Brad is quite good."

"That sounds like a fine idea. Invite us to dinner, darlin'."

"Consider it done."

"I won't let you forget that," he remarked.

Later, when they rose to leave, Jennings asked, "What now?"

"I'm afraid I have to get home and study for my exams."

"I knew you were going to tell me that, but like they say, hope springs eternal in the human heart." His arm fell into place over her shoulder, drawing Veronica in to his side as they walked back to the car.

"Why, what did you want to do?"

"Drive up into the mountains and park."

"There are some lovely views up there."

"What I had on the agenda had nothing to do with the view," he remarked, scraping his thumb across her neck.

"Jay, my friend, it sounds to me like you've been in the company of an adolescent boy too long," she laughed, wrapping an arm around his waist. "First the sexy slow dancing and now parking up in the mountains. Really! What next?" she challenged, her fingers finding his belt. Veronica linked one thumb underneath and was delighted to learn his shirt had ridden up in the back, allowing her to meet smooth bare skin there.

"Dunno. Guess I could borrow a surfboard and take you down to Malibu to catch a few waves," he suggested.

"No, thanks. I'd probably catch a cold if I don't drown first."

"Then I'll try to think of something less extreme," he agreed. Jennings unlocked the door for her, brushing a kiss across her face that was like morning dew easing from a blade of grass to the ground, smooth and easy and not making a sound.

"You do that." By the time they reached her home

at half past one Veronica found it difficult to believe the day had begun on such an unfortunate note, with bitter words exchanged between her and her oldest son and her regrettable act of striking the boy, who towered nearly six inches above her, physically more a man than a boy now. "Well, here we are," she said unnecessarily as he parked the car in the driveway.

"May I step inside for a while?" Jennings asked with the thought in mind that her youngest son would be in school and that the two others had a one thirty appointment with the dean. He was all too aware she might well decline his request, intimidated by the prospect of the romantic interlude that was likely to ensue.

"Jay, I don't know," she said slowly. When they were apart, he haunted her thoughts. She could think of nothing other than making love to him when she went to bed at night, yet there in the flesh she found herself in retreat from him. "I need more time to sort all this out."

He couldn't stand to see her fettered to the past, for her own sake as much as his. Jennings kissed her hand. "You take all the time you need, little darlin'. I won't come in now. When can I see you again?"

"I don't know. I have exams coming up this weekend. I have to study."

"How about lunch next week, then?" he suggested. "Or maybe a movie sometime?"

"I'll think about it. We'll talk about it when you phone tonight. You are going to call, aren't you?"

"You know I will." He left the car to open the door for her, allowing himself one discreet kiss on her lips before saying good-bye.

Chapter Nine

When Veronica seemed reluctant to set a date with him
during their several phone conversations the previous
week, Jennings decided to force the issue by meeting
her at work one afternoon. He showed up in her office
on Friday, a brilliant bouquet of mixed flowers in hand
and a halfway apologetic smile for arriving unan-
nounced.

Veronica was sitting at the desk, munching a roast
beef sandwich and reviewing a grant she'd been asked
to type up before she left for the weekend. "Jay! I
didn't expect you!" she exclaimed, too delighted to see
him to feel any real annoyance for a visit she'd not
consented to.

Jennings gave her the flowers. "You know what they
say about the mountain and Muhammad, darlin'."

Veronica stood and laughed, patting her waistline.
"Hey, watch that. I'll have you know my latest diet is a
total success and I've alreay lost ten pounds. Oh, these
are lovely. Thank you so much."

Jennings made a sound of personal disgust, shaking
his head at his own insensitivity. In his eyes she'd
never be unattractive, but he knew the few extra
pounds bothered her, and in the past she had taken a
good-natured offense at any remarks pertaining to her

figure. "You look wonderful," he said, concluding that an apology would exacerbate the matter and perhaps compound her embarrassment. He glanced over to Sara's desk and saw a floral arrangement similar to one he'd given to Vee. "I see spring is in the air all around this place."

Veronica frowned when she remembered she hadn't removed the card from the bouquet on Sara's desk. The arrangement had actually been sent to Veronica by a faculty member from an East Coast college who did his sabbatical at Cal Tech a year ago and grew very fond of her with absolutely no encouragement from her. She'd never dated the man and had all but forgotten him until the flowers were delivered earlier that day with a memo that the literature professor, Harold Jones, would be in town for a seminar soon. "Yes, so it would seem."

Jennings took a closer look at the flowers while Vee searched for another vase. "These must have been sent from the same florist," he remarked. "Well, all I can say is I hope Sara's friend is having better luck than I am. You evaded me all week long on the subject of that dinner date of ours."

Veronica sensed that attention from another man would bother Jay, and all he had to do was take another step toward Sara's desk to see the card. "Actually, those flowers were sent to me. I didn't want them."

"Are mine going to wind up over there too?" he asked lightly, well aware they wouldn't from the expression on her face. Since Vee had repeatedly told him there hadn't been anyone in her life since Mike, Jennings was naturally curious as to the source of the flowers, and the fact that he may have competition for her affections troubled him to no small degree.

"Never!" Veronica was unable to find a vase and

excused herself to borrow one from an office down the hall.

Jennings resisted the temptation to read the card in her absence. Clearly it would be a violation of her privacy, but he couldn't dismiss the incident either. When Veronica returned he asked her about it, broaching the subject hesitantly. "Vee, if you don't mind—" he began.

"Can I get you a cup of coffee?" she interjected. "I'd love to take you down to the cafeteria for lunch, but I don't have the time. If I don't finish working on this grant, I'll have to take it home with me, and I have so many other things to do this weekend."

"I'm sorry. I should have called. Sit down. I'll get the coffee and then be on my way."

"I'm glad you came," she said truthfully, disturbed by her inordinate fear of going out with him in the evening. Veronica hadn't had a real nighttime date with a man for years. She and Mike rarely went out due to the demands of his schedule, and dating struck her as something very young people did, or people on their way to making a commitment to one another did— something anyone did, except for herself. She supposed Jay wasn't asking for much, and it was unfair of her to engage in long nightly phone conversations with him only to bow out when he wanted something as innocent as dinner and a movie.

"I'm not," he confessed with a baleful grin. "To tell you the truth, darlin', those flowers bother me." Jennings pushed his chair around to hers and took her hand.

"They shouldn't. If they meant anything to me, I certainly wouldn't have passed them along to Sara." Briefly she explained how a man she never saw outside of the campus, and there only on business-related matters, came to fancy himself in love with her and pressured her continuously to spend time with him. "He became a real pest," she concluded. "The man just wouldn't give up."

"Sounds like me," Jennings observed.

"Oh, no! There's no comparison! I've been attracted to you since the very first time we met. You do know that, don't you?"

"Sometimes I wonder," he admitted. "I'm sorry, Vee, I shouldn't have said that. I know you still need space, time to adjust to everything, but—"

"But an evening out isn't as though you're asking me to run away to Mexico," she filled in, echoing a sentiment he'd expressed earlier in the week.

"You're the only one who can decide that." Jennings was a jealous man by nature, yet a wave of sympathy for the other guy who wanted Vee passed through him, and he felt for the man. "Tell me something, little darlin', did that professor from New York drive you away by all his demands? Or was it more like you never cared for him at all?"

"Both. I thought it was a little strange when he started using the word love when I barely knew him. At first I thought it was some kind of a come-on to get me to bed, but now I don't know. He still calls once in a while."

"Tell him you're spoken for," Jennings suggested with a smile that he found an effort to maintain in light of her current revelation. As he had suspected, Vee wasn't interested at the present in either pledges of love or a more casual affair, and as his spirits plummeted, he tried to convince himself it was different with him. They did have a developing relationship; she just needed more time.

"I plan to," she said softly.

Jennings brushed his lips across her cheek and stood. "Well, I'm on my way with sincere apologies for interrupting your lunch."

"I can do to have my lunch interrupted more often," she quipped, not so much out of a desire to ridicule herself but to say something light to distract Jay. Clearly he was leaving the office far less cheerfully than when he'd entered fifteen minutes ago. Veronica wondered if it were solely the flowers or seeing her that made him so unhappy, she with her continual stance that held him at an arm's length the same time she beckoned him forward with late-night phone calls that promised a deepening relationship.

"Oh, you shush now, darlin'," he reproved. "When would be a good time to phone tonight?"

Veronica stood from her desk and rested a palm on his shoulder. "Would you think me terribly fickle if I accept your offer for dinner and a movie?"

His glum look was dispelled as quickly as the wind scattered ashes in the breeze; the gray was gone and the grass was green again. "Vee, that would be wonderful! Shall we bring the boys along?" he offered kindly, hoping it would be a means of setting her mind at ease.

Veronica giggled. "That sounds more like punishment than a date, Jay! But I understand why you suggested it. Thank you, but, no, I want to be alone with you."

"Six thirty okay?"

"Perfect."

Veronica surprised herself by the absence of second thoughts as the afternoon wore away, and as she typed, her mind strayed to what she would wear, how to comb her hair, and finally to the boys' reactions.

She had forgotten about the older boys' plans to attend a Friday night sporting event at the high school.

When they reminded her in the early evening after work, Veronica worried about leaving her twelve-year-old home alone until eleven.

"I don't see why you can't take him with you," she said when Brad failed to make the offer.

"I would, but he doesn't want to go," Brad replied. "Go see for yourself, Mom."

She found Keith in the living room watching television. "How do you feel about a soccer game at the high school tonight, honey?"

Keith made a face. "I don't like soccer, and it gets cold on the field at night. I heard you want to go out, Mom. I can stay here by myself. Tom Hayes's mother works nights and he's home alone all the time."

"Honey, I worry about you."

"Brad and Greg will be home by eleven. That's not late," he argued, rather pleased at the prospect of having the house to himself.

"I don't know," she sighed, recalling Jay's generous offer to allow the boys to accompany them. No, she didn't want it that way.

Greg entered the room with his math book in hand. "Mom, you haven't had a night out for a long time. I have a geometry test Monday. I really should stay home and study anyway."

"I don't need you to baby-sit for me, Greg," Keith complained.

"Then you can baby-sit for me, partner," Greg told him with a grin.

"Are you sure?" Veronica asked.

"Yes, no problem. Go out and have a nice time with Jay."

"Thank you, sweetie," she said with appreciation, rushing off to the shower.

Jennings arrived a few minutes before she was ready

and took a seat at the kitchen table where the three boys were eating dinner. He endured a little good-natured teasing from Brad because of the deep purple orchid he brought along in a clear plastic box, and didn't mind the smirks the boys exchanged when he jumped to his feet as Veronica entered the room. He wanted to tell her how lovely she was, but the boys inhibited him. "This is for you," he said instead, taking the flower from the box. "May I?"

"Please, and thank you. It's beautiful." She wore a light blue scoop-neck dress, and he pinned the corsage near her shoulder. "I'm ready, Jay. You boys behave yourself, now," she said before leaving.

Outside, he held open the car door for her. "My boys certainly seem to like you," she commented, sliding into the passenger side. He had on a three-piece suit. The dove gray color complimented his brown hair, noticeably longer since they'd first met and hanging in blunt locks over his off-white shirt. He wore an ascot rather than a tie, and in a wave of insecurity Veronica wondered if her appearance was too casual next to his strikingly handsome yet somewhat formal attire. He almost resembled a member of a wedding party, and she hardly considered herself dressed as a bridesmaid.

"They think I'm a sentimental fool for bringing you the corsage."

"Oh, no. Did they say anything to you?" she asked, blushing at the thought of one of her boys embarrassing Jay.

Jennings patted her shoulder reassuringly. "Of course not, but I could tell. I got the same treatment from J.J. Give them a few years and they'll be asking me where I buy flowers." He noticed her frown and assumed it was because of reservations about dating him. "How are you doing, darlin'?"

"Fine. Jay," she said hesitantly, "am I dressed all right for where we're going? You look so much more formal than I do."

"Nonsense," he scoffed. "It's all an illusion because of my aristocratic nose. My parents suggested a place in Santa Monica for dinner. It's a bit off the beaten track, away from the maddening crowd, if you will. Is that satisfactory to you?"

She assured him it was, a prediction that was confirmed when they stepped into the low-key seafood restaurant where women in furs sat at tables near college students in blue jeans and T-shirts.

"Only in California," Jennings quipped when he saw a girl of eighteen or nineteen, wearing denims studded with diamonds, enter with an old man in a tuxedo.

"Those jeans probably cost her what I make in a year," Veronica replied. The service was good and they were handed menus after less than five minutes. As a working woman who seldom ate out, her eyes scanned the right side before reading the selections. "Everything's so expensive," she said before her intellect could censure the gauche statement.

High color shaded her cheekbones, and Jennings thought he had never found her more lovely. "Actually they're not bad," he said with a lazy smile, going on to put her at ease with a discussion of some restaurants he'd visited around the world. "'Course it was on my expense account," he concluded.

"Tell me about your overseas assignments," she requested, surprised when the waiter placed a bottle of champagne on the table.

"I ordered it when I made the reservations," Jennings explained, launching into a light-hearted account of his adventures, which had taken him to most of Europe and Asia.

"I have a feeling it wasn't all fun and games," Veronica remarked, pausing to swallow a bite of the red snapper she and Jay had both ordered. "From what I understand, you were involved in fairly serious business."

"I'm only telling you the good parts to impress you. Am I succeeding?"

"You, my dear, are impressive without saying a word," she admitted candidly.

"I do my best."

Veronica found herself more and more relaxed as the evening passed, and her only source of discomfort was that Jay seemed intent upon entertaining her with amusing anecdotes and cheerful conversation, anything that probably struck him as safe and comfortable subjects for her, carefully avoiding the topic of Mike and her adjustment to his death or touching upon her fear of involvement with another man, things they often spoke of on the phone. He was reserved in his display of physical affection as well, and she could see the effort this required on his behalf. After they left the restaurant, she was certain he was about to kiss her in the car, but instead he brushed one hand down the side of her face and started up the ignition.

Jennings took her to a huge theater in Hollywood that housed four separate movie auditoriums and asked her to choose one. She selected the same one he liked, and as soon as the lights dimmed, he took her hand.

Veronica sat with her fingers entwined through his and her head on Jay's shoulder, ignoring the fact she could only see half the screen in such a position because of the tall woman in front. Jay's shoulder was far more appealing than any movie could ever be.

"J.J. and I used to have a dog like that," Jennings

remarked when an animal of indeterminate breed scampered off after a burglar in the film.

"What dog?" she murmured dreamily, her hand resting easily on his thigh now.

Jennings tilted his head down. "That one."

Veronica shifted upward to see the screen. "Oh, he's cute."

"Are you having trouble seeing?"

"I don't care. It's okay," she said, returning to her former position.

Jennings stood. "Try the aisle seat."

"No, really, it's all right. You need the room because your legs are longer." She hastily changed places when the couple behind them began to grumble. "Thanks," she whispered.

"Did you enjoy the movie?" Jennings asked afterward.

"No, I thought it was awful, but I sure liked sitting there holding your hand," she confessed with a grin as they walked to the parking lot.

Jennings chuckled. "Think how much fun it'll be when they show a decent film. I didn't care for it myself. Would you like to stop for dessert? Maybe another drink?"

"Jay, I would love to, but I want to get back to my kids. It's nearly eleven."

"Would you mind stopping at my house for a few minutes?" Jennings bent over the open door as she slid in. "Don't worry, little darlin', I just want you to meet my folks," he said in response to her frown.

She chastised herself for even thinking Jay would attempt to take her off to some private place to make love to her after all the consideration he'd displayed throughout the evening, but the prospect of meeting his parents seemed too much of a prelude to a serious relationship to gain her immediate consent. Veronica was troubled by her ambiguity. Why did signs of commitment disturb her so greatly? Surely the thought that theirs was a casual relationship that would never go anywhere was an untenable one. She saw herself growing closer to him with each passing day, but these outward signs of a deepening relationship still frightened her, forcing her to retreat from him.

"Jay, I've had a marvelous time tonight, but I'd prefer to meet your parents some other day, not tonight. I promise you, soon I'll have the four of you over to dinner. How does that sound?"

"Wonderful," he said with all the enthusiasm he could muster. Jennings had been on needles and pins with her all evening, trying to play the part of the low-pressure suitor, the friend, when all along his heart was swelling with love of her, and he was hard pressed to think of anything more innocent, less threatening, than meeting his parents. Surely Vee should have enough sense to realize he'd never try to get her into bed there of all places, with his son and folks home. "I'm looking forward to it."

She sensed his displeasure and didn't know how to handle it, and sat next to him in silent amazement when Jay resumed his light inconsequential chatter, never ceasing his efforts to make her feel at ease in his company.

"Well, here we are, darlin'," Jay said when they reached her home. "I see the porch light is on, and all seems fine on the home front. Let me walk you to the door."

"Not so quick," Veronica answered, placing a restraining hand on his when he tried to open the door. "You haven't done everything right tonight, Mr. Jennings."

Her caressing tone didn't give him cause for alarm. "Darlin', I gave it my best shot. If something's wrong, you're going to have to spell it out for me."

She eased in closer to him on the seat, wrapping her arms around his neck. "Jay, my dear, whoever heard of the perfect date without the perfect good-night kiss?"

"I was saving that for the porch."

They were parked beneath a towering oak with low hanging branches that blocked visibility between the car and house. "I prefer the privacy here."

"You have a point there," he said happily. Jennings cupped her face in his hands and tried to keep the kiss as light and undemanding as the evening had been, but it was no good. As soon as her tongue swept over his upper lip, Jay opened his mouth to take it inside, savoring the sweetness like a famished man approaching the banquet table, too hungry for decorum, a victim of a greed he never wanted to know. He supposed that if he could make a conscious choice it would be not to love her, not to want her so intensely, but all that was academic now. He couldn't stop loving her and desiring her any more than the sun could set in the east.

"How's that?" he asked huskily, tearing his mouth from hers.

"I can't be certain. Do it again." Before he could answer, Veronica assaulted his lips with a tender passion that drew his breath out in a long sigh. She felt his palms press into her back and moved her hands from his shoulders to the sides of his face where the clean-shaven skin was smooth like highly polished mahogany beneath her fingertips. Her breasts were pressed flat against the soft fabric of his jacket, and as the kiss deepened and Jay ran his palms along her body, occasionally sweeping past the sides of her bust, she felt a tortuous ache there, a longing that would know surcease only in the touch of his hand.

"Jay, Jay," she got out in ragged sigh when he began to kiss her neck. Veronica grasped his open hand and placed it on her breast. She allowed him to caress her briefly, realizing she'd miscalculated as to the relief she would find when he took her breast into his hand, stroked the engorged tips. The yearning, the need for him was a hundred times stronger now, coursing throughout her entire being, radiating warmly from an incendiary heat in her lower body. "I have to go inside, Jay," she murmured, pressing his hand to her breast once before removing it.

Jennings stared into her eyes. "I understand. Let me walk you to the door." He only had a fraction of what he wanted from her, but that trust and added intimacy made him a far happier man than he'd been in a long time. "Is it too late to call you tonight?"

"No, call as soon as you get home. I'll be waiting, angel."

Chapter Ten

The Mediterranean-like winter eased almost imperceptibly into spring and Jay continued to court Veronica with charm, grace, and a great deal of patience.

He met her at Cal Tech at least three times a week for lunch, and took her to dinner, to the theater, or to a movie, wherever she wanted to go on the weekends when she didn't have to study or tend to her children. And he endured the maddening frustration of her impassioned kisses on the front porch or in his car because he had no alternative. Veronica wasn't ready for a full-fledged affair, and he made good on his promise never to pressure her, something that became more difficult with every passing day as his love grew.

She surprised him one day in early April by inviting him into the house while the boys were still in school. He detected the ambivalence in her invitation and questioned her.

"Don't be silly, Jay. It's all right," she replied hesitantly, checking the clock on his dashboard and wondering what would happen in the next hour before the boys were due home.

Jennings took her hand and kissed the tip of her thumb. "If there's any problem, I understand."

"Why should there be a problem?" she asked glibly,

well aware Jay wasn't referring to her study schedule. Veronica was unused to discussions about sex and how it made her feel. It was okay to flirt with Jay, to hold his hand, to rest hers on his thigh, but anything else made her uncomfortable and he knew it.

"No reason," he said pleasantly. "I just thought you might have things to do. I know how busy you are."

She gave in to a desire to kiss his cheek. "Come inside, Jay," she invited, "and let me open my own door. We'll get there faster that way."

"To hell with chivalry with an incentive like that," he rejoined, opening his side after she'd exited.

Jay went through the stack of law books on her dining room table while Veronica fed the hungry stray cat Brad had found out in the ravine behind the house. "I don't see how you do all the things you do," he said with admiration when she emerged from the next room. "This definitely isn't pleasure reading."

"You'd be surprised, sometimes it is. I really enjoy it. I find the criminal law a bit on the dull side, but I'm enjoying the readings in constitutional law."

"Need any help studying?" he offered with a wink. Jay spun her around into his arms and kissed the top of her head.

"Do you honestly think I'd get anything done like this?" Veronica rested her palms on his chest and smiled up into eyes that had all the color of lush grass speckled with daffodils.

"To be perfectly honest, no. But think of all the fun you'd have blowing it," he teased in the slow articulation that seemed made for bedtime talk.

"I can do without that kind of fun," she replied breathlessly as the splayed fingers behind her back descended, stopping indiscernibly close to the rise of her buttocks.

"Spoilsport." Jennings had made himself a promise not to kiss her until it was time to say good-bye so he stood there dueling with his desire, the outstretched hands tense, frozen immobile between the heaven of her soft flesh and the hell of the self-discipline he battled.

"Who, me?" she asked flirtatiously. "I've always thought of myself as a good sport."

She leaned into the fire of his loins with an incendiary gesture, and the seductiveness of her act combined with the innocence of her uptilted grin brought his love for her to the fore of Jennings's mind. "Maybe you are, Vee, but this ain't no tennis match."

The tenor of his statement conveyed much to her, and Veronica stepped back. "I'm sorry, I didn't mean to play with you."

Jay stared down at her with a great longing in his heart. "No, play with me all you want," he said, returning her to where she had been, so near yet so far from his body, locked in the tension of an embrace that struggled to maintain a level keel in the storm of his passion for her.

"I can't handle all this," she despaired in a small voice.

"Handle what?" he hedged, unwilling to second guess her and put words into her mouth.

"You know, Jay, this, all this. This dating, this courtship, this getting to know someone, touching them."

"You're doing it just fine, Vee, just fine. One word of advice," he soothed.

"What's that?"

"Get that plural usage out of here. Don't touch *them,* touch *me.*"

"How... How do I know..."

"Go on, little darlin'."

"How do I know you won't misconstrue my intentions and think I'm ready for more than I am?" she got out. "I really don't want to tease you, Jay."

He chuckled and led her into the living room, his arm locked around her waist. "Sit down here," he said, offering Veronica her own sofa and sitting by her side. "I'm glad you brought that up."

"You are?"

"Definitely. In all good conscience, there's something I must warn you about," he started, one hand on her shoulder and the other playing havoc with her senses by the way it traveled over her cheeks.

"Oh?" she asked with concern, until Jay was betrayed by a devilish gleam and the hint of a smile impossible to suppress. "Tell me about it."

"You have just cause to worry about, ah ... Shall we say, optimistic expectations on my behalf. You see, when my satyrlike appetite fails to get its full, I've been known to go totally berserk, lose control, and vent my animal lust on the nearest available woman. Now, you wouldn't want that to happen to you, would you?" he teased fondly.

"There have been days around the house and office when I'd welcome the distraction," she admitted, not entirely in jest.

"Oh, yeah? Well, I'm on call."

Veronica laughed and then asked him to be serious. "I guess I'm just not making any sense at all, right?"

He shook his head in a manner that discounted her statement. "You're making a great deal of sense. I hear what you're saying. From the neck up, anyway," he added candidly. "The rest of me is less amenable to logic, but I'll try to keep my body under control. If I get out of hand, Vee, just slap my wrist and I'll understand."

"You understand, then?" she asked, raising his palm to her mouth and kissing the crisscross of deep lines.

"As much as I can. Unlike you, I've never been faithful all my life to one person and then lost that person under such tragic circumstances. I can only imagine how difficult it must be for you, and I don't want to make it any harder on you. I'll wait for you," he promised, his fingers tangled through her downcast head, the mouth still driving him insane from those little kisses she continued to rain all over his hand. Jennings tried to remember if a woman had ever kissed him that way, with so much pent-up passion in the tender play of her lips on his palm, next his fingers, moving now and then to his wrist, and couldn't. Not likely, he concluded. How in the hell could a man forget something like this?

"Thank you, Jay." Her head rose and she flung her arms around his neck, nearly toppling him over with the momentum of the plunge as her mouth covered his. Veronica made a hungry foray of the parted lips, the tongue as soft as melting snow and twice as wet, only it wasn't cold, the wet hot heat was almost unbearable, deliciously unbearable.

Jennings didn't know what to do with his hands at first. His natural inclination would have made a mockery of his pledge to wait for her, so he placed them benignly around her waist, running both up and down the safe territory of her back. Safe for her maybe, but not for him, he soon learned. No matter where he touched her, he was off like a shooting star, soaring incandescent and freely with no knowledge of the laws of gravity, flying through the void without an anchor. God, the silk of her dress was like angel dust under his fingers, and when he chanced on something hard, the clasp of her brassiere, Jennings groaned in frustration, wanting so much to release her breasts from the confines of the garment and into his hands, into his lips like manna to the faithful wandering in the desert.

The kiss went on, Veronica kissing him with so much intensity that Jennings found himself struggling to maintain an upright position on the couch, a paradoxical battle since there was a time when he'd give his very soul to have her fall down atop his receptive body, press all her want into him, absorb her intensity like forest loam swallowing the first rain of autumn.

"Easy, easy, honey," he cautioned when she finally tore her lips away and began to nibble at his neck.

Veronica ceased at once, jerking her face up, and came close to hitting him under the chin with her head. "Oh, Jay, did I hurt you?"

"No," he replied with an expression that mystified her, staring into her eyes with a sense of wonderment as though he were an exile gazing on paradise for the first time in his life. Jennings took her face between his hands and kissed her with enough tenderness to make her want to cry, making a valiant attempt to plummet their passion back to the point where he could stand up and say good-bye, but it was impossible. Her breasts were full and oh, so soft against his chest, pressed in like sails just meeting a shift in the wind, all except for those diamond tips searing his skin, warm and impatient beneath the layers of clothing he wished he could cast aside in order to feel her better. He kissed her harder and she responded in kind.

The thought that she was a woman in her mid-thirties who had never been properly kissed by a man until now managed to impress itself upon her heightened senses, and Veronica shuddered in his arms, alive with anticipation and overwhelmed by the essence of him. That crazy, ostentatious cologne his son kept giving him and he wore out of kindness had metamorphosed by now in Veronica's eyes to an airborne aphrodisiac that could tempt a goddess made of stone, and she stifled the silly thought to keep a bottle by her bedside, a nighttime reminder of this moment with Jay. She partook of his mouth until she had to come up for air, and then tasted his eyelids, the tiny hairs of his lashes springy beneath her lips, the coarser brows glorious next to her mouth.

Jennings's hands continued to move up and down her arms, her back, the sides of her face, behind her neck, stifling the urge to touch her more intimately, finally taking both her hands in his, relying on Veronica to keep them in the right place. God only knew he couldn't do it much longer. He clasped their arms somewhat rigidly at her side and began to kiss her neck, moving upward to her eyes and doing what she'd done to him, delighting in the husky little sounds coming from her throat. The throaty music led him back to its source; Jennings kissed her neck again, descending lower into the scooped top of her dress, drifting downward as much as the limitations she needed now and the fabric would allow. He faltered when Veronica shifted on the sofa, one knee coming to rest between his legs. Jennings grasped her breasts from beneath, over the deep purple material, and opened his mouth on the rigid rise in the cloth and suckled there while she held his head to her body.

Veronica snuggled in to Jay, easing back when she realized where her knee had landed, more from concern of pushing in closer and hurting him than from modesty. The wet heat of his moist kiss had long since penetrated her clothing, and those shock waves of desire were consuming her. Veronica regretted her choice of clothing as he turned his attention to her other breast. If she wore a blouse, she would have raised it, but to stand and undo a dress that zipped in back she couldn't do, not now.

With his head slightly sideways, his mouth fixated on her breast, Jennings toyed with the other nipple between his fingertips, and was crashed back to reality when he saw the large dark patch of his own making around the hard peak. "Oh, Vee, look what I did," he said, reluctantly shifting his position. "I'm sorry. I ruined your dress."

Veronica glanced at her bust. The deep shade accentuated the color contrast between the wet and dry cloth. "Jay, it's nothing. It'll dry just fine."

"Are you sure?"

"Sure I'm sure, unless you have some hitherto unknown chemical in your saliva," she said, adjusting the dress where it had ridden past her knees. Her words were breathless from want of him.

"Not that I know of," he said. The time came for decorum. Jennings straightened his tie and stood. "What time are the kids due back?"

Veronica looked at the clock. "Any minute."

"I'd better go now, and you'd better change your dress. I can't imagine how any woman could ever explain away something like that." He pulled her to her feet. "When can I see you again? I thought we could have dinner and go to a movie over the weekend, unless there's someplace else you'd like to go."

"Knowing you, it'll probably be a drive-in movie." She linked her arm through his elbow to escort him to the door.

Jennings patted her hand and laughed. "I'm one step ahead of you."

"Oh?"

"I had home movies in mind. My parents are taking J.J. up to the snow and I'm staying here to house hunt."

"Jay, I've made plans with my boys. I can't see you this weekend, but I'll be thinking about you every minute."

His face fell. "And I suppose the next few days are out because of your studies?"

"Afraid so. Will you call me?"

"Every night."

She stood on her tiptoes to kiss him good-bye. "Whereabouts are you looking for a house?"

"I was hoping to find one next door to you," he said, pushing her over the threshold and back into the house when she stepped out.

"What are you doing?" Veronica demanded.

"Vee, go and change. I don't want everyone on the block to know how I've been drooling over you, especially if I move into this neighborhood."

"You're serious? You really would move into this area?" she asked, standing in the doorway.

"I'll call you after dinner. Go get decent now, okay?"

"Okay, one more kiss."

He brushed his lips across her forehead and left whistling.

Chapter Eleven

Her need to progress slowly on the relationship forced Veronica and Jay apart countless hours during late April and most of May. She managed to rise above most of the anxiety the separation induced and progressed so well in her studies that she opted to take the June exams early, giving her three weeks of free time from the courses to spend with her family and the man who had come to mean so much to her in the five months since Christmas. She awoke on the morning the exams were to be taken at the judge's house in high spirits, and in an impulsive act dialed Jennings's number. It was 6:00 A.M. on a Saturday, and she knew he was certain to be sound asleep.

"Jennings here," came the groggy response to her ring.

"Good morning, Jennings," she purred into his ear.

He'd been woken from a deep slumber and the sensual quality of her voice failed to register on his senses. Jay bolted up in his bed. "Vee, anything wrong?"

"No, everything's right. I just called to say hello."

"So, say hello, darlin'."

"Hello."

"Hi. All ready for the exams today?"

"More than ready. I'll be home by six."

"Let's go out and celebrate," he suggested with a prolonged yawn.

"We're always going out and celebrating," she answered in reference to all the places he had taken her in the last several months. "Not that I'm complaining. I love it."

"Well, what do you want to do?"

"I thought that since the days are starting to get so long, we could buy a bottle of good wine and climb up into the hills out back and drink it. How does that sound?"

"Well worth having you wake me up in the middle of the night to tell me about."

"It's not the middle of the night, but I'll let you get back to sleep. Good night, angel." She hung up and ate breakfast over her study notes, shaking her head in amazement at the sight of the newly waxed kitchen floor and the shining knotty pine cabinets.

The unlikely trio of two teenage boys and a twelve-year-old had freed Veronica from many household chores for months now, promising her more of the same in the future. The boys had always had their share of responsibility around the house, but the bulk of work usually fell upon their mother's shoulders. However, all that had changed in recent months. Brad had given Veronica his solemn pledge that she need never step foot into the kitchen again on weekdays for as long as she held down the job at Cal Tech and studied law, a proclamation Veronica took as a mixed blessing, feeling pride in Brad's newfound sense of responsibility and loyalty to his mother but concern because more and more it seemed Brad had taken on his father's role around the house.

Brad continued to be a serious young man, spending his weekends alone in the backyard either reading the classics, those of a more serious nature, which his mother found almost morbid, or else lying there on the hammock staring out to San Gabriels until night came and took away the view. He was courteous to her at all times, unfailingly thoughtful of her every need and those of his two younger brothers, but distant now to all of them, and Veronica couldn't reach him. He seemed to have gone into himself, and she was patient, knowing about the place where he had gone to, for she had been there herself. Brad was mourning the loss of the most important person in his life all over again, and there was nothing Veronica could do right now but be there and love him. It had always been apparent to her that Mike favored his firstborn, the blue-eyed baby with corn silk blond hair who resembled him in so many ways, so she supposed it was only natural for a special affinity to have evolved between the two, for Brad to mourn his father most of all.

Veronica went out in the yard to say good-bye to him before leaving for her examinations and found Brad gazing off into the foothills. She put her hand on his shoulder and he jumped. "Brad, it's only me."

"I'm sorry, Mom, I didn't hear you coming. Ready to go now?" he asked, still staring straight ahead.

"Yes. I just came to say good-bye and thank you again for everything you've been doing around the house. It's been such a help. I don't think I would have been in a position to take my tests early if it weren't for you." Veronica stepped around to follow the line of his vision. "Whatcha see out there in those mountains, Brad?" she asked quietly.

He shrugged. "Oh, nothing," he said commiseratively.

"You must see something."

"I was thinking of one time Dad took Greg and I

camping up there, right above the snow line. We came poorly prepared for snow camping because it was so warm down here that December, somehow we thought the snow was an illusion or something. Greg and I were miserable and Dad was miserable, but we were all trying to pretend we were having a great time, because we didn't want to disappoint each other. This went on for about two days, and finally Dad said, 'Let's get the hell out of here and go stay at the Disneyland Hotel, guys. If I'm going to freeze my ass off I might as well do it in comfort.' So then I asked him how you could freeze your ass off in comfort, and Dad laughed and said he didn't know, but on the way down the mountain we'd think of something."

Veronica shook her head and laughed. "Did you ever think of a way?"

"No, I'm still working on the problem." Brad checked his watch for the time. "You'd better go over to the judge's house now, Mom. You'll be late. Good luck on the exams, and don't worry about anything here. I'll take Keith to the dentist on the bus, and have dinner ready by six, okay?"

"Okay. Thank you," she said, forcing down the thickness that rose in her throat. "I love you," Veronica called over her shoulder as she walked away.

Brad turned and grinned a bashful smile before resuming his meditations. "'Bye, Mom," he said, looking beyond the foothills to high peaks above, his glance fixated on a large bird of prey he hoped would get the diamondback rattlesnake that had crept into their camp one summer, nearly biting his dad before they chased it off with the end of a shotgun.

"I'll call you if I get hung up," Veronica said as she neared the back door, but Brad was beyond hearing anything, and she let him be. She considered his introspective behavior on the short drive to Judge McCue's home in South Pasadena. Brad was going to be okay, just fine, she knew it as certainly as she had ever known anything, and her eyes shone with pride because of Brad as she pulled into the McCue driveway.

Mrs. McCue, a picture-pretty silver-haired woman in her late seventies, was on the porch tending to her spring annuals, bright purple and pink petunias and red pansies. "Veronica! All ready for the big exam?"

"You bet I am," Veronica enthused, kissing her cheek. "What beautiful flowers! I haven't had much time this year to plant any myself." She glanced over to several potted poinsettias that looked as beautiful as a Christmas display. "How did you manage to keep those in bloom through the winter?"

"What winter?" she scoffed, flinging up hands speckled with dark potting soil. "There aren't any winters in Southern California, you've been here long enough to know that, Veronica."

"You have a point there, Mrs. McCue." Veronica dropped to her feet to hand Mrs. McCue a spade that had slipped from between her fingers. "How's the judge?"

"Fit as a fiddle, and waiting for you. I'm so happy you decided to ask Melvin to proctor your law school tests. Now that he's retired from both the bench and teaching you're his only pupil. I'm surprised he didn't ask me to set up the guest room for you so you could fall into it after he chews off your ear until four in the morning!"

"Having the judge as my proctor is an honor. I honestly don't think I would be doing nearly so well with my studies if it weren't for all the discussions we've had about law," Veronica said sincerely, pleased to be the recipient of sixty years of experience from Judge

McCue, who had been a leading prosecutor in the district attorney's office for ten years before a former governor of the state appointed him to a seat in the Superior Court of Los Angeles County almost fifty years ago.

"Oh, come now! A bright young woman like you doesn't need conversations with an old coot like Melvin to get by! You'd do just fine. Speaking of the old coot, here he is," she said, handing her husband a potted plant. "I've run out of space for this. Take it out back, will you, Melvin?"

"Later, dear. I'm giving exams this morning. Let me get Veronica started and then I'll do it." He reached out and shook Veronica's hand, then began to shoot an artillery of legal questions at her.

Veronica was on the verge of suggesting they get on with the examination that had been recently mailed to Judge McCue when his wife intervened on her behalf. "For land's sake, Melvin, don't exhaust the girl before she even sits down to the tests. Go inside and get her started," she ordered. "Veronica, I left cookies and lemonade in the study. Coffee is on the stove, all ready."

"Thank you so much. Shall we, Judge?" she asked, taking his arm.

"Yes, very well. Did you read everything I gave you before Easter?"

"Every word, even the ones that were so dry I thought the papers were going to catch on fire."

"I know what you mean, but a well-rounded knowledge of the law is the foundation of it all, you can't do anything without the basics," he said didactically as they walked to the study.

"I know." She sat down at the desk while the judge opened the sealed envelopes. "No fair looking," she reprimanded gently when he sneaked a peek at the first test. The honor system of the correspondence school was such that the proctor didn't open the sealed envelopes sent to him or her, nor did the examiner read them afterward. The judge had always resisted his urges in regard to the former, but occasionally slipped on the latter requirement.

"I'm just making sure all the pages are here," he said, dismissing her comment. "Remember the time they left out page three?"

"Yes," Veronica replied with an indulgent smile. "How does it look?"

"All the papers are here." He set them down on the walnut burl map table in his study. "And you're a shoe-in to pass this one with the highest scores. Don't forget what we talked about the week before Easter," he advised.

"I never forget what we discuss," she laughed, ushering him out of the room before he reminded her and violated the rules of an honor system she guarded so carefully.

"You have three hours. Shall I give you a half hour warning when the time is almost up?" he asked, leaning into one of the two canes he used and tapping the other on the wall.

"Why? Something wrong with the clock?"

"Not that I know of, but last time you got so involved with one question you forgot the time and didn't complete part of the test," he reminded her. "Fortunately you did so well on the rest, you still received an A."

"So I did. Yes, please, Judge, let me know when I only have half an hour left. And thank you and Mrs. McCue so much for everything."

"It's our pleasure, dear." He finally left to join his

wife on the front porch and Veronica got down to business.

"I don't believe it!" she exclaimed two and a half hours later when he reentered the room. "I just sat down!"

"It can and it is, my dear. How are you doing? Almost finished?" He sat a cup of coffee on the table. "This is from Mrs. McCue. I wanted to bring it in sooner, but she wouldn't let me. The old coot," he said with affection. He leaned over Veronica's shoulder and glanced at the test. "Good, very good."

"Thanks. It's a bit more difficult than I had anticipated, but so far I think I've answered everything correctly. I only have one more short essay to go," she said, sipping the coffee.

"Good girl. I'll be back in twenty-seven minutes," he replied. He grabbed one of the macaroons his wife had made and excused himself, returning as the clock struck high noon.

"I'll take that," he said, eagerly snatching the exam from Veronica's hands and looking over the pages.

"Tch, tch, you of all people reading that, Judge McCue. It is against the rules, you know," she teased fondly.

"Read this," the judge replied, hobbling over to one of the massive floor-to-ceiling bookcases that lined the study walls and removing a volume. "Better yet, take it home and keep it."

Veronica read the title and laughed. It was a collection of classic essays on civil disobedience, many of which were penned by the old man himself. "Thank you. How does the exam look to you?"

"Right on," he remarked, turning to the next section.

"Where did you pick up an expression like that?" she laughed.

"From my great grandchildren. Good, good, uh-oh, we have to talk about that," he mused, turning to the next section. "Naomi has lunch ready for you, and then I want you back here by one thirty for the patent law exam. Are you certain you want to take constitutional law tomorrow? You might want to rest up a bit."

"No, unless it's any problem for you and Mrs. McCue, I'm ready to take it tomorrow. Won't you be joining us for lunch?" she asked, well pleased by the approval evident in his expression.

"In a bit. Naomi is in the front yard. Tell her I'll be there briefly," he asked, his attention spellbound by the examination in his hands.

The test succeeded in holding his interest until it was time for Veronica to begin another. "You missed a nice lunch," she said to him when she returned to the study.

"I'm sure I'll hear about it from now to doomsday," he remarked, patting her on the shoulder. "Very good, young lady, very good," the judge said in a fatherly tone. "I found your impressions of the Long case a bit on the shallow side, but then, that's to be expected. You've hardly had a chance to sink your teeth into the law, much less digest it. Bring your boys over to dinner sometime, and we'll go over the decision. I'll never forget the day it came down from the Supreme Court for as long as I live," he began and Veronica headed him off at the pass.

"I'd love to have dinner with you and Mrs. McCue. You name the time, and we'll be here. How about the next exam now?" she asked politely.

He gave her the patent law test. "I didn't know your school had a course in patent law, Veronica," he mentioned as she settled into the desk.

"They don't. I arranged a special tutorial with one of

the professors. Next semester I'm doing an individual study in protection of intellectual property."

"You have a strong interest in that field, don't you? It's an unusual area for a young lady to be interested in; women usually go into family practice or probate law, something more down to earth. I think it suits their natures better," he said, and she let the sexist comment pass out of respect for the man, his age, and all that he had accomplished in his lifetime of service to the county of Los Angeles.

"Well, I have my special reasons," she replied, not elaborating. She'd never taken the judge into her confidence regarding Mike's death.

"I'd like to hear them someday, but you have to get to work now, young lady. I'll bring you a cup of coffee and give you a half hour warning at four."

"Thank you so much." The second exam was far more difficult than the first, and by the time she'd finished, Veronica had chewed the erasers from six pencils and worn out three of the erasable ballpoint pens she had. Her concentration was so intense that she barely noticed the judge when he tiptoed in and out of the room at four.

"A tough one, huh?" Judge McCue asked later when the time was up. "Did you finish?"

She shook her head. "Not quite, but if I did okay on what I could do, I'll pass. That is, I'll probably pass," she decided, modifying her original statement. "That was the shortest three hours I've ever sat through."

"Veronica, I wish I could give you another half hour, but I never did it with my own students at Loyola, so I can't do it now," he said sadly, taking the exam and leafing through the sheets.

"Oh, no! I wouldn't dream of such a thing, Judge McCue! I wasn't hinting for more time."

"Of course you weren't," he hastened to reassure her. Judge McCue reached for a brandy glass on his desk. "How about a little one to take these jitters away? You've had a tense six hours. You could use one."

She tried to decline his offer. "I'd love to, but I have to drive home soon. I never could handle liquor. Why, a single glass of wine, and I'm done for," she laughed.

The old man wasn't about to let a chance for stimulating conversation slip by so easily. "Oh, pshaw! A strapping thing like you can handle a tiny shot. Come sit down." He propelled her to his desk as best he could, leaning into Veronica with a cane in his hand. "By the way, from what I saw of the second exam, you did an excellent job. Congratulations. I can call the law school next week and squeeze the results from them a little sooner than you could probably get the information, if you're worried about the scores."

"Could you really? Do you know the staff?"

"Some of them. Vernon Oxford was one of my students at Loyola years ago. He had a promising career before him but wound up falling into the bottom of a whiskey bottle in his late thirties. Since then he's taught part-time at one unaccredited institution after another," he said, relishing in the gossip. "I'll give him a call for you roundabout next Wednesday."

"With that information I'll buy him a bottle of Seagram's and get the scores from him by Monday," she quipped, accepting the brandy snifter because she didn't know how to refuse it with the old man sitting there so expectantly, the two undimmable brown eyes glowing and waiting to talk about what he loved most in the world.

"It would probably work, knowing Oxford. I noticed they asked you about the Fitzsimmons case. I observed part of that one. I came close to presiding over it but had to disqualify myself because Sean Fitzsimmons was my friend."

"You're kidding! You knew him?" she asked, taking a dainty sip of the brandy because any more would be certain to make her eyes tear.

"Very well. He was one of the finest men I ever met in my life, Veronica, but I wish to hell I'd never laid eyes on him, because I could have rendered a fair decision," he began, spiriting her away into a fascinating tale of legal maneuvering that held her spellbound as she sipped the fine old brandy, which seemed to mellow with each taste. The judge's wife finally joined them to tell Veronica one of her sons was on the line.

Naomi McCue looked at the half-empty brandy decanter and shook her head. "Shame on you, Melvin, getting this girl stupefied so she'll sit through your long drawn-out stories!"

Veronica gasped when she saw the time. "Oh, my God! It's after seven and I told my boys I'd be there by six! Where's the phone, Mrs. McCue?" Veronica had been dieting all week, and that, combined with the high-level tension of the lengthy examinations, intensified the effect of the brandy, potent enough on its own. She rose on uneasy feet and the judge's wife asked her to be seated.

"I'll bring the phone to you," Mrs. McCue said, casting a disparaging glance at her husband. "You old coot, at least I don't have to worry about what you do with a girl when you get her drunk anymore."

The judge laughed. "She never had to worry and she knows it."

"Really?" Veronica asked, rubbing her temples and wondering how she was going to get home. Driving was out of the question, both for her and the judge. Mrs.

McCue returned almost immediately with the phone, giving her little time to consider transportation.

"Hello, Brad?"

"Yeah, Mom. We were worried about you. Usually when you say six, it's no later than six thirty, unless you phone. Is everything okay?"

"You sound like my mother," she said, giggling uncontrollably.

"I'd prefer to sound more like your father than your mother. Grandma has a squeaky old-lady voice," he said. "How did your tests go? Think you passed?"

"Sure do," she got out, pressing her hand to her forehead as a wave of nausea came and went.

Brad heard the unusual inflection in his mother's voice, and it took him all of five seconds to figure out she had been drinking. He wasn't shocked, though he had never known her to be intoxicated, not even the least bit tipsy the way his dad used to be once in a while. If anyone had a right to hang loose once in a while, it was his mom, because she worked so hard and had endured the same irreplaceable loss he had. "I'm glad you passed your tests. So, what are you doing now?"

"Just sitting around talking to Judge McCue. He's a brilliant man," she mentioned, the content crystal clear in her head but somehow lost in the transition from mind to mouth. "Brad, do you think I could be a judge someday?"

"No sweat. You can be anything you want. What are you and the judge talking about?" he asked, playing for time while a plan formulated in his mind. He listened until he had one. "Hey, Mom, I just remembered something. It's real important."

"What?"

"Mom, listen to me. Remember when I tuned up the car last time?"

"Yes, darling, you did such a good job."

"Listen, I didn't do such a knock-up job. I've been thinking about it all day. Something's wrong in the distributor and the car's not safe to take out on the freeway. You can't drive the car, Mom," he said, stressing the words as though he were talking to a child or a deaf person. "You have to let me borrow a car and come and get you."

There was silence from Veronica's end. As much as she had been drinking, she was sober enough to follow Brad's thoughts, bless his heart and damn her for getting drunk with the old man. Damn her even more for lying to him, but pride had to reign over truth. "The car has a problem? Well, don't worry about it, Brad. You see, I never meant to drive it from here anyway."

"It's a long hike back home, Mom, and they didn't let the judge or his wife renew their licenses this year because of their eyesight. What did you plan to do?" he asked in the tone of a patient parent.

"Ah...ah...Jay and I had kind of a date for tonight. He was going to pick me up here," she explained with the jackhammers pounding away in her head.

Brad was wary of the story she asked him to buy. "Mom, how come you never told us? I said I was fixing dinner at six, didn't I?"

Veronica hated lies, most of all lies with the ones she loved the most, and God, she loved Brad so much, but the die had been cast; she couldn't renege now. "I didn't, baby? I guess I forgot. You know how hectic it's been. I really appreciate all you're doing for me, Brad. You mad at me for going out with Jay?"

Brad shook his head in frustration. She had left him with little alternative other than to call Jay Jennings and confirm what she said. "No, I like the man. Dad always talked about him when we went camping."

"He did?" Veronica asked, trying hard to grasp upon a crumb of knowledge about the man her hazy mind said she was falling more and more in love with each day. Mike had rarely spoken about Jay to her, and until she met the man he had remained a shadow figure in her mind. Jay Jennings had never existed for Veronica in the flesh and blood until he held her in his arms. "Brad, tell me, your father never spoke much about his war buddies with me. What did he say about Jay? Did he talk to you?"

"Yeah, there were times he did, but... but I really don't want to think about that now. All I can say is that he really loved this Jennings guy, so that's why I love him too."

"Oh, Brad."

"You get back to your talks with the judge now, and I'll see you later."

"I love you," she repeated.

"Yeah, Mom. I'm glad you did well on your tests."

"I'll be home soon, son." She hung up the receiver and turned to the judge, who seemed on the verge of falling asleep in his chair. "Oh, I just lied like hell. I guess I should call a cab, huh?"

Melvin McCue hadn't missed a beat. "It sounds to me like you'd far prefer to see your man. Do you mind a bit of advice from a man who's been on this planet probably much too long for everyone's good?"

She held his hand. "Oh, shut up—with all due respect, Judge. What's your advice, anyway?"

"Pride has its place with one's offspring, but there are times when it's less appropriate."

"Oh? And you're an expert on these things?" she giggled, looking at the purple veins on his hand that seemed poised for flight, so high and taut.

"How can a man be married for sixty-one years and not be an expert on these things?"

She discounted his case. "Small sample. Not enough information."

"Veronica, my dear, you'd be surprised."

"Nothing would surprise me anymore."

"Shush, listen to me, since you criticize limited information."

"I'm listening," she answered, reaching for the brandy decanter and paying as much attention to how the old lead crystal lamp on the table made rainbows on the wall as she did to her mentor.

"Call your young man, because sometimes the soundest of decisions are rendered on the smallest grain of evidence. It's always veracity, the truth that counts, not how many facts you can add up." He passed her the phone and exited, shaking as he made his way to the door like the lone Joshua tree atop barren rock in a fall storm, bowing to the wind yet twice as solid as the stone itself.

"Well, I was going to call him myself," she muttered, the most blissful of smiles lighting up her face.

Chapter Twelve

"Brad, what's going on?" Greg demanded as his brother stood there in the hallway, tossing the telephone receiver from hand to hand. "Did you get in touch with Mom?"

He nodded and looked around for the telephone book. "Greg, do you know where Jay Jennings lives? He was supposed to meet Mom at the judge's house and didn't show up. I thought I'd give him a call."

"Is that why she's late?"

"Yeah. Do you know if she has his phone number written down anywhere?" he asked when he remembered Jennings hadn't lived in the area long enough to have a listing in the book.

"I think I saw it on the bulletin board in the kitchen. This doesn't make much sense. Why wouldn't Mom have told us she was going out and why would she ask you to call Jay?" he questioned suspiciously. Brad had been acting strange lately, barely speaking to him anymore in the room they had shared nearly all of his life. Greg had never forgotten the sarcastic remark Brad threw out to their mother that time she hit him, the one about she and Jennings, though his older brother seemed to like the man well enough now.

"Because she left the phone number here," Brad

tried, racing downstairs to the kitchen with Greg at his heels.

"So, why didn't you give it to her?" he persisted. "I'm sure Mom's going to ask you to talk to a guy if he stands her up, especially Jay, whom she knows so well. And he's crazy about her and would never forget a date with her. Besides that, Mom must have his number memorized. She calls him all the time."

"Maybe she forgot it."

"Come on, Brad, gimme a break, huh?"

"Just shut up, will ya?" he ground out, dialing Jennings's number.

"No, I won't. I'm getting sick and tired of you acting so high and mighty around this house. You're only a little over a year older than me, and you act like it's ten most of the time. I've had about all I can take of you trying to play father with me, and I'm not going to let you louse up anything for Mom. Put the phone down, or explain to me exactly why you want to talk to Jay." Greg made a lunge for the buttons, disconnecting the call as Brad dialed.

"Cool it, Greg," Brad said calmly. "Just get out of here, okay? This is none of your business."

"And I suppose calling Mom's date is your business?" he challenged, making an unsuccessful attempt to grab the receiver from Brad's hand.

"You don't understand, Greg."

"Then tell me."

"Okay, you win. I'll tell you what's happening. Mom drank too much over at the judge's house, so I told her the car isn't running right and not to take it on the freeway. She told me she had a date with Jay and wouldn't be driving anyway, but I think she just said that so we wouldn't worry. So I thought I'd give Jay a call and ask him to pick her up."

Greg hung up the phone. "That doesn't sound like Mom," he said unhappily. "What if she gets mad at us for telling Jay she's been drinking?"

"I've already thought about that. We won't come right out and tell him."

"She'll kill us."

"Would you rather have her killed on the freeway or something?"

Greg winced. "Don't be stupid. She'll take a cab or something."

"I have to make sure she's all right. I'm calling Jay," Brad insisted.

"Why don't you just borrow his car and we can get her?" Greg suggested.

"Because she would be embarrassed for us to know she's been drinking. Don't worry, she'll understand why we called. Remember what Dad always used to say about Jay?"

"Dad said a lot of things about Jay."

"I was thinking about how he used to say whenever he needed help or advice, Jennings was always there and he loved him like a brother," Brad said.

Greg laughed. "That's not saying much, given the way I've felt about you lately." He passed the receiver to his brother. "I guess you'd better call Jay. I know he'd want to see Mom anyway from some of the conversations I've overheard between them. He calls her at least twice a day. Do you think they're sleeping together?"

"That's none of our business, Greg. Help me think of something to say. I can't just tell Jay Mom's drunk and I want him to take her home. She'd be so embarrassed," he predicted.

Greg and Brad rehearsed a statement and the oldest dialed the number, relieved when Jennings answered the phone, identifying himself at once as though he were in a business office instead of at home. "Mr. Jennings, this is Brad Dubcek, sir."

Jennings flicked off his television set with the remote control unit and leaped to his feet. He couldn't think of any reason for the boy to phone him unless something was wrong with his mother. "Brad, how are you?"

"Fine, sir."

"And how is your mother? I understand she had exams at the judge's house today. She's back now, isn't she?" Jennings asked as calmly as possible. He'd been checking his clock all evening, second-guessing the time she would be home, and allowing her a while to have dinner and rest up before he phoned to congratulate her and see when she wanted to take a stroll into the hills beyond her home.

"No, sir, she isn't. I understand you and she had a date for tonight?"

"I, ah..."

Brad jumped back in before Jennings could say anything else. "Well, I thought that since you were picking her up there shortly, you could give her a message for me. I hate to bother her there. You know how it is, she and the judge sit around having a few brandies and talking about law after the exams, and they really get into it and don't like distractions. I talked to Mom earlier in the day when she called to check on Keith, and she said you'd be there by eight."

Jay frowned. The boy thought his mother needed him, of that much he was certain, but why then the circuitous route? Jennings was on the verge of reminding Veronica's son that the shortest distance between two points was a straight line when the boy cut in again.

"Mr. Jennings? Would you mind giving Mom the

message? You are going to the judge's house, aren't you?" he asked urgently, while his brother stared intently on.

"Of course, Brad. I was just on my way. What's the message?"

"Tell her we couldn't do the laundry because the machine isn't working."

Jay suppressed a smile. "I see. Look, Brad, I'm not all that familiar with the L.A. area. Tell me the best way to get to the judge's house," he asked, not having the slightest idea where the old man lived.

Brad breathed a sigh of relief and flashed Greg the victory sign. "The house is in South Pasadena, sir," he began.

"Brad call me Jay, please. I knew it was in South Pasadena," he lied, "what's the best way to get there?"

"Where are you?"

"I'm at my parents' home in Glendale." Jay removed a pen from his shirt pocket and prepared to write on the newspaper he'd been reading while he watched television.

"Do you have a pencil handy? It gets a little tricky."

"Sure do," Jennings replied, making hasty notes while the boy gave him instructions. "I have it, thanks a lot, Brad. How are you boys doing?" he asked hastily, anxious to be on his way to Veronica.

"Just fine. What time do you and my mother expect to be home?"

Jennings chuckled. "Why, does she have a curfew?"

"It depends on who she's with and what she's doing," Brad shot back in a tone that made Jay stop laughing and his younger brother frown.

"I see, son. We won't be late. I would imagine your mother will be very tired after six hours of law exams. Talk to you later," he said indulgently.

"Yes, and Jay?"

"Yes, I'm still here."

"Thank you."

"Thank you," he said sincerely, with stress on the second word. "Later, Brad."

Speeding eastbound as quickly as the law and traffic would allow and then some, Jennings replayed the conversation with Brad, his vehicle gliding down a stretch of the myriad of freeways that crisscrossed the county like the tracks of skiers in hard snow, easy beneath his wheels. But his mind flowed with no such fluidity. What had happened to Vee? Had she failed the test and phoned her sons in a disconsolate mood? No, not Vee. Vee had endured so much, had she failed the exams she would call it a day, go home, and take them some other time. She would never fall apart and quit over that. Had Brad misunderstood his mother? Uh-oh, he worried, picking up Highway 134. What if she had a date with someone else, and he barged in? No, unlikely, he concluded, hoping he hadn't allowed himself the indulgence of wishful thinking to assume he was the only man in her life—but dammit, he was. He had to be.

Then what was it? "The judge and Mom sit around and have a few brandies," Jennings murmured aloud. "Aha!" He slapped his hand on the steering wheel in an exuberant burst of energy. That was it. Vee had had a long week, between trying to get her exams out of the way earlier and working in the office at Cal Tech. It would be more than enough to make any woman with her schedule want to kick back a little on Saturday night when the tests were over. Bless Brad for calling him.

Jennings was hard pressed to think of anything he would rather have delivered into his arms unexpectedly than one Veronica Dubcek, and a not so sober Veronica at that. Would she? Could he? Jennings mused with a sleepytime smile on his face that would probably have been enough to distract the most conscientious of female motorists on the road were his features not bathed in darkness. No, what she would do under the circumstances was academic, because he wasn't going to lay a hand on her. The first time with Vee was going to be beautiful, not the possible result of her diminished capacities that would undoubtedly make her hate him as much the next day as he would hate himself for taking advantage of her.

Jay castigated himself for thinking the thoughts any man may have considered, and then let them pass, the image of her brandy-sweet mouth on his, the scent and taste of her lips devouring his face in greedy little nibbles. Jay knew that when it happened it would be good for her, perfect for her, ecstatic for her, and since it would be all those things to Vee, it would be so much more to him. Dubcek's ghost would return to the grave where he belonged and Vee would be his.

Jay found the spacious hillside home easily, charmed the Great Dane on the porch, and rang the bell. No one answered, and he rang again, hoping the kid hadn't given him the wrong number or that Vee and the judge hadn't gone elsewhere to do their drinking. The door flung open as he raised his hand to ring for the third time.

"Jay! What are you doing here?" Veronica asked in amazement. There was a fancy blue glass in her hand and Jennings took it.

"Didn't you hear, Vee? The judge and I had an appointment for tonight. Good stuff," he remarked after sampling the brandy.

She stared at him, blankly at first and then with skepticism. "About what? How come neither of you mentioned it to me?"

"Think we have to tell you everything?" he said beguilingly in a low tone, trying to gauge her condition. Two and a half sheets into the wind, Jennings decided. He couldn't bring her right home, probably not to a public place either. They would have to go home to his parents' house. *Oh, God, Vee, why are you torturing me like this?* he silently implored, looking at her standing there barefoot, her luminescent blue eyes the color of midnight in the darkened landing, her cheeks flushed the same rose shade they would be soon, soon when he took Vee in his arms the way he longed to and made her his.

"No, but I don't believe you, not for one minute, Jay Jennings," she flirted, inserting her forefinger in the neckline of his shirt and playing with the little springy hairs that grew near his Adam's apple.

Jay removed her hand and held it. "You don't believe me, huh? Why not?"

"'Cause," she said, falling into his arms and kissing him full on the lips. She molded her body to his, delighted by the instantaneous response she felt against her hips.

Jennings sighed and withdrew from her caress. "Little darlin', how do you expect me to teach my kids manners if I get busted for making love on a judge's front porch?"

"They fell asleep, both of them. Let's go inside," she suggested. "I'll give you some brandy."

"I don't want any brandy," he told her. "One of us has to drive, and it won't be you, sweetheart. Get your shoes on and let's go."

"Where are we going?" she asked, pulling him into the house and dragging him to the study by the hand.

"Home to my place."

"Are your parents home?" Veronica asked, snuggling by his side and wrapping an arm around Jennings's waist.

The question had been posed as though addressed to a five-year-old, and Jennings responded in kind. "No," he said, stressing the word, "Mommy and Daddy are gone for the weekend."

"Oh, shame on you, inviting girls in when your parents are away!" she laughed.

"Unfortunately, I don't have anything shameful on the agenda," he replied rather melancholically. "Will you please sit down and put your shoes on?" he ordered when he saw the sleeping judge. "This place gives me the creeps. How old is that guy, anyway?"

"Eighty-two."

He shuddered and took in the garish late Victorian style of the room, the dark pattered wallpaper, walnut woodwork, and heavy drapes on all the windows. "God, that old skeleton and this entire place reminds me of a scene from a horror movie." Jennings forced her into a chair and knelt to slip on her shoes, pausing reverently to kiss her ankle.

No one had ever kissed her there before and Veronica giggled. "Why did you do that?"

"Because I like to kiss you," he said simply.

"But my foot?"

"I'll kiss whatever I can get my lips on. Did you bring anything else?"

The waves of nausea kept fading in and out and one caught her as she stood. Veronica clasped both hands to her forehead and moaned. "I don't feel good."

Jennings took her in his arms and patted her head, which he held cradled under his chin. "I know, darlin', it'll all be better soon." He looked around for her other things and saw a red leather purse on the chair near the bay window. "Is this yours, Vee?" He led her to the bag and held it out for her inspection.

"Yeah, I don't remember where they put my sweater."

"It's okay, we can get it later. Come along." Jay took one more look at the sleeping judge and wondered if he lived to be eighty-two whether he'd pass out in the company of a desirable woman like Vee after a few brandies. He'd just as soon be dead, he concluded, holding her closer to his side. "I hope the ride doesn't make you any sicker. If you start to feel worse, let me know and I'll pull over for a while."

"Thank you," she said miserably, crossing her arms over her chest as a brisk breeze came down from the mountains. Veronica shivered in her thin cotton blouse.

Jennings removed his camel-colored jacket and put it over her shoulders. "Here, darlin'. Now you be sure to tell me if I have to stop," he instructed, opening the door and helping her into the front seat.

"Okay."

The combination of nausea and pleasantly cool night air had a sobering effect on Veronica as they made their way back to Glendale. "Oh, hell," she complained.

"Feeling sick again?"

"No, feeling like a fool," she corrected sadly as she recalled the scene at the door when she'd uninhibitedly thrown herself at him.

"You've had a long hard week. Drinking a few on a Saturday night is nothing to be ashamed of," he consoled, taking hold of her hand and placing it on his thigh, his fingers entwined through hers.

"That's not entirely it, although I do feel badly about that too. It's what I did after drinking that bothers me," she admitted with chagrin. Veronica rolled down the window and let the crisp air bathe her flushed face.

"If you're going to tell me you did something with the judge you wouldn't do with me, I'm going to stop this car and make you walk home."

She mustered a weary smile. "No, it's the way I... Oh, you know."

Jay was perceptive enough to surmise the cause of her discomfort. "Vee, my darlin', your greeting on the porch was the high point of my day, maybe even the thrill of my life."

"I could tell how overjoyed you were, fending me off like I was contagious," she grumbled, sliding down into the seat.

He chuckled and drew her in to his body, hating the stick shift that kept them apart. He was driving his father's car and not his own, since J.J. had wanted to take the better-equipped vehicle up to the mountains.

"That wasn't why and you know it," he murmured into her ear. "The first time we make love it will be with moonlight and roses, not brandy and the old man snoring inside."

"Oh, Jay," she sighed, "you make it sound so beautiful. Curse my blasted middle-class morality that keeps you from my bed."

He patted her knee. "Don't worry, it's all coming together."

She lapsed into silence until he pulled off the main road. "Is this where you live?" she asked when he parked the car in front of a wood frame bungalow. "It's a nice house."

"Thank you. Come on inside for coffee."

Her head spun when she stood. "Oh, God, I think I'm going to be sick." Veronica pushed Jay away when he offered her the support of his hands on her shoulders. "I don't want to throw up on you."

"It wouldn't be the first time," he remarked, easing

back in and refusing to let go of her. Jennings rested his hands on her shoulder and held her from behind until the nausea seemed to have passed. "Better?"

"Much."

"Let's go inside and get you more comfortable."

"When was the last time someone threw up on you?" she asked out of curiosity as he unlocked the door.

"I guess it must have been when J.J. got sick in Manila last year." He sat her down in the living room, stretching her legs out on the sofa and propping several pillows behind her back. "How's this?"

"Wonderful, but make the room stop spinning, will you?" Veronica slid down until she was nearly flat on her back. "Can you get me some aspirins and coffee, please?"

"I don't know if you can handle them yet. Let's give your stomach a chance to settle, okay?" he suggested. "Just relax for a minute and I'll get you an ice pack." Jennings couldn't find one and returned to her with a plastic bread bag filled with ice and wrapped in a kitchen towel. "This will have to do." He held it over her forehead.

"Oh, that's wonderful," she said appreciatively. "Thank you so much for everything, Jay."

They stayed that way in silence until Jennings asked her how she felt about fifteen minutes later. "Too bad," he replied when she said nearly sober and much better.

Veronica opened her eyes. "What do you mean, 'too bad'?"

"I kinda liked it when you were drunk and falling all over me," he teased. Jennings kissed the hand he held on his lap.

"Liar! You hated it!"

"Not entirely," he said sincerely, recalling the bittersweet pleasure of the brandy-flavored kisses and the feel of her body pressed into his. "Not entirely by a long shot." He released her hand and stood, pausing to shift the ice pack and brush his lips over her cold forehead. "Vee, you're frigid."

"Only on the outside," she returned lightly. Veronica elevated herself enough to kiss his cheek and fell back onto the stack of cushions. "How about that cup of coffee now?"

"Coming up."

Veronica held the bag of ice to her head and bemoaned her fate while Jay was busy in the kitchen. She had some explaining to do to her boys, to Jay, and to herself, and her head wasn't up to the task. Not now.

"Why the frown?" he asked when he returned. He pushed the coffee table in closer to the sofa and placed her cup on it.

"I don't want to think about it. I take milk in my coffee, do you have any?"

"Sorry, I forgot. I'm sure we have some. Hang on a minute."

"I'm not going anywhere for a while."

He poured the milk into her cup. "Say when."

"When. Oh, Jay, what are my kids going to think? Brad called you, didn't he?" she asked, having long since put two and two together and coming up with the inevitable four.

Jennings took a sip of the coffee he drank black and nodded. "Yes, and I'm so glad he did."

"I wouldn't have done anything irresponsible like drive home in my condition. I thought of calling a cab, but then I changed my mind," she confided.

"I know you wouldn't have done anything foolish, darlin'. I just wanted to be with you tonight. What were you going to do?"

"Phone you. The judge actually suggested it."

"Bless the old goat's heart."

Veronica grinned. "He's a sweetheart. I love him."

"So I've gathered." Jennings left his position on the other side of the coffee table and sat on the end of the sofa, taking Veronica's legs and resting them in his lap. "Tell me something, little darlin', does a man have to be eighty-two with over sixty years of legal experience behind him to gain your love and admiration?"

"No," she demurred shyly, swirling the hot liquid with her spoon to cool it.

"Excellent," he enthused. Jennings stroked her toes while he spoke. "Don't worry about your image in front of Brad and the other kids. It's okay, really it is. They understand."

"But I don't usually do things like this. I'm embarrassed."

"Don't be, it's all right. Don't give it a second thought. You're only human, you know, and you've had a difficult time of it lately. Everything's going to be better soon," he assured her, still massaging her feet. "How did the exams go?"

"I'm sure I passed them both. The judge always checks them over before he seals the envelope." The pain in her head and abdomen wasn't enough to diminish the pleasant sensation of his hands on her feet. Veronica snuggled lower into the pillows with a contented smile.

Jennings was pleased to see her feeling better. "I thought that was against the rules."

"It is. The judge cheats," she sighed as Jay's hand moved along her lower leg, gingerly brushing up and down the shin. "Were you serious the other day about finding a house in Pasadena?"

"I was. J.J. is going to Cal Tech, it's ten minutes

away from downtown Los Angeles where I work, and the house I have in mind has a lovely view," he explained while continuing to massage her knees and cursing the hose that kept him from touching her bare skin.

"Um, that's nice. There are several places in Pasadena with truly spectacular views. Are you talking about the San Gabriel Mountains?"

"No, your bedroom window."

"You're kidding!"

"Afraid not. Buying a house is a big decision. I have to look for things that will make me happy in the long run."

"Wait a minute, there aren't any houses behind mine," she said, "with the exception of one high on the ridge and surrounded by trees."

"I didn't say it was right behind your house. The one I have in mind is up the street a little, but the lot extends into the hills. Yesterday when I walked to the highest point, I could see into your bedroom. Pity you weren't there." His hands continued to move along her legs.

The area behind Veronica's knee was ticklish. She giggled as his thumb brushed there. "Stop it, Jay. You're tickling me."

Jennings removed his hand to her upper leg. "Does the thought of having me for a neighbor tickle you?"

Veronica strongly suspected the location of the house Jay was interested in wasn't coincidental. It struck her as a strategic movement in a well thought-out courtship, and all the trouble he seemed willing to go through on her account endeared him to her immensely. "Oh, I don't know. I suppose it depends on how pesky you'd be," she teased.

"Who, me a pest? Never," he disclaimed, his hand

rising above her thigh. "Whatever happened to garter belts?" Jennings grumbled when he continued to meet the thin layer of nylon separating her flesh from his hand.

"They're uncomfortable."

"Not for me, they're not."

"Fine, I'll get you one sometime. Be a sweetheart and pour me another cup of coffee," she requested as his hand ascended her thigh.

"Sure." Jennings lifted her legs from his lap and did as she asked. "How are you feeling?"

"The nausea has passed, but my head is killing me."

"Maybe we should try some aspirins now. I think you should be able to keep them down." He fixed her coffee the way she took it and excused himself to get the medication.

"There you go. I brought you some ginger ale to take them with. It's easier on a sick stomach than water."

"Thank you." Veronica gulped down the tablets, her stomach coming close to rebelling from the icy liquid. "Oh, God, why did I drink so much brandy without any dinner?" she moaned unhappily.

"Poor baby, didn't have dinner? Feel up to some?" Jennings took the soda glass from her hand and placed it on the coffee table.

"No, I'd probably upchuck it all."

"We don't want that happening. Vee, did I tell you DOD called early this morning, around seven? I'm flying back to Washington in a few days."

Her eyes snapped open. "No, you didn't mention it." She asked him how long he would be gone.

"About two weeks. DOD needs me to brief some new people on one of the projects I worked on in Beirut."

"Oh, what was that?"

"How's your security clearance?" he asked with a lopsided grin.

Veronica looked at him blankly. "I beg your pardon?"

"It's classified information. I can't tell you anything. Probably saying I was going in regards to DOD was saying too much already."

"Your secret is safe with me," she said with a mock salute. "I'll miss you, you know."

"And I'll miss you. I'll phone every day if I can. Maybe by the time I get back we'll be neighbors," he said wistfully, wondering if any other man would buy a house he didn't particularly care for to be near the woman he wanted.

"You're talking about the Stewart place, aren't you, Jay?" It was an old barn of a house in need of numerous repairs and had been on the market for years. "I never did like that house, but I suppose it can be remodeled," she said when he nodded.

"It has all kind of potential," he said, his eyes sweeping the full rise of her bust as he spoke.

"Potential for what?" she asked in a sultry tone when confronted by his eyelids.

"For many a wondrous thing," he replied with the same inflection. "I expect to get very close to my neighbors for starters." Jennings reached over and briefly caressed her breast.

Her head was hurting too much to do anything but smile. Veronica decided it was time to go home to bed. She leaned to kiss his cheek, yawned, and left the comfort of Jay's sofa. "I'd better be on my way now. Thank you so much for everything."

"It was my pleasure. Veronica..." he said hesitantly as he helped her into her shoes, one hand resting on each of her ankles.

Veronica placed a palm on the side of his face, wondering how he could possibly implore her with such beseeching eyes after all he had done for her. "What, Jay?"

"I was kind of hoping for an invitation to your home for dinner before I left for Washington on Tuesday," he said expectantly. "Perhaps followed by that hike into the foothills." Jennings rotated his head and kissed her splayed fingers, one at a time.

Veronica put her other hand on his face, cupping the lean cheekbones between the two. "Done," she said softly, stooping to kiss his forehead.

Chapter Thirteen

Jay Jennings was a man unused to long periods of celibacy, and as spring came and went, fading gracelessly into an unseasonably warm summer, he found himself restless and discontent, the heat inside his body knowing as little surcease as the tulips in his yard down the block from Veronica's house, wilting daily under the onslaught of a merciless June sun.

He honestly didn't know how much more he could hold out like this; it had been difficult enough to want her so badly and not to know the pleasures of her body when he merely desired her, both in the flesh for several months and in the meanderings of his erotic consciousness over the years, but now that he loved her, had loved her since very early in the winter, the way it had to be between them was becoming tortuous, all consuming, untenable. Jennings had learned her unspoken cues. He knew all too well when he could touch her, how and where he could touch her, but the progression of their intimacy had halted months ago, frustratingly short of where he so desperately needed her to be, beneath his body, joined to him, a part of his life forever.

He hadn't told her of his feelings, afraid she would retreat from him, expect him to become demanding of what he needed with diminishing hope of ever receiving, as the days passed and he fell more and more into the role of best friend and confidant instead of that of lover, though the impassioned embraces erupted at regular intervals. They were flash floods in a dry land, never remaining long enough to nurture the promised growth. They were like mirages to Jennings; he saw the welcome waters that could soothe the fires of his discontent, he could almost feel the sweet relief as the images flooded his senses. But Vee denied him every time, she took it away, plummeting him to the depths of despair with her nonverbal messages, those little hands jerking and freezing on his chest or back, the mouth so recently receptive of his tightening, a spiritual retreat he felt in his soul.

The phone rang just as Jay and his son were preparing to walk down the block for dinner at the Dubceks. Time was when he resented the company of the four boys, but this evening they were welcome. Jennings had had enough of being driven to the brink of physical release while he caressed her for a while, the both of them fully clothed on her sofa like a pair of young lovers half their age. It had happened again, just a few days ago, and he couldn't endure what it did to the two of them, not until they had to run through it one more time.

"Dad, it's for you," J.J. called out from the living room. "It's Gabrielle. She's in town."

Jennings cursed himself for the first thing that came into his head. He and Gavi had always been good together in bed, damn good. They had been coworkers in the DOD until he left the agency, never in love, but always the best of friends and, when neither was involved with someone else, the best of lovers. Hearing from her now seemed to be an act of fate, a sign.

Maybe he could remove some of the pressure from him and Vee this way, he reasoned, hating himself for the self-serving logic.

"Gavi! How are you?" he asked enthusiastically.

J.J. eyed his father with disbelief, stunned that he could sound so overjoyed to hear from an old lover when he had a new one, as poorly suited as he felt the Dubcek widow to be for his father. J.J. smiled. Maybe this would be it; his father would finally turn to someone who would return his affection.

Jennings placed his hand over the receiver. "Can I do something for you?" he asked sharply.

"No, sir, I'll wait for you on the porch."

Gavi laughed into the phone. "Still giving that boy a hard time, Jay?"

"It's more like the other way around. Where are you, Gavi?"

"At the airport. Last minute assignment from DOD, or I would have given you advance warning."

"Advance warning of what?" he asked invitingly.

Gavi had never been one to pull punches. "Jay, my friend, I'll take your bed over the Holiday Inn any time. Invite me over to that great big house you bought in Pasadena a few months ago. I've been dying to see it! I find it difficult as hell to imagine you in upper middle class Southern California suburbia."

Jennings debated with his libido and his loyalty to Veronica. "Ah, Gavi, I'd love to see you, but..."

"There's another woman?" she interjected when he faltered.

"What else could keep me from jumping at an offer like yours?"

"I'm happy for you. You need someone. Look, forget what I said about spending the night there. I'll be in town until Monday. Can you meet me sometime? I want to hear all about the lady in your life, and there's some new gossip about DOD I know you'd love to hear."

Jennings thought of all the good times he and Gavi had shared together, of the sensation of her body next to his between cool sheets that wound up damp and kicked to the foot of the bed before dawn, and he weakened. "Gavi, I have a very large house. Stay here."

"Would that be all right with your lady?"

Lately Veronica had astutely avoided his home, afraid of the romantic encounters that were all too likely to ensue. They usually met at her place, where one or more of her three sons unknowingly played the role of chaperon. "Yes, quite sure. I have a dinner engagement and should be back by ten. I'll leave the back door open." She agreed at once to his suggestion and Jennings gave her instructions to his home.

"Ready?" he asked J.J., who was sitting on the porch reading a book.

"As ready as I'll ever be," he complained. "You know, Dad, I'd much rather stay home and work on a computer project than go to the Dubceks for dinner. They're nice people and all, but I get a little bored sitting around with those kids."

Jennings chuckled and rested his hand on J.J.'s shoulder. "Son, the oldest is only a year or so younger than you, and the next one is only two years younger. Is it that much of a difference?"

"It is when we have nothing in common. The only mutual interest I can think of when I'm with them is the way you and I tried to figure out how their father's software programs leaked out to the UK, and I don't think the topic would go over big with any of them, especially since we couldn't come up with a way to get Dubcek off the hook."

Jennings and his son had given up a few months ago on exonerating Mike Dubcek, though neither ever doubted his innocence, the father because he knew the man, and the son because he knew his father. At best, they decided Mike had generated the code from numbers signifying some personal or professional memento and had inadvertently passed the information along to an unscrupulous party who had the skill to generate the decoding key from whatever data may have slipped from Mike's lips. It was the only theory that made any sense. "I know, J.J. It's a damn shame we couldn't figure out what went wrong."

"Well, yeah, Dad," J.J. said philosophically, "but Dubcek's dead. Nothing we could find would ever bring him back. So what did Gabrielle have to say? Is she on assignment here?"

"Yes. J.J.,," he confided, "she's staying at our house for a few days. Don't mention it to any of the Dubceks, okay?"

The young man smiled meaningfully. "You didn't have to tell me that. I'm surprised, though."

"Why?"

"I thought you were in love with Vee. What do you need Gabrielle for?"

"Just to talk over old times. She's not sleeping with me."

"Who? Vee or Gabrielle?" he said pointedly, dropping the topic because his father's tone brooked no further discourse about that or anything else. J.J. had lived with a seldom displayed aspect of his father's personality lately, and it seemed to have begun almost from the very moment he had telephoned Veronica Dubcek on Christmas Eve. He was all too often brooding and unhappy around the house, morose at times and going for hours without speaking to him. Initially J.J. attributed his father's disposition to the news of his friend's tragic death, but as the weeks passed and the mood darkened, he deduced the widow was at fault, and he resented Veronica because of the power she had over his father's emotions. He couldn't imagine any woman not returning Jay Jennings's love and wished his father would stop wasting his time on her. If Veronica Dubcek wanted to wallow in her grief and self-pity for the rest of her life, let her. J.J.'s only wish was that she would jump on the funeral pyre and be done with it, instead of torturing his beloved father the way she did. "Dad," he said, trying to dispel Jay's introspective mood, "when Dubcek was younger, didn't he play a lot of chess?"

"Yes, he sure did. Mike played in several international tournaments before he gave it all up. Remember when we used to play?"

"Yeah, I noticed some pretty fancy chess sets in Brad and Greg's room. Maybe I'll challenge one of them to a game. It would beat tossing basketballs in their driveway for most of the evening."

"Do they still play?"

"They said some. Maybe you and I can start playing again," he said hopefully, wanting to add it would be a pleasant change from watching his father sit around and brood about his unrequited love for Veronica Dubcek, but not daring to say a word.

"That sounds good," Jay muttered distractedly, his eyes fixated on the Dubcek house as they walked down the street.

The front door opened and the son watched his father's face brighten as Veronica stood there with a sunshiny smile and glowing blue eyes. He wondered what kind of game she was playing while he forced his frown away and grinned. "Good evening, Vee," he said, but she was barely aware of his existence, having eyes only for the man whose spirits she had just elevated from gloom to joy by her very presence. J.J. brushed past them on the porch and went to find the other boys.

"Hello, there," Jennings said softly, sweeping her into his arms and kissing her cheek. "How's my darlin'?" He gave her a bouquet of mixed flowers: irises, daisies, roses, and daffodils.

"Thank you." She beamed up into his eyes, standing so close to him that the rainbow spectrum of blues, yellows, and greens seemed to blur and merge into a wonderful continuum of nature's favorite colors, the green of verdant fields and hillsides, the blue of the sea and sky, the yellow shade of the sun and the moon, of every heavenly body known and yet to be discovered. "I'm fine, angel, how are you?" She kissed the cleft of his chin, inhaled the sweet scent of whatever soap he had just used in the shower.

"Good, Vee, very good." Jennings crushed her to his chest for a while longer and then led her inside, his arm around her waist. "Need any help in the kitchen?"

"No, but come talk to me while I stir the gravy. I can't believe that we live three houses away from each other and haven't been face to face for nearly a week."

Jay had been extremely busy at DataBank, and she had been doing some extra reading for a law course she wanted to take in the fall. The reading progressed slowly because her thoughts were always with Jay. At last Veronica felt she had truly come to terms with the relationship after so many months of uncertainty. She loved him unquestionably, and since she was now certain of that, she would tell him soon.

Jay took a chair and pushed it over to the stove where she stood, stirring a thick beef gravy.

"Too tired to stand?" she teased fondly, stifling a yawn.

"No, you are. Sit down and let me do this." He removed the spoon from her hand. "You didn't sleep much this week, did you?"

"I had some reading to do," she replied. "I'm so glad it's summer. Tell me about your week."

He chuckled. "I called you every night this week on the phone. There's really not much more to say. I've hardly lived a James Bond existence since I've resigned from DOD."

"You miss it, don't you?" she asked. "All the excitement and glamour and everything."

"Yes, I do miss DOD. By and large, the work was routine, but it had its moments." He squashed a lump of flour in the gravy with the spoon and glanced at Vee. "You're the only woman I ever knew who could manage to look exhausted and ecstatic at the same time," he remarked, wishing the fatigue had derived from a source other than her studies. He assumed the pleased expression was self-satisfaction from a job well done, because it sure wasn't from any emotions he induced within her. Jennings was beginning to come to the unhappy conclusion Vee simply didn't love him. Had she loved him, all her inhibitions about giving herself to him would have vanished a long time ago, melted and flowed away like the snow on the San Gabriels down to the valley rivers. At times he thought his interpretation of her behavior was a simplistic one, but he was at a loss to come up with anything more plausible.

"Oh, I am happy," she effervesced, standing to place her arms around his waist and rest her head on his back. The linen of his dove-gray jacket was cool beneath her cheek, but the heat outside and in her kitchen was sweltering, and the scent of his sweat rose to her nostrils. "Jay, for goodness' sake, take off this jacket. You've known me for so long, you don't have to dress when you come to dinner."

"I'm fine. I'm used to far warmer climates than this."

She stood on her tiptoes and kissed the damp little waves that barely touched his collar in back. "You're perspiring."

"It's not from the stove, darlin'." Jennings shifted the spoon to his other hand and placed his palm face up behind his back, clasping her breast. She wore a light-weight cotton shift, one that reminded him of an African caftan with its brilliant and bold geometric print, and Jennings was surprised to find she wasn't wearing a bra from the way she felt in his hand. "Did you forget something, Vee?" he drawled in the accent that went to the heart of her every time.

"It was so warm. I took it off," she said, the words coming out in a breathless sigh as his thumb and fore-finger found her nipple. "Easy, angel, you're doing things that will call attention to my informal attire," she said, mimicking his accent.

Jennings turned from the stove and lusted over the gorgeous sight of her low-hung breasts, full and tumes-cent under the red and green dress, and accentuated the effect by pulling the cloth tightly behind her back. "Good, then we'll be even."

Veronica heard footsteps approaching the kitchen and eased his hands from her body. "Even for what?" she whispered.

"For all the times I had to crawl home through the ravine out back so the state of my feelings for you wouldn't be known to the entire world," he teased, gently caressing her derriere.

"Liar!" Veronica laughed.

"Don't I wish, little darlin'. Shush, I hear the kids."

It was J.J. and Greg. "Dad, we're setting up two chessboards inside. How about if I challenge Brad, you take Greg, and winners play each other?"

"Are you any good, Greg?" Jennings asked.

"Not really, Brad and I haven't played since..." His voice trailed off and he glanced anxiously at his mother, relieved that she didn't appear disturbed by what he had nearly said. "We haven't played for two or three years, and even then, my father and Brad were better than me."

"Then it sounds like we're evenly matched, Greg. I was never much good at it myself."

"How long did you play?" Veronica asked, taking the spoon from Jay's hand.

"Off and on for five years. When will dinner be ready?"

"Very soon. You'd better wait until afterward. Greg, did you set the table?"

"Brad and J.J. did. Is there anything else you want us to do?"

Veronica looked around the kitchen. "Well, yes. Everything is ready but this gravy. It still needs a few minutes. Why don't you take the rest of the stuff into the dining room?"

As usual Jay was a congenial host, sitting at the head of the table where Mike sat on those rare occasions when he had time to dine with his family, speaking to all of them, with something special to say to all three of her boys, asking about their summer plans and how the school year had ended.

Veronica noticed J.J. seemed quieter than usual and tried to dispel the obtrusive thought that he didn't particularly care for her and his presence had been forced by Jay. She knew the young man to be reserved by nature, and he never had been overtly rude to her, yet there were times when an eerie feeling crept over Veronica when they shared the same table. The silent disapproval J.J. projected was very reminiscent of how her husband had been at times, and Veronica couldn't say why. It wasn't solely what he did, or what she felt him to do, and it certainly wasn't his appearance. There was an intangible essence about his attitude, and as she sat there watching him, Veronica became chilled to the bone. Her appetite failed her. She set her fork aside, a smile plastered to her face as Jay told the boys about a new game program DataBank was scheduled to develop before Christmas time.

The more she observed J.J., the more Veronica was convinced she had not freed herself from ghosts of the past. It was almost as though Mike's spirit had come back from the grave to haunt her, to warn her away from the man who was J.J.'s father and had been her husband's best friend, the man he had forbade her to love long before she did indeed come to love him.

Her careful scrutiny drew J.J.'s gaze to hers. The boy tried to manage a courteous smile and wound up with a frigid line across his lips. One might almost call it a sneer, though he tried to correct the cold image he projected. In an uncharacteristic gesture J.J. excused himself from the table.

Veronica gasped, but Jennings was too involved in relating a mildly off-color joke to her three sons to notice. *My God,* Veronica thought to herself, trying to deny it, *either I'm going insane for seeing so much of Mike in this boy or this boy was not fathered by Jay Jennings.* Neither was a highly appealing alternative. She had to get away from the table. "Gentlemen, if you'll excuse me, I have to check on dessert."

"Need any help?" Jay asked, jumping to his feet as she stood.

"No, thank you. Everything's under control. Why

don't all of you go inside and start the chess tournament? I'll bring in the pie shortly."

"Sounds good," he agreed. "If you need any help, holler, and leave the dishes on the table. We'll get to them soon."

She thanked him hastily and ran outside to the sanctuary of the gazebo on the hillside beyond the redwood deck, and it all came to her at once, a discordant collage of images and impressions of Jay's son. The first time the boy had ever smiled to her at the Silvers' party on Christmas Eve, months before he came to resent her, her first thought had been of the similarity between J.J.'s smile and those of her sons. People always said the boys had their father's smile, the ever so slightly undershot jaw, the way the teeth never showed much, as though the smile were reserved, always controlled, even when she knew otherwise. Veronica struggled to remember J.J.'s eyes. No, they weren't blue like Mike's and her boys, but they weren't like Jay's either. They were dark, nearly black, and she suspected his mother's genes would have dominated over those of the boy's American father, whomever he may be. The more she thought of J.J., the less of Jay she saw in his physical appearance and the more she saw of Mike.

She swung herself slowly on a swing suspended from the rafters of the structure and shed a few tears, neither for herself, J.J., or Mike, but for Jay. Never, not even with her own husband or father and brothers, had she seen a more tender and intense father-son relationship, and something inside told her Jay would be destroyed to learn the truth. Well, Veronica vowed, he'd never know of what she so strongly suspected from her, never.

She predicted Jay and the three boys would be lost in their chess game for hours, so Veronica lingered in the gazebo where the air was cooler than in the house as dusk fell on the mountain range, transmuting the green of the foothill chaparral to blue, to gray, then to night, the absence of color, and she wondered how to win J.J. over. For so many years there had been just him and his father; Veronica supposed it was only natural for him to resent the role she had come to play in Jay's life, and the future concerned her, for that role was about to change drastically. She loved J.J.'s father with all her heart and soul, her ghosts had been put to rest, and though he had never told her so, Veronica felt Jay loved her as well.

Veronica had always known she was a rational woman, easily able to put two and two together and come up with four, and now that she did so, there was no other explanation for Jay's kindness and patience all those months, and she was ready to alter their relationship, to be his lover, his wife—whatever Jay wanted, she would be. With all his talk about the first time being right between them, she'd not told him of the feelings that had solidified during the last several weeks.

She would tell him soon, and together they would handle the problem with J.J. Though Jay had never hinted at the possibility, Veronica was certain now that their relationship was responsible for the shift in the boy's disposition. It concerned her greatly, but never would it deter her from the pursuit of a life with Jay. Singularly and together they had endured so much beyond the recalcitrance of a juvenile boy, and they would prevail over this too. They had to, because J.J. was so much her own, as much hers had he been born of her, the brother of her sons and the son in soul, if not flesh, of the man she loved, and fathered by the man she had once loved.

"Hey, whatever happened to our apple pie?" a voice called from beyond the hydrangeas.

"On its way," she replied, rising from the seat of the swing, which was just as well because of the long unrepaired slant that sat so uncomfortably under her bottom. Veronica rubbed her rear end as she stood.

"Having problems, Vee?" Jay asked sympathetically, his eyes following the movement of her hands.

"Nothing I can't handle," she replied contentedly, falling into the haven of his embrace.

"Well, it's nothing I can't handle either," Jennings answered back, familiarly massaging the full rise of her buttocks and mildly surprised when she didn't give him the inevitable Stop sign after a few moments of the pleasure of her flesh in his hands. "Damn you, Vee," he murmured pleasantly into her ear.

"Oh, what, Jay?"

"Why did you have to go and lose it all before I even had a chance to see it?" he demanded wistfully, one hand on the slope of her hip and the other on her right breast. "Just how much weight have you lost since Christmas?"

"Enough," she said evasively. "Why, Jay, do you have a fixation on big-breasted women with large tail ends?" Veronica laughed.

"No, I'm fixed on you. I would have taken you anyway I could," he said sincerely, leaving her to wonder at his use of the past tense.

Veronica frowned. Now wasn't the magical moment to tell him of her love. Jay seemed distracted, probably preoccupied with his work, and the four boys were in the house. "How did the chess game go?"

"You mean chess games," he corrected, removing his hands from the places he coveted just about the most of all, and ushering her into the house.

"Was I away that long?"

"Yeah, but with all due respect, no one missed you."

"Thanks! So the games went well?"

"Very well. J.J. is onto something, and I don't know what."

"I'm not following you. What kind of things do you mean?"

"You know, I really don't know myself what he's onto yet. J.J. usually only gets this hyped up over the solution to intellectual problems, you know, debugging the program that seemed perfect down to the final wire, that sort of thing. I can't understand why he's off over a game of chess with your boys. He keeps asking them about Ruy Lopez. Does the name mean anything to you?"

"Ruy Lopez?" she asked, and frowned as the memory returned. The Ruy Lopez openings had been a favorite of Mike's, years ago. No one had mentioned the name to her for years, but now that it came up she suspected the plays would be known to her oldest sons.

"It's a chess play, that much I can tell. Why should J.J. get so excited about it?"

"Jay, that was Mike's favorite opening. He used it almost all the time back in the days when he played a lot of chess. Ruy Lopez was a Spanish clergyman in the middle of the sixteenth century. He either evolved or wrote down a series of opening moves, probably both. I don't know much about chess, but the offense is aimed at gaining control of the center of the board as quickly in the game as possible. Mike loved to use the Lopez moves; I think there were several variations. Maybe J.J. is regaining an interest in chess and wants to learn them. Like I said, I don't know much about the game, but Mike swore by the moves."

"No, there's more to it than that," Jennings said, stealing a quick kiss on her lips before they passed into the kitchen to cut and serve the apple pie.

"Well, whatever it is, we have a copy of the original Lopez manuscript, translated to English of course, and some other texts in which the moves are analyzed in detail. J.J. is welcome to take them all home and study the books."

Jennings cut the pie while Veronica spread out dessert plates on the dining room table. "I think Brad already fetched the books for him. When the last game ended, J.J. was long gone and reading about Lopez on your front porch. I hope he doesn't appear to be insufferably rude. I'll make him come in for the pie."

Veronica placed a cautionary hand on Jay's arm. "No, let him be, Jay."

"Why? He spends enough time alone. I think it would be nice if he got to know his neighbors some," Jennings disagreed, kissing the top of her head.

"He's been getting to know us for the last six or seven months, angel. Lighten up some, will you?"

Jennings considered her proposition. No one, and he meant no one, had ever told him how to handle his boy, neither mother nor wife, not a soul, because he knew in his guts how to raise that boy and had always followed his natural instincts, even on the subject of infant feeding schedules years ago. Jennings had strongly disagreed with his mother when she wanted to feed the baby on a strict four-hour schedule, and the boy's 3:00 A.M. howls used to cut through his soul, so he would rise to feed the baby himself, and his own lack of sleep then was the last thing on his mind. "Well, if you think it's best, Vee," he agreed at length. "Maybe I'll just see what he's all jazzed up about and bring him a piece of pie, if you don't mind."

"Mind? Sweetheart, I insist. Take him a big one."

"Thanks," he said, accepting the oversized section

of pie. "I'll be in soon." Jennings found his son sitting on the porch beneath a low-watt yellow bulb, scribbling feverishly onto a paper napkin. "Watcha doing?" Jennings gave him the apple pie.

"Dad, forget the pie. I'm onto a big one," he said with a preternatural look his father knew well. J.J.'s body was on earth but his soul had ascended to the heights.

Jennings sat down on the red brick porch. "Tell me about it, son. What's with this Lopez guy? Vee told me he was a medieval Spanish priest who documented and invented some opening moves. What is the significance of all of that to you now?"

"Dad, get this." He held the book to the light and pointed out a series of lettered numbers that indicated the chess plays.

"I'm still not following you."

"See these numbers? They're the ones Dubcek used to generate the decoding sequence. Remember? Old Long John gave us the original sequence; otherwise I never would have figured it out."

"Don't be modest, J.J.," his father said, knowing there must be more to the story. "Out with it all."

"Okay, Dad, get this. You know Synfo in London?"

"Sure, they're the company that marketed the disks before DataBank could. What about them?"

"Well, the chief engineer in charge of developing new programs is Wilson Townsend," he announced triumphantly.

Jennings was at a loss to follow his boy. "So?"

"So! Listen, Dad. Townsend and Dubcek were opponents at several tournaments in the midseventies. Dubcek always opened because he was better, and he always used the Ruy Lopez moves. They fascinated him for some reason, and years later when he tried to generate the encoding sequence, good 'ol Lopez came to mind. Got it, Dad?"

"With crystal clarity. When Townsend heard Mike was affiliated with a company whose work he wanted to steal, he took a shot in the dark and came up on target. Congratulations for figuring all that out. I'm impressed."

"Thanks. I'm convinced my theory is correct. It has to be, Dad, it fits all the data. Dubcek knew he was guilty of an error in judgment by generating a code someone else could figure out, and when Silvers and the rest of them confronted him with stealing the programs, he felt he might as well have given them away," J.J. said after a poignant pause. "Oh, Dad, sometimes everything is so sad, isn't it? I mean the whole thing with Dubcek's death seems to have been such a fluke, like you said, a random thing, what with Townsend taking a shot in the dark."

Jennings hugged the boy. "Yeah, it is, J.J., but sometimes the random shot in the dark doesn't end in tragedy at all. Sometimes it turns into a nova and then the whole world glitters."

J.J. clasped his father's shoulders and stepped back. "I'll have to think about that one, Dad. Are you going to tell the Dubceks about our Lopez theory?"

He heard the boy's use of the first person plural and smiled. "Do you think we should?"

"Yes, I think it would be a good thing."

"Then let's go inside, Sherlock Holmes."

Chapter Fourteen

Veronica believed J.J.'s theory and found some measure of relief in knowing for certain now Mike had not intentionally defrauded DataBank. The Dubcek boys shared their mother's feelings, but the revelation sent the family into a tailspin of what-ifs, and the evening ended on a somber note, with Brad and Greg taking positions as a pair of melancholic sentinels in the backyard, sadly conversing to one another, and Veronica unnerved to have the past resurrected so untimely, on the night when she had meant to arrange a romantic lovers' rendezvous with the man she wanted. Only Keith seemed uneffected, going off to the den to watch television after a laconic "I knew Dad never did anything wrong."

Jennings had given J.J. permission to precede him home, so he could have a few minutes alone with Veronica on the front porch. "Perhaps J.J. and I should have waited before telling you about his Lopez hypothesis, Vee. It certainly seems to have put the damper on the evening around here." He pressed her palms together, raised them to his lips, and kissed the ridge of her knuckles.

"No, angel, it's okay. Brad had already figured out what J.J. was driving at before he told us the code came from the twenty-third variation of the Lopez moves. I think right now he feels more cheated than the rest of us by the randomness of life. Just think, if Townsend hadn't been at the London tournament and played with Mike years ago, or if..."

Jennings silenced her with a thumb across her lips, his fingers cradling her face. "Shush, darlin', no more ifs. They can drive a person crazy if you keep up with them long enough. Brad's a survivor, he'll get over this, and I know he needed to feel Mike died because he couldn't live with the dishonor of a strategical error in judgment, not because he had acted unethically and was found out," he consoled.

"It was all so senseless," she persisted. "You knew he had to be innocent all the time, I mean innocent of any willful wrongdoing, didn't you?" On the dimly lit landing the rainbow eyes were dark with luminescent flashes shining through, like a pinpricked sheet of black velvet cloth held up to the sun.

"Yes, he had to be," Jennings asserted once more. "I'm sorry the evening turned out the way it did. You seemed so happy at first, scintillating, I would say. Any particular reason? You know, I got so involved with the chess games, we didn't have much time to spend together."

"I'm happy because of you."

"I thought it was just finishing your courses for the semester."

"That too," she conceded, "but mostly I'm happy because of you. Jay, I want us to take a vacation together this summer, soon, as soon as we could arrange it."

Jennings thought of a frustrating trip her family and his had made to Death Valley around Easter time, he and the three oldest boys in a four-person tent, and

Veronica and Keith in the pup tent next door. He'd spent three sleepless nights, wanting her desperately in the cool black desert air, but there was no way he could go to her. "The six of us, darlin'?" he asked without enthusiasm.

She laughed against his neck. "No, the two of us. Just you and me."

Jennings wasn't particularly excited by that prospect either. They'd gone through that one before, he and Vee off together, she insisting on separate rooms, once after a promise to come to his bed. "Vee, darlin', it sounds good," he said noncommittally. "I don't know when I can get away though."

She hid her disappointment. "I thought you said something about a week off in mid-June."

"That's right, but I made plans to go backpacking in the Rockies with J.J. and I can't change that now."

"How about a weekend, then? We can drive up the coast to Big Sur," she tried, alarmed by his blasé reaction to her suggestion. Had she tried his patience too long?

"We'll see, love. Kiss me good night, I have to get home now." He kissed her reverently and without passion.

Veronica didn't know if he'd done so in deference to her subdued mood over the code or if his response heralded a change in their relationship. She didn't think she could bear it if Jay moved away at the same time she had decided to go to him. "Good night. Are you coming by for brunch in the gazebo tomorrow?"

"I think I'll pass on that. An old friend of mine from DOD is passing through town and we're getting together to compare notes."

"Oh, well, he's welcome to come over too."

Jennings frowned but didn't correct her. "Most of

what we have to discuss is classified information. I'll give you a call later in the day." He brushed his mouth across hers and strolled down the street.

Jennings walked home like a man going to the gallows. Why in the hell had he offered Gavi use of his home, knowing his invitation wasn't as innocuous as he had phrased it, knowing Gavi had known, and would come to his bed if he wanted her, with open arms and an open heart, half of which he could get from Vee and the absence of the other half making him ache with the want of it. Her promises of a weekend together hadn't lulled him into a false security about the relationship working out the way he would have it be. They'd played that game before, with both of them coming up losers. Jennings was sick of moonlit evenings with the woman he loved so desperately throwing him down the stairs after just a taste of what he needed. You might as well let a starving man sniff a Thanksgiving dinner for all the good it did him, he thought gloomily. Maybe, just maybe, sweet Gavi could make his wait more tenable, because Jennings knew he would continue to wait until Vee told him to go away. He loved her too much to ever leave of his own volition.

Gavi was sitting on the porch with J.J., laughing over a mutual friend neither of them particularly liked. Eight years older than Jennings and in her midforties, she was still a very attractive woman. She stood when she saw him. "Jay!"

"Gavi!" They fell into one another's arms, and J.J. discreetly excused himself.

"How are you, honey?" she asked, clinging to him.

"Can't complain. Let's go inside and have a drink," he suggested, figuring it'd be just his luck to have one of the Dubcek boys skateboard past his house right about now.

Gabrielle laughed. "Worried about the neighbors?"

"What makes you say that?" Jennings asked with a sideways glance.

"J.J. and I had some time to talk while you were down the street. Come on! The kid is pulling my leg. Did you really buy this house to be near a chubby widow up the block?"

"Yeah, I did," he admitted with a rueful grin, his eyes sweeping over her scantily clad body in shorts and a halter top. "But I wouldn't call her chubby."

"How's it working out?" She knew what Jennings liked to drink, and made a double screwdriver for him and another for herself before curling up on the sofa. "Sit down, honey. You look beat."

"Thanks, babe," he said, taking the drink. "It's not going so well."

"You're in love with her?" she probed.

"Yes, more than I ever thought anyone could love anyone," he said, downing the liquor in three sips.

"How long's this been going on?"

Jennings smiled to himself. "I don't know how to answer that one," he finally offered. More than once, he wondered if he had always loved her, loved her since those godawful days in Nam when all he had was her image to sustain him in a long journey through hell and back. "I had a crush on her years ago, and we met for the first time around Christmas."

"Is this the lady whose picture you took from the locker wall in Vietnam? The one who was married to your best friend and always sent salami and crackers and cheesecake photos of herself?"

Jennings head jerked from the bar where he'd gone to prepare another drink. "How 'n the hell did you know all of that?"

"You got drunk and told me in Lebanon, around ten

years ago, I think. Don't you remember?" she asked, smiling at the memory. "And then again in Greece, and once in Brazil. Now that I think of it, you always used to talk about her when you got bombed. You even called me Veronica once while we were making love. Remember?"

"No, I don't, and incidentally, there weren't any cheesecake photos. Forget it, Gavi," he said sternly when she opened her mouth to disagree.

"So, you found the lady of your dreams after all these years, Jay?" she asked softly. "Wherein lies the rub?" she said when he nodded unhappily.

"She's not in love with me and won't let me make love to her, Gavi. She really gets me down at times."

"Poor Jay," she consoled, "that's rough. What are you going to do?"

"What can I do?" he asked rhetorically. "Keep on loving and wanting her, I suppose."

"Maybe you should come back to DOD and forget her. Sounds to me like any woman who doesn't love you and won't let you touch her has a few screws missing."

Jennings shook his head and chuckled. "You're just what I need tonight, Gavi, a one-woman fan club. Come here."

She went to his side without question, sitting on the arm of his chair briefly before Jennings pushed her down to his lap. Gavi heard footsteps in the next room and kissed his forehead before standing.

"What are you doing?" Jennings demanded gruffly when she left.

"Honey, your son is around."

"So, he's seen you on my lap before, Gavi. Come back."

"It's different now. He's not a child anymore. Hold

your horses, will ya?" She began a voluble discourse about the latest political maneuvers in DOD while J.J. looked around in the next room for a book he had misplaced. "You miss it, Jay, I know you do. Get away from this sunny suburb and your frigid widow and come back to us. We need you," she concluded fervently, after yelling out a raucous good night to J.J.

"I could never leave her," he said simply. "Besides, I made the decision to resign from DOD before I met Vee," he said when Gavi raised a cynical eyebrow to his devotion to Veronica.

"Hum. How's the work at DataBank?"

"Interesting. Did J.J. fill you in on Dubcek's suicide and the Lopez moves?"

"Yes, he did. I'm sorry, Jay. I know how much Mike Dubcek meant to you. It's a rotten shame, the whole thing. There was a suicide in the department last July. Did you hear about it?" she asked, refilling her glass, and then dumping the contents into Jennings's before making another.

"Who?"

"Lance Beecher."

"That crooked guy? I can't say as I'll do much mourning for him, but I sure do feel for his wife. She was a good woman."

"I know, I always liked Joyce too." Gavi settled onto the arm of his chair, facing him, her hand resting lightly on his chest. "Honey, let's go upstairs."

She allowed him to caress her breasts. There was a decided lack of passion in the way he touched her, and Gavi wondered if it was because he had been drinking heavily or because he was in love with another woman. She kissed his mouth and was met with the same ambivalent response. "Come on."

Jennings let her lead him to his bedroom and watched

her undress beneath the harsh light of an overhead Spanish-style chandelier, heavy with black wrought iron and amber glass. She smiled and walked toward the door, and had the nude woman approaching him been Vee, Jennings knew as certainly as he had ever known anything in his life that he wouldn't be standing there, confused and impotent, straining against the winds of desire like a windmill without blades, useless. Totally useless to anyone.

Gavi saw his anguish and didn't know quite what to make of it, but it was better to let Jay stop than she; he'd been rejected enough for any man already. She took him into her arms, unfastening his belt and burying her lips on his neck since that frozen mouth didn't invite a woman's kiss.

His arms hung limply at his sides, and the image of Veronica smothering his face with hot little kisses, the repressed passion of a lifetime waiting for him there, flooded his senses like a Canadian blizzard; everything that had been before was obliterated in its wake, and one all-pervasive color blanketed the earth, the way images of Vee colored every nuance of his life now. Vee was part of his soul and it wouldn't work with someone else, not yet at any rate. "Gavi, I can't. Please forgive me." He took his dark brown robe that hung on the hook behind where he stood and covered her.

"I forgive you, my friend. My only hope is that you can forgive yourself," she whispered. "Good night, we'll talk tomorrow," Gavi said, closing the door as he walked away.

Jennings needed a breath of fresh air and sat on the porch until the phone rang. He had sobered rapidly after the incident with Gavi. "Hello?" he ground out.

"Jay? Are you all right?" Veronica asked, alarmed by his harsh tone.

"Vee!" he exclaimed. It was so rare for her to call him around midnight. "Anything wrong?"

"Nothing we can't make right again. Jay, I'm coming over." To hell with the opportune moment, Veronica had decided in the hour or so since Jay had left her home. He may have talked about the first time bathed in moonlight and red roses, but she needed him now, and his bed would be the most romantic place in the world for her.

"Vee, it's awfully late." He thought of the naked woman in his bed and flinched.

"I know, angel, but not too late. Stay where you are. We have to talk."

"Vee, I've been drinking and I have a headache," he hedged.

"I'll take care of you. See you in a jiffy." Veronica slammed down the receiver and, running to the door, raced to his house.

"Oh, Lord, help me," Jennings implored, snatching up the halter top he'd stripped from Gavi and stashing it in the desk drawer. There wasn't time to shove his old friend out the back door since Vee would be there in a matter of seconds, and even if she didn't live so close neither he nor Gavi were capable of driving anywhere in their condition. As lucid as Jennings felt after the encounter with the other woman and subsequent conversation with Veronica, he didn't trust himself behind the steering wheel of a car with his hands shaking like dry leaves in an autumn breeze.

Jennings buried his head in his hands and when he looked up, he saw Veronica standing in the hallway, right beyond the living room entrance.

"Hi, angel. I knocked softly, and just came in when you didn't answer," she said, rushing to his arms.

"Hello, Vee," he said somberly. "Have a seat." He

ejected her from his arms, feeling he didn't deserve to hold her for a while.

"Jay?" she asked quizzically, "what's wrong? You seem so tense." Veronica recalled all the times she had refused him when he wanted her with a passion she could taste in her every pore and assumed he was afraid of the frustration that so often ensued from their intimate encounters.

"Nothing, I'm just tired. Let's sit in the yard. It's hot as hell in here. Can I get you anything? Would you like a drink?"

"No, thank you."

"It's just as well, I drank enough for the both of us," he replied.

"You don't seem like you've been drinking," she observed as they walked into his backyard. A full moon was slung low on the horizon and the scent of orange blossoms permeated the night air.

He didn't sit on the half log bench with her as was his habit, but chose to lean into a massive palm tree. "I sobered up mighty fast tonight."

"Anything happen?"

"Almost," he said cryptically. "What did you want to talk about, Vee?"

"I don't know if I can now. You seem so distant." She left the redwood bench and grasped his hand.

"No, I'm right here." He clutched her to his chest, cursing himself for going to Gavi the way he had. Somehow it seemed to desecrate this moment, but he forced the incident from his mind, intoxicated all over again from the feel of Vee next to his body. "Say whatever you came to say, darlin'." Pitter-patter kisses rained down on her face; Jennings nibbled on her nose, her closed eyes, the soft forehead, everywhere.

"It's really not very complicated."

"Few things are when you get right down to it."

"Oh, I love you so much!"

He had waited a lifetime to hear her say those words to him. "Vee, what did you say?"

"I said I love you so much," she repeated, easing back enough to look up into his face. "Do you love me?"

"Love you?" he said in awe. "I more than love you, whatever that is." Neither spoke for a while, Jennings too overcome by the realization he had what he wanted most from life now, and Veronica enchanted by his beatific expression. It didn't seem possible her love could make him glow that way in the moonlit garden, but it did, the plethora of wondrous thoughts bathing his features as though he were a man long adrift in the world who had stumbled quite unexpectantly into Paradise. "Oh, God, how I love you." He lifted her hands from his chest and kissed the palms, the kisses long and moist on her skin.

"Jay, darling, I'm sorry it took so long to work everything out. Thank you for being so patient with me." She cupped his face between her hands when he released them so he could hold her in his arms.

"I would have waited forever for you, Vee." Jennings kissed her mouth, spinning her around in the garden so that his bedroom came into her line of vision.

She saw a naked woman go to the window. The woman yawned and then opened the shutters to admit the night air. "Oh, Jay," Veronica said sadly. The sound seemed wrenched from her soul.

Jennings followed her glance and sighed, marveling at how a man could descend from heaven to hell in such a short period of time. "It's not what you think. Come sit down and I'll do my best to explain."

She knew where his bedroom was, knew of it from the hours they had kissed and touched one another there like a pair of young lovers saving their chastity for the altar. "What's there to explain?" she asked bitterly. "No wonder you were in such a hurry to get home tonight, and then didn't want me to come over. I suppose I thanked you prematurely for your patience. It must have been fairly easy to wait with her in your bed." She jerked her hand from his when he reached for her. "I'm going home, you'd better get back to your friend."

"You're not going anywhere until we work this out. Sit down," he demanded, forcing her bodily back to the bench.

"I don't want to talk to you now."

"Then listen, dammit."

"I swear, if you lie to me now, I'll never forgive you."

"I won't lie to you, Vee. I never have and I never will."

"So, how long have you been going to her for—for relief after you leave me?" she said harshly.

"Vee, I haven't gone to bed with another woman since I met you, and that's the God's honest truth."

"Do you do it standing up?" she demanded angrily.

"Stop it, Vee, and just listen. The woman you saw in my room is an old friend. I haven't seen her since before Christmas."

"And just how friendly were the two of you?"

Jennings sighed and told her the truth. "We were lovers at one time, if that's what you want to know. We worked together for years at DOD, and went to bed together when... when it was mutually convenient," he settled upon.

Her anger had yet to be mollified, as much as she understood all the frustration she had caused Jay over the last several months. "Well, it certainly must have been very convenient for you to have her drop into town when old Veronica's been holding out on you, Jay. How was it?"

"Nothing happened. I thought it might, but I couldn't."

She looked at him suspiciously. "But I suppose she was ready and able to give you a hand."

"Gavi would have made love to me, yes."

"So, what happened? Did I phone at an inopportune moment?"

"No. I knew before you called I couldn't do it."

"What do you mean, you couldn't do it?"

He despaired, his patience growing thin. "Do I have to draw you a picture, Vee? Physically and emotionally I just didn't want her."

"Why?"

"Why in the hell do you think? Because I love you."

"But not enough to wait."

"I did wait," he contradicted. "I just weakened somewhere along the way, that's all." He stopped his pacing and returned to the bench where she sat wringing her hands. "There's really nothing I can do now but apologize, and say how much I love you and how sorry I am."

"Would you have told me about this had I not come over and seen her?"

"I don't know. Probably not. There isn't much to say," he said unhappily.

Her jealousy and anger detonated like a keg of gun powder hit by a flying bullet. Veronica was spent, and in the wake of the explosion she tried to collect her scattered thoughts. "So you never touched her?"

"No, I didn't even begin to make love to her," he hedged. "I told you, I was incapable of it."

Veronica sat there silently and forgave him. "Oh, Jay!" She threw herself into his arms. "It's over and done with, let's just forget the whole thing now."

"There's nothing I'd prefer," Jennings murmured, infinitely relieved to see the sunshine restored to her face.

"Come here." She extended her hand and led him to a secluded part of the property, onto a hillside that overlooked a densely wooded ravine.

"Vee, what are you doing?" Jennings asked when she stripped off the caftan and spread it out on the ragged Bermuda grass.

She wore nothing beneath save a pair of pale blue nylon briefs. "Has it been so long you've forgotten?" she laughed, pressing herself against his body. "I tell you, I almost have."

His splayed fingers found the soft rise of her buttocks. Jennings molded her to his pelvis, the surging desire there to greet her. "No, I remember. It's nearly all I've thought about since I met you."

Veronica was stunned when he released her and retrieved her dress from the ground. "Jay, don't you want me?"

He drank in the sight of her. "That's the understatement of the year. I want you more than anything on earth, but not right here. Remember, I said the first time has to be perfect." He tossed the dress over his shoulder and surrendered to the uncontrollable impulse to drop to his knees and kiss her midriff, easing down the elastic waistband and running his lips over where the soft hair met the smooth flesh of her lower abdomen.

She grasped his head and sighed, "Jay, this is perfect! It's a beautiful night, warm, a soft breeze, enough moonlight to see one another. Put the dress back on the grass and make love to me," she urged. "No, don't stop," she pleaded when he rose to his feet. Veronica reached out to him. "Oh, please, Jay."

With Spartan discipline Jennings removed her hand from his body and pressed her palm into his chest. "Darlin', listen to me, your oldest son walks in these hills sometimes at night, and—"

"Oh, my God!" She snatched the dress from his shoulder and slipped it over her head. "Why didn't you say something sooner?"

"I was too distracted," he smiled.

"I knew he walked here early in the morning. I didn't realize he went out in the night as well," she remarked, wanting to ask Jay more about her son, but too caught up in the passion of the moment. "Let's go inside, then," she suggested.

"No, not with Gavi and J.J. around."

"Then come to my house. All the boys are sound asleep. They won't come into my bedroom."

"No, I know of something better yet," he insisted, kissing the tip of her upturned nose. "Come with me. There's a pretty stretch of land past that gully in front of my house, to the right. No one ever goes there because the only way to get down to it is through my front lawn."

"Take me there," she said softly. "Do you go there often?"

"Fairly often. When I want to be alone." His fingers tightened around her hand as he led her back to the house and then out front.

"What do you think about when you're alone there?"

"Do you really want to know?"

"More than anything in the world," she asserted.

"I wish I were home with you, and you were my wife," he confessed.

She halted her pace and threw herself into his arms. "Do you still feel that way?"

"Do you have to ask?" Jennings replied in amazement. "Of course I do."

"Let's get married Monday morning, then!"

"How long would it take to get married? Could we really arrange it so soon?"

"I don't see why not," she said dreamily while her heart swelled with happiness.

"What about blood tests and all that?"

"Rebecca Silvers is a doctor. I know she'd open the clinic for us and do it tomorrow."

"Wonderful. Well, here we are. What do you think, Vee?"

Veronica peered up to the moon, barely visible through the canopy of dense foliage. It was darker here than out back, and when her eyes adjusted to the dimness, she saw Jay had strung a hammock between two oak trees. "It's lovely! Oh, Jay, love, listen to the sound of the wind blowing the branches. It almost sounds like the ocean."

Jennings eased the loose-fitting dress over her head and stretched it out on the grass as Veronica had done. "Darlin', that roar you hear right about now is the rush of blood through my veins."

She was oddly humbled by the beatific luster that transfixed his gaze as he stooped to remove her panties, pausing to see what he had uncovered, easing her to a place on the ground where a shaft of moonlight penetrated the growth overhead.

"Oh, Vee, you're so beautiful and I love you so much," Jennings proclaimed in an awed tone. "I can't believe all of this is happening to me. I keep thinking it's some kind of a dream and I'm going to wake up at any minute."

"Jay," she whispered, weaving his hair through her fingers. "From now on we'll be together when we wake up." She was sitting up, with Jay on bended knee, kissing the full underside of her right breast. When he shifted his head, she eased the tip into his open mouth, cradling him against her body.

Jennings grazed his lips upward until he found hers again, pulling back after he kissed her to stare into her eyes. Too overcome to speak, he stood to undress.

Veronica shifted to watch him in the pale moonlight. He was splendid, and the light on his body moved with the swaying branches, dancing along the planes and hollows, the downed and smooth places, and she loved him so much she wanted to cry.

Arched over her, Jennings paused to kiss away a single fragile teardrop. "I still can't believe all this is finally happening to me," he whispered reverently.

She held out her arms and drew him to her side, her voice spirited away at first by that transcendental gaze of his, the one that didn't seem to be of this earth. "It is, and it's happening to both of us, love."

He was lying halfway atop her, and never had she borne a more precious burden, the weight of his lean body flattening the softness of her breasts. Veronica raked her fingers through his hair, the brown shade nearly black in the night. Lovingly she cherished the wiry wisps of sideburns, sweeping her stroke inward to absorb every contour of his face, to etch him indelibly upon her soul forever.

Jennings uttered her name in a ragged sigh as he tore his mouth from hers, burying his lips in the scented hollow of her throat, taking possession of her there with voracious little kisses that left her breathless. When his hand grasped her breast it was as though she were entirely his, had always been his, and he rained the most tender and provocative deluge of lingering moist kisses down on her, and iike an unrelenting shower, no place was left untouched.

Veronica's hand strayed to his chest and trembled, not from uncertainty but from the intensity of all the glorious emotions raging through her like rampant white water waves in some wild unseen river, coursing inevitably to an end somewhere, to be absorbed by a sea a thousand times bigger than itself. Tenderly she ran her forefinger in a circle around the dark hair that swirled about the taut nipple and then tasted of the sweetness there. One hand rested on his shoulder until Jay lifted it to his mouth, and she allowed the other to drift down his abdomen, following the enticing line of springy hair that descended along his body.

Jennings made a sound of deep contentment and profound desire, easing himself atop her supine form with one hand on her breast and the other at the small of her back, the long fingers crunched against the rise of her buttocks, kneading the smooth flesh with firm and loving strokes. The kiss deepened until Veronica gasped for air, and he moved his mouth from hers, covering her upper body with brief eager kisses.

"Oh, Jay, my love."

"Yes, yes, darlin', I'm here for you, always." He kissed her mouth once more. "I still can't believe all this is real," he repeated.

"Oh, love, yes, yes."

Jennings knew very soon it all had to be. No shadowy dream lover, the Veronica of a thousand fantasies had never been like this woman in his arms when they consummated their vows of love. The glorious mirage did not fade as he neared the shore this time; the waters glittered, became more and more resplendent until he plunged in, a jubilant cry heard as he bathed and was reborn in the warm mysterious depths of her.

Chapter Fifteen

"Happy, Mrs. Jennings?" A brisk ocean breeze swept up the landing and he immediately removed the dove-gray jacket he had worn at the wedding and placed it over Veronica's shoulders.

For a man to do that when they would be inside in a matter of seconds was such a typical Jay-like gesture that she had to smile, marveling once more over his unfailing consideration for her. "Oh, yes, angel, very happy. This place is divine." Veronica rested her palm on his back while he opened the door. They were honeymooning at a Santa Monica beachhouse and the mighty Pacific rolled just below them, where a taupe-colored rocky bluff met the pale beige sand. She rushed to the window and drew the drapes. The sea was spectacular in the setting sun, a fiery sphere easing into the horizon, lending a final crimson glow to the darkening sky.

"Jay, look at the view! I'm still amazed that J.J. gave us a weekend here as a wedding present! I had expected something a bit more modest though. We must have divested him of his entire life's saving. I did try to talk him out of it, you know."

"Yes, you told me, Vee, but there's no talking that boy out of anything he really wants to do."

"I know, Jay. But it makes me feel bad. He'd been saving for a daisy wheel printer since Christmas. He didn't have to do all this, you know. The conversations we had were all I ever wanted from him," she said, recalling her amazement at J.J.'s unconcealed happiness when he learned she and Jay were to be married as soon as possible.

After the euphoria of their first night together Veronica's mind had begun to turn to practical matters, and the prospect of sharing a home with a young man who held her in low esteem was too important to overlook. She'd shared her fears with Jay the next morning when they awoke in her bed. Veronica was surprised to learn Jay knew of his son's resentment toward her, and skeptical when Jay told her it was truly a thing of the past. J.J. simply wanted to see his father happy, and was too young to hold her blameless for not making a commitment to him sooner.

Jennings loosened the ascot he wore around his neck and placed their suitcases next to the bed. They were a handsome pair of brown leather cases, a gift from the Silvers family, and given to them the day before their Friday afternoon wedding. As it turned out, they were unable to schedule the wedding for Monday morning; Rebecca was unavailable due to an emergency at the hospital, Jay had to see to a job interview, and after waiting so long to be together, they both decided Friday was as good as Monday.

"Don't worry about J.J. I think it was important for him to show you he approves of our wedding, and he feels a little guilty for his behavior in the past."

"Yes, he told me as much. Here, let me help you," she offered, unbuttoning his shirt. When his chest was exposed, she reverently kissed it.

Jennings shuddered. "Yes, I noticed the two of you were involved in some pretty heavy discussions out there in the kitchen."

"Did he ever tell you he's interested in law school?"

"No, this is something new. You must have inspired him. Talking about law school, have you decided yet about quitting your job at Cal Tech and enrolling in a regular law school? I know you could get into Loyola, and your present schedule is just too much for anyone."

"Yes, I think that's the way to go. Have you made up your mind about putting your house on the market and moving in with me?"

"Yes, you're right, I should do that. Your boys have lived in the house all their lives, and neither J.J. nor I am particularly attached to our place down the block. I still don't like the idea of using the same room you and Mike shared all those years, though. Mind if we turn it over to my son and get a contractor in to build another master bedroom and bathroom next to the deck out back? It would give us much more privacy, and a spectacular view of the mountains," he suggested. That bed of hers had always bothered him when he had held Veronica and caressed her there on the few times when she allowed it. Jennings supposed he was being silly about the whole thing, but as long as Veronica was agreeable, he wanted a new room with new furnishings.

"That would be wonderful. But let's work the details out later, not now of all times." Veronica sat on the bed to remove her shoes, and Jay immediately came to her assistance. "Thank you, love. Oh, Jay, I'm so happy! The boys get on so well together, don't they?"

"Yes, I never had any reservations in that area," Jennings murmured, swirling her around so he could unbutton her dress after he'd removed the shoes. "Did you?"

"No, not really. Even though J.J. didn't seem to care for me at times, he always related well to my boys. I hope they're doing okay at home. Mind if I give them a call?"

Jennings eased the ivory silk dress from her shoulders and chuckled. "You worry too much, darlin'. J.J. is nearly eighteen, and your two oldest can take care of themselves, don't worry." He initiated a tender assault of her back, bathing it with slow wet kisses.

Veronica sighed. "I know. I'm being silly. I know how mature J.J. is and how insulted he and Brad got when I suggested having your parents stay there, but this is the first time I've ever left my kids alone overnight."

Jennings patted her bottom and dialed the phone. "I understand, darlin'. Don't forget my parents are visiting them tomorrow."

The phone rang three times before it was answered. "Hello, Brad? This is Mom. How's everything at home?"

J.J. laughed into the receiver. "Vee, this is J.J. Would you like me to get Brad? He's watching television."

"J.J.!" she exclaimed, a hot flush warming her cheeks. "No, just tell him I said hello. I forgot there's something on Friday nights he hates to miss. How is everything?" After J.J. reassured her everyone was fine, Veronica spoke to her two other children, pleased when Brad came to the phone. She said good night and hung up with her incorrect identification of J.J.'s voice ringing in her ears. Since Jay had never mentioned any suspicions about the boy's paternity, the last thing she wanted was to say or do anything to make him uncomfortable. As far as she was concerned it didn't matter except in the potential to wound Jay or the boy.

Jennings took in her agitation and understood at once. "Those kids do sound a lot alike on the phone, don't they?"

"Oh, all teenage boys sound the same to me," she

dissembled. "I speak to hundreds of them every day at the university and can't tell one from the next."

Jennings smiled at her kindness. "Darlin', sit down. There's something I've been meaning to tell you, but the timing wasn't right. It's about J.J. Don't ever be embarrassed to note there's very little of me in him, physically, I mean. You see, there's no way he could be my biological son."

Veronica sat on the bed, pulling him down to her. "Jay, angel, it seems to make you unhappy. You don't have to tell me anything."

"You're my wife, and I want you to know. It's something I've never told anyone, not even Sally. I suppose I should tell my boy someday, but I haven't been able to. I guess it's sheer ego on my behalf."

"Are you certain, Jay? Maybe he is yours. Did you have blood tests or anything like that done?"

"No, I never have."

"Then how do you know?"

Jennings squeezed her hand. "Because I never slept with his mother. I never went to bed with any of the native women in Nam. I told the guys I did. They all did it, you know, and I didn't want anyone to think I was strange, so I lied, and afterward I continued the lie because I wanted everyone to think I was the boy's father. Most of all I wanted him to know he had a father. But as far as his mother went, I barely knew her. I used to slip a few supplies to her for all those brothers and sisters she had, and after J.J. was born she wanted to turn him into an orphanage where he'd be lucky to get a single meal a day. I took him, and I guess you know the rest."

She raised her palm to the side of his face. "Jay, do you know who his father is?"

"Not really. I always figured he could have belonged to any guy in the unit," Jennings said, hastily correcting himself. "Except for the two married guys, Mike and John Silvers."

Mike Dubcek had always been his number-one choice when it came to such speculations, and he had no desire to desecrate his memory before the woman who had waited for him back home. More and more during the last six months Jennings had seen the similarity in mannerisms between his son and the others. They walked alike, they smiled alike, they even sounded the same on the telephone as Vee had just observed, and all four, J.J. and Brad most of all, recalled the young Mike Dubcek to his mind, the Mike he had forgotten in the sense of the physical impression he made on one until the past several months.

Veronica smiled at his delicacy. Mike had confessed his infidelities to her in a rambling letter sent from Tokyo, one he either forgot about or chose never to mention again once he returned home, and she had forgiven him for what he did. You couldn't expect a man to behave civilly under the most uncivil circumstances of all. "I don't think John Silvers would be a very likely suspect, angel. J.J.'s obviously not half black."

"No, he's not, darlin'. Do you think I'm wrong in letting him think I'm his real father?"

"You are his real father, Jay," she reassured him, "but wouldn't it be marvelous if Mike had been . . . responsible?"

Jennings looked at her and knew for certain now that she suspected the same thing he did. Her acceptance shocked him. "How so, darlin'?"

"Oh, nothing, it's just some sentimentalism on my behalf, I suppose. You see, he would be more mine that way, the brother of my sons and all. Not that he's anything less," she hastened to say.

"Then it wouldn't hurt you?"

"Not at all."

"Vee, the thought has occurred to me that your suspicions may be correct, but I really don't want to know the truth, if it's all the same to you. Can we forget this conversation?"

"Forgotten. I just didn't want the two of us to tiptoe around the similarities we've each noticed privately among the boys, and always be afraid of hurting the other," she explained.

"So you've suspected for a long time?"

"Yes. Oh, sweetheart, I was so happy to find out he didn't really hate me," she said, changing the subject because of the pain it caused her husband.

"How could anyone ever hate you?" he wondered. "He just couldn't stand to see me suffer the slings and arrows of unrequited love," he said lightly. Jennings spun the gold wedding band on her ring finger around a few times and the joy was restored to his face.

"I realize that now. At first I thought it was because he resented the time we spent together," she explained, realizing she was repeating herself, but eager to take his mind from unpleasant memories.

"No, darlin', never. You should have talked to me about it sooner. J.J. just got tired of seeing dear old dad moping around the house day and night, but you know all that now. I'm glad he told you himself this week."

"Poor angel. I'm so sorry for taking so long about everything. I've just always associated lovemaking with love, marriage and, forever after, and had to be sure. That must have struck you as a ridiculous attitude in this day and age."

"It struck me as the most wonderful attitude in the world. As frustrating as it was at times, I always respected you and the values you lived by. And," Jennings said, resting both palms on her breasts, "you didn't make me suffer so much that you can't make it up to me," he finished with a disarming smile that made her rise from the bed.

"What do I have to do?" she asked in a hushed tone.

"Be my wife and love me forever."

"I will, I will." There was a faraway expression on his face as he helped her undress, and Veronica couldn't resist asking him about it. "What are you thinking, love?"

"Nothing," he lied, his mind years and miles from where they were as he thought of the village girls in a country nearly a world away whom he couldn't go to even in his most dire hours of need because all the desire and love he was capable of back then had been given to Veronica. It was she who kept him faithful to a dream, she who made all others pale in comparison, and he wondered if he dared to tell her.

"You mean nothing you'd want me to know about," she said gently. "You're a very secretive man, Jay Jennings."

He lay down next to her in the bed. "I promise to tell you all my secrets tomorrow. Tonight I just want to hold you tight."

"Hold me tight from now on until forever."

"Oh, I will, but let me tell you something, little darlin', I've been holding you close for a long, long time, longer than you ever thought possible."

Veronica smiled and hugged him fiercely to her body. "Oh, I think I'm going to like your secrets, love."

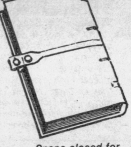

Share the joys and sorrows
of real-life love with
Harlequin American Romance!™

GET THIS BOOK FREE as your introduction to
Harlequin American Romance — an exciting series of romance novels written especially for the American woman of today.

Mail to:
Harlequin Reader Service

In the U.S.
2504 West Southern Ave.
Tempe, AZ 85282

In Canada
P.O. Box 2800, Postal Station A
5170 Yonge St., Willowdale, Ont. M2N 6J3

YES! I want to be one of the first to discover
Harlequin American Romance. Send me FREE and without obligation *Twice in a Lifetime.* If you do not hear from me after I have examined my FREE book, please send me the 4 new **Harlequin American Romances** each month as soon as they come off the presses. I understand that I will be billed only $2.25 for each book (total $9.00). There are no shipping or handling charges. There is no minimum number of books that I have to purchase. In fact, I may cancel this arrangement at any time. *Twice in a Lifetime* is mine to keep as a FREE gift, even if I do not buy any additional books.

154-BPA-NAWB

Name _____
(please print)

Address _____ Apt. no. _____

City _____ State/Prov. _____ Zip/Postal Code _____

Signature (If under 18, parent or guardian must sign.)

This offer is limited to one order per household and not valid to current Harlequin American Romance subscribers. We reserve the right to exercise discretion in granting membership. If price changes are necessary, you will be notified.

Offer expires January 31, 1985.

AMR-SUB-1